LORD RAVENSCAR'S INCONVENIENT BETROTHAL

Lara Temple

MILLS & BOON

Published in Great Britain 2018
by Mills & Boon, an imprint of HarperCollins*Publishers*
1 London Bridge Street, London, SE1 9GF

© 2018 Ilana Treston

ISBN: 978-0-263-93273-7

MIX
Paper from
responsible sources
FSC® C007454

This book is produced from independently certified FSC™ paper
to ensure responsible forest management.
For more information visit www.harpercollins.co.uk/green.

Printed and bound in Spain
by CPI, Barcelona

To my fearless editor Nic Caws,
who swoops in and saves me from myself
and my babies from creative quicksand.

Raven and Lily are particularly grateful
for your superpowers.

Chapter One

Alan Rothwell, Lord Ravenscar, drew his team of black purebreds to a stop on the uneven drive of Hollywell House. It was fitting that each mile passed on the road from Bath had added a shade of grey to the clouds. It suited his mood and it certainly suited the gloom of the sooty stone and unkempt lawn of Hollywell House.

The estate had seen better days and with any luck would see them again, but first he would have to buy the place. The only problem was that he had no idea from whom. The news that Albert Curtis had dropped dead in church in the middle of his sermon after recovering from a bout of fever was doubly unwelcome—now Alan would have to renegotiate the purchase with whoever inherited the house.

'What now, Captain?' His groom tilted his head to inspect the clouds and Alan handed him the reins and jumped down, avoiding a muddy rut. Even the gravel was thin on the ground and the drive in worse shape than the country lane leading up from Keynsham. No wonder poor Albert had wanted to escape to a mission in the jungle; he had not been cut out to be a landlord.

'The door's open. Perhaps the new heir is inside, come to inspect his new domain. Walk the horses while I see what I can do about this setback, Jem.'

'Matter of time before we get soaked, Captain.'

'Isn't it time you stopped calling me Captain? It's been six years since we sold out. Don't think I don't notice you only revert to rank when you're annoyed with me, Sergeant.'

'It's coming through this stretch of Somerset, Captain. Always makes you jittery.'

'With good reason. What's *your* excuse?'

'Your foul temper the closer you come to Lady Ravenscar's territory, Captain.'

Jem grinned and tapped the whip to the leader's back, setting the curricle in motion before Alan could respond to his old sergeant's provocation.

Jem was right, of course. His temper was never one of his strong points, but it undeniably deteriorated the closer he came to Ravenscar

Hall. Stanton had warned him to steer clear of Hollywell and find another property, preferably on the other side of Bristol, and Stanton had a damn annoying tendency to be right. No doubt he would tell him it served him right for trying to poke one in his grandmother's eye. The satisfaction of imagining her reaction to his plans for Hollywell House was fast losing its appeal the closer he came to his childhood home.

No, not home. It had never been a true home. He had been six when he, his parents and his sister had left Ravenscar Hall for the first time, but old enough to be grateful it was behind him. The last thing he had wanted was to be dragged back there with Cat when his parents died, but at least he had spent most of those long years away at school rather than at Ravenscar, and the moment Cat had married, he had enlisted and sworn never to return as long as his grandparents were alive.

Hollywell House was another matter altogether. He had been here only last month on his return from Bristol, but his strongest memories of Hollywell were still those of a boy. For an angry and grieving twelve-year-old, Jasper and Mary Curtis's library had been a sanctuary from the brutality of his grandfather's tyranny. It was the library that had sparked the idea to acquire Hollywell for the Hope House foundation; it was light enough and large enough to make a fine memory room like the one they had established in London. After the fire at the old structure they had been using for Hope House in Bristol, it was no longer merely a good idea, it was a necessity. Whatever pressure he had to bring to bear on Albert's heir, he would do so.

He took one step into the library and stopped abruptly.

Just last month he and Albert Curtis had shared a glass of brandy in what had been a perfectly ordinary and orderly library. The only unusual features were Harry and Falstaff, two weapon-wielding suits of armour which had taken pride of place in the centre of the room, standing guard over what was once a small ornate bookcase where old Jasper had kept his favourite books, and a pair of worn leather armchairs he had brought from France before the revolution. This unusual if pleasant arrangement had been reduced to a pile of tangled steel breastplates, helmets and books, and at the edge of the chaos stood a young woman wielding a very large flanged mace which had once been held confidently in Falstaff's metal gloves.

'Did you do this?' she demanded.

The absurdity of her question when it was apparent she was not only the author of this destruction but probably also mad roused him from his shock. He surveyed the room again. And then her, more leisurely. She must be quite strong, because though the mace was substantial, she held it aloft very steadily, rather like a cricketer waiting for him to bowl. She was also reasonably pretty, so it was a pity she was mad.

'Why would I do this?' he temporised. 'You can put that mace down, by the way. I'm not coming near you, believe me.'

The tip of the mace hit the floor with a thump that shook the room, but she didn't release the handle.

'Who are you and what are you doing here?'

'What I am doing is giving you a wide berth at the moment. Is your mania general or is it directed against anything medieval?'

She looked around the room for a moment and her mouth drooped.

'I don't understand. Why would anyone do this? It makes no sense.'

'That is the definition of madness, isn't it?'

She frowned at him.

'I'm not mad. You still haven't explained who you are and what you are doing here.'

'Nor have you.'

'I don't have to. This is my house and you are trespassing.'

'You are Curtis's heir?'

She nodded, her mouth quirking at the incredulity in his voice.

'Albert Curtis was my cousin, or rather he was my mother's cousin. Are you with Mr Prosper?'

'No, I represent the people who were about to acquire the house from Albert before he inconveniently passed away.'

'That's not very nice. I think his death is much more inconvenient for him than for you,' she said, a sudden and surprising smile flickering over her face and tilting her eyes up at the corners, transforming her looks from passable to exotic. He noticed the hair peeping out from her fashionable bonnet was auburn or reddish brown, which suited the honeyed hazel of her eyes. Warm colours. He was partial to light-haired women, but he could always widen his range. He moved into the room, just a couple steps so as not to alarm her.

'Not at all. He's dead. Nothing can inconvenience him now.'

He really shouldn't be trying to shock the woman he now had to convince to sell them her legacy, but teasing a mace-wielding young woman was a temptation hard to ignore. She might be mad, but she was definitely entertaining.

'You can't possibly be a solicitor. I've met dozens and not one of them would dare say something like that.'

'Dozens? You are perhaps a criminal, then?'

'Worse. So if you're not a solicitor, what kind of representing are you doing? And why are you pursuing it now Albert is dead?'

Worse? Perhaps she *was* mad. She didn't seem addled, but neither did she seem very affected by her cousin's recent death or even by being alone in a vandalised and empty house and in the presence of a stranger. Ravenscar knew his worth when it came to women and he wasn't used to being treated with such cavalier insouciance; Rakehell Raven usually caused a much more gratifying response. Women either ran from him or ran to him, they rarely held their ground.

He nudged one of the books at the edge of the tumbled bookcase with the toe of his boot. *On Customs of the Dje-Dje Tribes of the African Plain* by Reverend John Summerly. That must have been Albert's, poor man.

'I didn't know he had died until a few days ago.'

'That still doesn't explain why you entered, knowing full well you had no business here anymore. Why?'

He took another couple steps and bent to pick up a copy of Aurelius's *Meditations* from under

Harry's gauntlet with a satisfied sigh. The spine had split, but that could be fixed. He tucked it under his arm and returned his attention to the young woman and her peculiar comments. She was still watching him with suspicion, but without a glimmer of real fear. Did she really think that mace would do an ounce of good against him if he chose to divest her of it?

'What's worse than a criminal, then? A nun?' he asked.

Her eyes widened.

'On what scale is a nun worse than a criminal? And please return that book. It's mine.'

'On the scale of flirtation material. I don't flirt with nuns. Criminals are fair game.'

Her eyes widened further, the honey even more apparent the closer he came. Her skin also had a warm cast to it. This was no milk-and-water miss, despite her clothes. There was also just the faintest musical lilt in her voice which was neither London nor West Country. Perhaps she wasn't as proper as she looked, which would present some interesting possibilities...

'You are standing in what closely resembles the ruins of Carthage, facing a woman armed with a mace, and you are considering flirtation? You don't look addled, but I'm beginning to suspect you are. Either that or quite desperate. Please put down that book. It's mine.'

'So you pointed out, but my advice is that you might not want to argue with someone you suspect is either addled or desperate or both.'

'Thank you kindly for that advice. Now put down the book and step back.'

He moved closer, making his way around the pile of books.

'Not until you tell me what you believe is worse than a criminal. Somehow I can't quite see you as a nun.'

Her smile flickered again, but she mastered it. She raised the mace slightly and let it hit the ground again with an ominous thump. He stopped.

'I shall take that as a compliment, though I am certain most would disagree. You have three chances to guess. If you do, I will make you a present of Marcus Aurelius. If not, you leave quietly.'

He put his hands on his hips, amused by the challenge. This unusual creature was brightening up a dreary afternoon quite nicely. He would very much like the truth to be that she was a very permissive courtesan so he could see if she could wield something other than a mace in those surprisingly strong hands, but her dress certainly wasn't supporting that theory. He considered the bronze-coloured pelisse with just an edge of a muslin flounce embroidered with yellow flowers peeping out beneath. Simple but very elegant and expensively made. Her bonnet, too, though unadorned by all the frills and gewgaws young women favoured, looked very costly. Had he met her in an assembly hall or a London drawing room, aside from avoiding her like the plague as another one of those horrible breed of marriageable young women, he would have presumed she was perfectly respectable. But respectable young women did not wander through empty estates on their own, even if they had inherited them, and they didn't threaten strange men with maces. They came accompanied and in such circumstances they swooned or burst into tears.

'Let me see. You're an actress. Your last role was Dido and you are reprising. I don't think the mace is historically accurate, though.'

'No, an ox hide would be more apt, but I feel safer with a mace. Try again.'

His brow rose. He added well educated to his assessment. Not many women…not many people knew the tale of Dido's clever manipulation of calculus to capture land from the Berber king.

'A bluestocking with a penchant for the medieval.'

She considered.

'I would consider that a compliment, but that isn't quite accurate and certainly not what I was referring to. One last try.'

Before he could respond, the door opened and Alan turned to face an exceedingly burly man. The mace hit the ground definitively as the young woman let it go.

'Finally. Where have you been, Jackson? Distracting him is tiring work. I thought he might be the one who did this, but probably not, so do escort him out. Oh, and please leave the book as you exit, sir. You haven't earned it yet.'

Alan considered the glowering man. *She* might not be a criminal, but her henchman certainly looked the part. He added it to his collection of facts about her, but he still drew a blank.

'I have one last try, don't I? Just like that fairy tale with the spinning wheel, no?'

She laughed and nudged the mace with one pale yellow kid shoe. An expensive one, he noted. He should know, he had paid for enough female garments.

'That's true,' she conceded. 'I'm nothing like that silly woman, though. Who on earth would barter with their unborn child's life? I would have either thought of some better way out of that fix or something less valuable to bargain with. Well? One last try, sir.'

He moved towards her, ignoring the movement behind him. Her head lowered and she looked more wary now than when they had been alone in the room together. At first glance he had thought her pretty but unexceptional, but either closer examination or her peculiar chatter had affected his judgement. Her warm hazel-brown eyes, like honeyed wood, captivated him, and when she smiled, her mouth was practically an invitation to explore the soft coral-pink curve. She would taste sweet and sultry, honey and a hint of spice, he thought. It was a pity she was one of the most despised subcategories of the already despised species known as respectable young women. His only consolation was that they usually feared him almost as much as he wished to avoid them.

'Very well,' he replied. 'My last chance at Aurelius. You're a member of that dreaded breed of females who believe themselves deserving of all forms of homage and adoration for qualities that they have done nothing to deserve. You are, in short, an heiress.'

He had expected outrage, not amusement. She might be respectable, but she was not predictable. That at least might be a point in his favour when it came to negotiating the purchase of Hollywell House.

'How do you know I have done nothing to deserve it? I'll have you know being an heiress is hard work and not just for me as Jackson here will attest.'

'Does this bruiser keep fortune hunters at bay, then?'

'In a manner of speaking. Well, you have earned your Aurelius. Goodbye, sir.'

'In a moment. We still have the matter of the sale of the house to discuss. We will offer you the same price as we did your cousin. It is quite generous, I assure you.'

'As you pointed out, until after probate is granted, there is no point in discussing anything. Who is "we", by the way? I thought you said you merely represented the prospective buyers. The use of the pronoun "we" seems to indicate otherwise.'

For a moment he debated telling her the truth about Hope House. She was just unconventional enough that she might not see it as a disadvantage, but he and his friends had long ago learned to keep their involvement in the Hope House foundation for war veterans private. It was no one's business and certainly not the business of a pert and overly perceptive heiress he was still not convinced wasn't also a little unhinged. Intelligence and madness often went hand in hand.

'Does it matter, as long as we offer you fair price? You can't possibly live here.'

Her mouth flattened and a light entered her eyes that in a man would have conveyed a distinct physical menace. Perhaps he had misstepped.

'Do you hear that, Jackson? Here is another man who has an opinion about what I can and cannot do.'

The giant clucked his tongue.

'I heard, miss. Shame.'

Alan tried not to smile.

'I dare say now you are going to tell me the last fool who dared do so is buried under the floorboards?'

'No, but I am very tempted to be able to tell the next fool precisely that. The door is behind you, sir.'

'Do you really think you could carry out that threat? Or is it just a variation on the age-old cry of the spoilt heiress when her will is thwarted?'

'You keep a civil tongue in your head around Miss Lily,' the giant rumbled behind him.

'Jackson, no!' she cried out as a bulky hand settled on Alan's shoulder.

Alan turned in time to intercept the anvil-sized fist heading his way. It wasn't hard to dodge and the counterblow he delivered to the giant's solar plexus was more by way of a warning than an attempt to do damage. But clearly this Jackson was in no mood to heed warnings. Even less did he appear to appreciate being tripped and sent sprawling on to the pile of books.

'Careful of the books,' the girl cried out with a great deal more concern for them than for her protector. The giant grunted, stood up, dusted himself off, smiled and lunged.

Alan did not in the least mind brawling. He and his friends often indulged in sparring either in the accepted mode at Jackson's Boxing Saloon or in the much less respectable tavern yards and village greens occasionally set aside for such sport. This giant clearly also appreciated the fancy, but despite, or perhaps because of, his size, he was used to winning by *force majeure* rather than by skill and it was no great stretch of Alan's skill to avoid or deflect most of his blows. He was just beginning to enjoy himself and was even considering offering the giant a pause so they could both take off their coats and make the most of this opportunity for some sport when the door opened and an elderly woman entered the library. But her shriek, either of shock or outrage, wasn't enough to stop Alan's fist from making contact with the giant's face.

'Alan Piers Cavendish Rothwell! What on earth is the meaning of this?'

Luckily the giant fell back under the blow and conveniently tripped over the books again, because the sight of his grandmother dealt Alan the stunning blow his opponent had failed to deliver.

Though they were a mere mile from his childhood home, the last person he had expected to see in the doorway of Hollywell's library was Lady Jezebel Ravenscar, the only woman on earth he could safely say he despised and who fully reciprocated his disdain and had done so ever since he could remember. The only person whom he disliked more was her thankfully defunct husband, his grandfather and the late and most unlamented Lord Ravenscar.

Before he could absorb and adjust to this ill-fated turn of events, the girl spoke.

'You needn't have come, Lady Ravenscar. I merely wanted to see the place before returning to the Hall. Here, Jackson, put your head back and hold this to your nose.' She wadded up a handkerchief and handed it to the giant.

Alan had no idea what connection existed between his grandmother and this young woman, but he could have told her there was no possible way his grandmother would let her off so lightly.

He was right. Lady Ravenscar turned her unsympathetic dark eyes to the young woman.

'When George Coachman told me you had directed your groom to stop at Hollywell on your way back from Keynsham, I instructed him to come here immediately. While you are a guest in my home, Miss Wallace, you are under my care and that means you cannot dash about the countryside unaccompanied as your departed parents clearly allowed. At the very least you should have taken your maid. You are no longer in the wilds of Brazil or Zanzibar or Timbuktu or wherever—'

'You were right the first time. Brazil,' the girl interrupted, her hands clasped in front of her in a parody of the obedient schoolgirl.

'Brazil. Yes. Well, this is England and young women do not...'

'Breathe without permission. Yes, I know. My schoolmistresses were very clear about what young women can and cannot do in English society and the latter list is leagues longer than the former. I even started writing them down in a journal. It is a marvel that any of our beleaguered species can still place one foot before the other of our own volition. My parents did me a grave disservice by raising me to be independent and an even graver disservice by dying before I was old enough for people to no longer care that I was.'

She bent to pick up the book Alan had dropped during the brawl and handed it to him.

'This is yours, I believe. I would have given it to you anyway. There was no need to break poor Jackson's nose.'

He shoved the book into his coat pocket, keeping a wary eye on his grandmother.

'It isn't broken.'

'Just drew my cork, miss,' Jackson mumbled behind the handkerchief. 'Thought you were a toff. You'll not get over my guard so easy a second time.'

The girl correctly interpreted Alan's expression.

'Don't encourage him, Jackson. This is my house now and I won't have you silly men brawling in it. There is enough disarray here as it is. If you want to beat each other senseless, kindly step outside.'

'It's not your house till after probate,' Alan couldn't resist pointing out. 'We will contact you presently about the sale.'

'Enough of this,' Lady Ravenscar announced, ramming her cane into the floor with as much force as the girl had smashed the mace into the worn floorboards. 'What is all this about a sale? And where are you going, Alan?'

'Back to Hades, Jezebel. You needn't worry I was thinking of contaminating the hallowed grounds of the Hall with my presence. That's the beauty of your husband forcing my father to break the entail. Believe me, I am as glad to be shot of the Hall as you are of me.'

'Nanny Brisbane is ill. I dare say if you are already in the vicinity, she would be grateful if you would show a modicum of respect and visit her.' Lady Ravenscar's tones were dismissive, but she didn't move from her position in the doorway. She didn't have to because he stopped in his tracks. Once again she had dealt him a very effective blow.

'Nanny Brisbane is ill?'

The girl glanced from him to his grandmother, her brow furrowed.

'Are you the rakehell?'

'Lily Wallace!' Lady Ravenscar all but bellowed and the girl shrugged.

'Sorry, the black sheep. Mrs Brisbane contracted the fever as well, but she is mending. Still, she would likely be happy for a visit, unless you mean to scowl at her like that and go around bashing things. You can't possibly be her Master Alan, you don't look in the least like the miniature of you and Catherine she keeps on her mantel, but then those are never very good likenesses.'

Alan abandoned the effort to determine if she was mad or not and moved towards the door again.

'I will see Nanny before I continue to Bristol.'

Lady Ravenscar hesitated and then moved aside to let him pass.

'Catherine and Nicola would no doubt expect you to pay your respects as well.'

He didn't stop.

'I don't need lessons from you on family loyalty, Jezebel. Though it is very typical of you to preach what you don't practise.'

As he climbed on to the curricle and took the reins from Jem, he cast a last look at the classical façade of Hollywell House with its pillared portico. He hated the burning resentment and anger his grandmother always dragged out of him, but it was his fault. It served him right for trying to exact a very petty revenge on her by trying to acquire Hollywell. In fact, he should have continued to avoid this particular corner of England like the plague just as he had for the past dozen years. Nothing good came of tempting the fates.

Chapter Two

'Lily, might I have a word with you for a moment?'

'Of course, Catherine.'

'Don't hover in the doorway, Catherine!' Lady Ravenscar snapped from the great winged armchair placed near the Rose Room's fireplace but angled so she could survey her domain. 'There is no call for secrets. If this is about your brother, you may share your information with the rest of us.'

Since Lady Ravenscar was the only other occupant of the room, her words were less a polite invitation than a command. Poor Catherine wavered and Lily stood, moving towards her.

'Is Nicky faring any better this morning, Catherine?'

Catherine met her eyes with a clear expression of gratitude.

'Her fever has diminished a little, but she is still restless. That is what I wanted to ask you. I have a basket to take to Nanny Brisbane, but I don't wish to leave Nicky with only a maid. Would you mind sitting with her until my return?'

'Of course,' Lily replied, ushering Catherine out of the room before Lady Ravenscar could react. Poor Catherine had no stomach for opposition to her imperious grandmother and it was not merely because she and her twelve-year-old daughter were financially dependent on Lady Ravenscar. Lily wondered if Catherine had always been this way or whether marriage to an impecunious parson, widowhood and now almost a decade under her grandmother's thumb had leached her will away. Looking at her reminded Lily why she had returned to England after her father's death in the first place.

Like the intrepid traveller Lady Hester Stanhope, Lily had discovered that life as her wealthy father's hostess was vastly different now that he was gone, but she had no ambition to end her life an indebted recluse like Lady Hester. She had spent her year of mourning in the house of an aged and distant cousin, which had been even more stultifying than the weeks since her arrival in England. Even after she had come out of mourning, she had discovered there was no role to be played by a young woman of marriageable age unless she handed herself over body and soul to some respectable duenna while society tutted over her advancing years. She didn't even have the freedom to manage her own inheritance—the lawyers managing the trust, who had obeyed her every word while her father lived, now balked and held her to the rigid letter of the trust. Her father's death had been a shock on so many levels Lily was still reeling from the loss of everything she valued.

'It has been three days since Mr Marston has been to visit you. Is he travelling?' Catherine asked as they climbed the curving staircase.

'Yes, on business to Birmingham and then he is bringing his daughter back to Bristol to prepare for her debut in the spring.' The words were stiff and she tried to smile.

'Are you worried whether she will like you?'

Lily almost wished she had not been tempted to share some of her story with Catherine. It made it so much more inescapable.

'Mr Marston said she is as lovely as an angel, but that is the least of my worries. I know his offer makes good sense. I had no idea how restrictive life could be when my father passed and it is even worse now I am out of mourning.

Everything the Kingston gossipmongers didn't say while he was alive, they happily whispered over his grave. The only thing that kept them from saying it to my face was the hope I will marry one of their sons. I cannot even carry on with my business concerns because Papa tied it up in a ridiculous trust when I was born and never thought to change it, because he believed he was indestructible. Right now the only thing I have any control over is Hollywell House, or at least I will after probate. I must marry or I shall go mad. Sometimes I wish Papa had left me on Isla Padrones in Brazil when my mother died instead of bringing me to Jamaica and forcing me to enter society. At least on the island I had become accustomed to being alone and having few expectations.'

'You could always stay here with us if you don't wish to marry. I know my grandmother isn't an easy person, but she is not quite as bad as she seems. When Nicola returns to school, it is just the two of us and it can be rather…lonely. I am certain she will agree.'

They stopped at the top of the stairs.

'That is very generous of you, but I already feel I have encroached too much on our very distant relation. It is only because Mr Marston's home is in Bristol…'

She touched the little gold pendant at her throat. She knew this feeling. The same one that would catch at her breath every time her father sailed away, leaving her and her mother on tiny Isla Padrones. The world closing on her, shutting her in, but also a sense of safety, of the world reduced to the familiar once more. The move to Jamaica when she had been fourteen had taken away that safety without really opening the world any wider. Her school and then Kingston society had been even more oppressive than the isolation of the island where she had run wild. She had not known how rare the freedom of being alone was until she had lost it.

'Perhaps I should remove to Hollywell House…'

Catherine's blue eyes widened.

'But, Lily, you could not live there on your own!'

'I could find someone to lend me countenance. My pin money is still generous enough to support a companion. Surely there must be an impecunious relative somewhere on the family tree who would be willing to…' She pulled herself to a halt at her selfishness. She might be scared of her future, but there were many women whose fates were indescribably worse than hers, or even than Catherine's.

She had seen that only too clearly the day she had walked into the brothel near the Kingston docks that her lawyers had tried to prevent her from visiting after her father's death. Any one of those eight women would have traded places with her at the bat of an eyelid. The worst was that the lawyers had made it clear that though she could evict the women from the structure her father had bought, under the trust she could not sign over the house to them. She had done the only thing she could think of—at least her mother's jewellery was hers outright and she had sold the most expensive necklace and given an equal share to each of the women, much to the lawyers' shock and dismay.

'You would do better to marry him, you know,' Catherine said in her quiet voice. 'He is handsome and intelligent and I can see you are fond of him and he is very fond of you and he respects you, which is just as important. Otherwise he would not be so very patient and accommodating. Believe me, waiting for a...for a perfect solution usually means waiting for ever.'

'I know. I probably shall. You should go to Nanny Brisbane before it begins raining again.

Catherine smiled. 'Grandmama was right, you know. I do want to take a basket to Nanny, but it is true I received a note from my brother. He is coming to visit Nanny and I would like to see him, but I didn't want to tell Grandmama.'

'Well, since she is the one who mentioned Mrs Brisbane's ill health to him at Hollywell House in the first place, she wouldn't be surprised.'

'Did she? Still, talking about him makes her so crotchety I really would rather not.'

'I am not surprised. The way he called her Lady Jezebel sounded like he hated her.'

'That is what Grandfather called her, never Jezebel or Lady Ravenscar. She was an earl's daughter, so Lady Jezebel was her courtesy title and my great-grandmama, the Dowager Marchioness, insisted Grandfather continue to call her that when they wed because she didn't want two Lady Ravenscars at the Hall. Then when we returned from Edinburgh, Alan refused to call her Grandmama and would call her Lady Jezebel just like Grandfather.' She sighed. 'They will never forgive each other. Nicky and I don't see him often enough, situated as we are. He did visit Nicky up at her school last month, but I wish...'

There was such weariness and pain in Catherine's voice Lily wished she could do something for her, at least say something reassuring, but she had never been good at polite lies. Then the moment passed and Catherine opened the door.

* * *

No twelve-year-old of any spirit enjoyed being confined to bed and Nicky was a very spirited twelve-year-old. The fact that she was leaning back against her pillows and allowing a maid to brush her hair was a testament to how weak she was. But when they entered, she sat up, frowning.

'Sue said Uncle Alan is staying at the Ship in Keynsham! Is it true, Mama?'

The maid blushed under Catherine's accusing eyes, curtsied and hurried away.

'Do lie down, Nicky. Lily has been kind enough to offer to sit with you while I take a basket to Nanny Brisbane.'

Lily picked up the book lying by Nicky's side and smiled.

'*The Mysteries of Udolpho*. I haven't read this in years.'

'I am halfway through, but my head hurts too much to read.' Nicky was distracted only for a moment. 'But, Mama…is Uncle Alan really in Keynsham? Will he come see me?'

'Nicky, you know your uncle doesn't come to the Hall.'

'Then I want to go to Keynsham.'

'My dear, you aren't well enough…perhaps when you are better…'

'No! By then he'll be gone and I shall return to school and I won't see him for months! It's not fair that Grandmama is so evil and has cut him off and is going to leave everything to some doddering, preachy old cousin of Grandpapa's we haven't even heard of and doesn't care a straw for the Hall! It's not fair!'

'Nicola!' Catherine scrubbed her palm over her forehead and then with a gesture of defeat she headed towards the door. 'We will discuss this later, but right now I must go. I will return very soon.'

Nicky watched the door close, her hands still fisted by her sides and her eyes red from unshed tears. Lily could feel the frustration and confused pain in her own bones. It was around this age that she had begun to actively resent her father's frequent disappearances. Her poor mother had borne the brunt of her temper as well.

She kicked off her kid slippers and curled up on the bed by the girl, picking up the discarded book.

'Where were you? Here? *"Surely, Annette,"* said Emily, starting, *'I heard a noise: listen.'* After a long pause... 'No, ma'mselle,' said Annette, 'it was only the wind in the gallery; I often hear it when it shakes the old doors.'"* Lily added a rattling groan for good measure and was rewarded by a faint smile. She kept going, investing as much melodramatic nonsense into the story as she could, rising to a distressed falsetto when Emily hurried to greet the man she thought was Valancourt and promptly fainted when it was not.

'What a great deal of fainting they do engage in!' she interjected. 'I haven't fainted once in my life, have you?'

Nicky giggled again. 'No, but perhaps that's because we haven't yet been in love.'

'What do you mean, "we"? How do you know I haven't?'

'Have you?'

Lily sighed.

'No, never. It's very disheartening, though I still doubt I will faint if ever I am foolish enough to fall in love.'

'Don't you want to be in love? I do!'

Lily considered Nicky's flushed cheeks and the dark eyes glistening with hope. *She is merely a girl, Lily. She has time enough to discover the futility of dreams.*

'Well, yes, but I don't think I shall be very good at it. I am not very suited to adore anyone, certainly not someone like Valancourt. Never mind, let's discover what horrors and creaking and groanings next lie in store for our intrepid and oft-faint Emily, shall we?'

'You're funny, Lily. I wish I had a sister like you.'

Nicky leaned her head momentarily against Lily's shoulder and Lily blinked against the peculiar burning over the bridge of her nose. Not a sister. A daughter, someone like Nicky who would curl up beside her while she read... And a son leaning against her as well until he was too old for such sentimental nonsense.

She would take them to Isla Padrones and teach them to swim like the gardener Joao had taught her after her father had sent her and her mother to live on the island. Her mother had been frail and despondent after the nervous illnesses that had plagued her in the jungles of Brazil, where her father had been searching for his precious gems, and the Jesuit doctor from the nearby mission had recommended sea air. He had probably meant one of the coastal towns, but her father's romantic soul had remembered a short visit to the islands of the Amazonian delta and had sent them to one of the smallest. They were supposed to be there only until her mother recovered, but perhaps her mother's realisation that she was healthiest when she didn't have to witness her husband's infidelities had turned a convalescent retreat into a permanent home, regardless of the impact of this isolation on their only child. Ten years after leaving the islands Lily could fully appreciate what was wonderful and horrible about their seclusion there. If… *When* she had children, she hoped she could show them the pleasures of being alone, but also create a broader world than her parents had provided.

'Well, so do I,' she replied lightly, thinking of how often she had prayed for a sibling during those long years. 'A sister like you, I mean. I always wanted a sister.'

Nicky snuggled closer and closed her eyes with a sigh.

'I always wanted an older brother, too. Someone like Uncle Alan. You know, dashing and dangerous so all the girls will want to be my friend just so they can flirt with him. Well, they already do even though he's so old.'

Lily tried not to laugh.

'Don't tell him that. The old part, at least. As for the flirting, I am certain he knows that already.'

'Oh, that's right, I forgot you have met him. Sue told me he was at Hollywell House when you and Grandmama were there.'

'Is there nothing the servants don't know?'

'Certainly nothing worth knowing. So, what

did you think of him? Isn't he handsome? The girls at school said he was the handsomest man they have ever seen!'

Nicky looked up at her, her face a study of curiosity, defiance and need. Lily tried to tread as carefully as possible over the ground of Nicky's hero worship and through the unsettling sensations that accompanied the resurgence of the memory of their encounter in the Hollywell House library.

It wasn't surprising she hadn't recognised him as Catherine's brother. She had heard a great deal about the notorious Rakehell Raven since her arrival, but she had still expected him to look more like his sister. Catherine herself was a very handsome woman, but there was a softness to her that had no echo in her brother's harsh, sculpted face, and though her hair was also near black, it was slightly warmed by mahogany lights rather than the jet sheen of her brother's that added credence to his Raven epithet.

The biggest difference was in the eyes. Catherine's were a clear sky blue, slightly chilled around the edges. Her brother's were a world away, a very dark grey she had at first thought as black as his hair. She had seen such colouring in the Venetian sailors who had manned the ship that brought her to England, but Lord Ravenscar's face was pure Celtic god—sharp-cut lines of a deity bent on the destruction of lesser mortals. Perhaps his eyes also were merely black and the impression of the complex shades of an evening sky were just an illusion that would dissipate if she had a longer look. Not that she would ever have the chance to examine the man's eyes, she reminded herself. After his visit to the old nanny, he would probably return to his gambling and womanising and whatever other dubious activities he enjoyed. She smiled at Nicky and told her what she wanted to hear.

'I think your uncle is very handsome and very aware of his charms.'

'Oh, it isn't just that he is so handsome. It is because of the Wild Hunt!'

'The what?'

'Haven't you heard of the Wild Hunt?' Nicky was practically shimmering with excitement, her ills and aches forgotten. 'It is said that when the dark huntsmen come riding through the night with their hounds, everyone should hide in their homes or be swept up in the hunt.'

'Is that what your uncle does? It sounds very tiring.'

'No, silly, those are just tales. But Uncle Alan and his friends were known as the Wild Hunt Club because they were all very wild and excellent riders and it was said that no woman's heart was safe around them and no man could win a race or a wager against them because they made a pact with the devil so they would always win. Not that I really believe that silly thing about the pact. That is just what people say when they are envious.'

Lily schooled her smile, a little envious herself—she knew all about the challenges of a girls' school.

'I am not the least bit surprised your friends at school are in love with him. I could definitely have used an older brother like him to smooth my path at the Kingston Academy for Young Ladies.'

'Were the girls horrid to you?'

Oh, God, how did one explain such things to a child? And why was she trying to? It wasn't like her to share her stories and to do so with a girl half her age...

'Not horrid, really. My mother had just died, you see, and my father sent me to a school where I knew no one. I was very used to being on my own and I was just a little...well, perhaps more than a little defensive. Like a cornered cat. I even tried to run away several times.'

Perhaps this was a little too much. Nicky's eyes were wide and compassionate, more like her mother now.

'That sounds sad.'

'It was, but it passed. Then I started making friends and it wasn't so lonely any longer.'

'I like school. I don't know any children my age here and at school I have lots of friends who like the same things I do.'

'Like novels with things that creak and groan and lots of swooning.'

Nicky grinned.

'Especially novels.'

'Shall we read some more, then?'

'Yes, please. And could you do those funny voices? The story is so much better that way. I can almost imagine I am there...'

Chapter Three

'You'll come by again tomorrow, Master Alan?' Nanny Brisbane struggled to keep her eyes open.

'Tomorrow,' Alan assented and her eyelids sank on a long childish sigh and her worn hand relaxed in his.

There was nothing for it. He could stay in Keynsham for another night, pay a visit to the Hollywell solicitor and come by in the morning before he continued to Bristol. It was the very least he could do for the woman who had all but raised him and his sister and almost lost her life doing so.

Even in sleep Nanny had the face of a devout elf, caught between mischief and adulation. She should have married and had a dozen children instead of being saddled with two sad specimens of the breed. The love that would have spread easily among her potential brood had been concentrated on them and his parents whenever they chose to come out of their little scholarly world and until their deaths from putrid fever when he and Cat were young.

Cat was waiting for him in the low-ceilinged parlour, tidying up the remains of the tea she had prepared for Nanny. He waited until they left the cottage before speaking.

'Are you certain she will be all right?'

Cat smiled and tucked her hand in his arm.

'She is over the worst of it and one of the tenants' wives, Mrs Mitchum, comes to tend to her every few hours.'

'She looks so frail…'

'She is getting old, Alan, but she is still strong. It is just this fever. Practically everyone in the region has fallen ill these past weeks, but it often passes as swiftly as it comes, sometimes as briefly as a day, and there have been very few deaths.'

'Few… Albert was one of them, though. Were you ill as well?'

'Grandmama and I were, at the same time. She was quick about it, but I was quite miserable for three days. Thank goodness Lily… Miss Wallace was here to help.'

'The heiress?' He couldn't keep the incredulity out of his voice.

'Why, yes. She may not be very easy-going, but she is utterly unshakeable, which is useful in a household descended into chaos.'

'Unshakeable. I noticed that. From my meeting with her I would have guessed you would dislike her thoroughly.'

'Well, you are not as clever as you think, Alan dear. Is it strange being back?'

'I'm not back, Cat. A visit to Nanny Brisbane is my concession to childhood debts. That is all.'

'Still, I thought you swore never to set foot on Rothwell territory as long as Grandmama is alive.'

'I was never a reliable fellow; why expect me to stand by my word now?'

'That's not true, Alan.'

'You're too soft, Cat.'

She sighed.

'I won't be so obvious as to say you are too hard. I'm still glad you came to see Nanny. She misses you. What did you think about your meeting with Miss Wallace?'

'*Meeting* isn't quite the word I would use. The only thing I nearly met was the business end of a mace. What on earth is someone like her doing at Ravenscar and how is she Albert's heir? This family is altogether too complicated. Is she another dreaded Rothwell? I thought they were all safely tucked away north of the wall.'

'Goodness, no. Her mother was a distant cousin on Grandmama's side and made what initially was a *mésalliance* with an impoverished young man, only to have him become one of the wealthiest men in South America. He died a year ago and now Miss Wallace has returned to England to marry... Oh, dear, I shouldn't say anything because it is not yet announced. You mustn't repeat that.'

'I couldn't be bothered to, Cat. It is no business of mine.'

'Well, it might not happen anyway. Mr Marston is...'

'Marston? She is to marry Philip Marston?'

'You know him?'

'Very well. We share ownership of several loom manufactories. This is a small world indeed. I had no idea he was contemplating marrying again, but I'm not surprised he has set his sights on an heiress. He is one of the savviest businessmen I know.'

'I believe he is truly fond of her.'

'Of course he is, Cat.'

She sighed.

'You would do well to take a page from his

book. Perhaps if you married, Grandmama would relent and change her will in your favour.'

'We all know Jezebel won't leave me a crust of bread, married or not. She and Grandfather were clear enough about that when I left.'

'She might if you only tried to…to be concili-ating and mend your ways. She has become much less rigid since Grandfather passed.'

He stopped for a moment, raising his brow, and Cat flushed.

'Sorry. I know it is none of my concern. Well, it is, but it isn't. But I think pride is a poor sub-stitute for all this. It isn't just the money, but the Hall. This is your home, Alan.'

Alan smiled grimly at her tenacity. Cat might not have the Rothwell temper, but she employed a water-dripping-on-stone approach to attain-ing her ends.

'No, it ceased to be my home over a decade ago, or longer before that, when Grandfather forced our father to break the entail and dis-owned him for wanting to be a doctor. Let's not rehash this. I have no intention of mending my ways, as you so quaintly phrase it. I like my ways and they like me. Since I have no intention of ever spawning heirs, the Hall would be wasted on me anyway. Our Hibernian cousins are welcome to the Hall and all things Rothwell. I have to go, Cat. I have some pressing affairs to see to.'

She tilted her head as they approached the stables where his gelding waited.

'You're probably wise not to linger with everyone feeling poorly. You wouldn't want to fall ill.'

'That's not why and you know it!'

'Nicky was feverish last night and woke up with a headache. I'm worried she might also have caught the infection. She begged me to let her see you in Keynsham before you disappear again, but I cannot risk her leaving her bed while she is so poorly.'

'Blast you, Cat. Very well, I will see her quickly, but I'm not staying. I don't know why you even stay here after what that old witch put us through.'

'To be fair, it was mostly Grandfather. Yes, I know you can't stand it when I defend her and she is a horrid old harpy sometimes, but Nicky actually cares for her and I have her future to think of; I cannot afford to be cut out of the will like you, Alan. It is my responsibility to make my peace with her for Nicky's sake.'

'I can provide for you. I have enough to leave you and Nicky comfortable when someone finally puts a bullet through me.'

Cat wrinkled her nose.

'All from that mill you won gambling.'

He laughed.

'How the devil is my sister such a prude? My money is quite the same colour as Jezebel's, believe me.'

'Even so, who's to say you might not marry, and then where will Nicky be?'

'Let's just say there's more likelihood of my forgiving Jezebel than of my willingly entering a state of matrimony, Cat.'

'Oh, good.'

He sighed.

'I surrender. Come, I will sit with Nicky for a while and then I must leave. But we are entering by the back door.'

The sight that confronted them when Cat opened the door to Nicky's bedroom was not entirely that of a sickroom. Nicky was indeed in her bed, propped up against a mountain of pillows, her dark brown hair down about her shoulders and a glass with a viscous liquid on a tray by the bed, but she was laughing and she wasn't the only occupant of the bed.

'That's just silly—' Nicky stopped when Cat and Alan entered the room, crying out joyously, 'Uncle Alan, you came!'

Alan directed a wary look at Miss Wallace,

who was leaning against the headboard with her feet tucked under her and a book in her lap. He walked around the other side of the bed and bent to kiss his niece on the forehead.

'Of course I came. Not that there seems to be much wrong with you, pumpkin.'

'My head feels like I'm wearing a bonnet three sizes too small and I can hardly hold up my book and I had a fever last night and Lily says fevers often worsen in the evening. Are you staying? Please say you are.'

Lily. The name was far too whimsical and delicate for the spoilt heiress who had addressed his harridan of a grandmother so impudently. He sat on the bed and took his niece's hand, wondering why the heiress was still sitting there. Anyone with the least manners would have removed herself. She didn't even make way for Cat. Clearly she was used to the world arranging itself to suit her rather than the other way around. He focused his attention on Nicky.

'I can't stay, Nicky.'

'Because of Grandmama? If I ask her, she might let you. Shall I ask her?'

'You saw me last month when I came by your school.'

'That was last month. Just for a little while? You must hear this story. It's called *The Myster-*

ies of Udolpho and it is even funnier than *The Romance of the Forest.*'

'I didn't realise Mrs Radcliffe wrote comedies.'

'Well, they aren't really, but Lily makes them so. Especially the swooning and the groaning.'

Alan raised his brows and turned to the heiress. Any normal, proper young woman would have been off the bed and out the room like a scalded cat the moment he entered; instead she was curled up like a kitten against the pillows, her fingers tracing the gilded lettering on the leather-bound book, and her honey-brown eyes warm with laughter. The presence of his niece in the bed as well should have made her look less like a very expensive mistress holding court in her boudoir, but his unruly imagination compensated. His mind had already pulled the pins and ribbons from her glossy hair and set it tumbling over her shoulders, cleared the room of his sister and niece, and significantly enlarged the bed. Now he was left to imagine what she might look like under the fine powder-blue sprigged muslin, if the sleek lines of her figure were spare or carried some pliant padding waiting to be warmed, softened.

Cat's assessment came back to him—unshakeable. It was a sad trait of his that he hadn't yet met a cage he didn't want to rattle and right now the thought of shaking this pert heiress out of her amused condescension was adding fuel to an undeniable physical curiosity. He caught her gaze with his.

'Groaning? Is it that kind of novel?'

If he had expected to finally shock her, the shimmer of laughter in her honey-gold eyes at his suggestive question sent that hope to grass. Here was the same gleam of mischief in her eyes he had glimpsed in Albert's library and it had the same impact on his hunting instincts. He reined them in reluctantly. This was a game without a prize.

'I don't know what novels you are wont to read, Lord Ravenscar, but in this book the groaning and creaking is confined to the castles,' she answered, and her voice, at least, was prim.

'Still, hardly suitable reading material for a girl of twelve, don't you think?'

'Oh, but everyone reads her novels at school, Uncle Alan,' Nicky interjected. 'There's even a girl who swoons when we read them at night.'

'I think it is a very healthy sign that a twelve-year-old finds such novels amusing,' the heiress added.

'Are you speaking from experience, Miss Wallace? Were you also a voracious novel reader as a schoolgirl, then? That might explain it.'

'Explain what?' Nicky asked.

'I think your uncle is referring to my flair for dramatics, Nicky.'

'I would amend that to histrionics.'

'Would you? I believe I was rather calm in the face of a ransacked library and an intruder with a punishing left hook.'

'If being calm is brandishing a mace at a stranger, then, yes, you qualify. Besides, you didn't know about my boxing prowess until your burly protector arrived.'

'That is true. I dare say you would have thought better of me had I shrieked and swooned like a heroine from a novel. Would that have gratified your male pride and preconceptions of proper female behaviour?'

'It would have certainly been less tiring. Conversing with you is like going ten rounds with Belcher.'

'Alan,' Cat admonished, but without much conviction.

'Who is Belcher?' Nicky giggled.

'Belcher is someone who would have given your uncle the black eye he deserves, Nicky.' Lily laughed and again he found himself wondering whether there was anything that could truly unsettle this peculiar young woman. Either her defences were legion or she was truly without any depth and took nothing seriously.

It shouldn't matter and he should know better than to treat her laughing dismissal of his barbs as a challenge, but he leaned towards her, his weight on his arm, his fingers just skimming the spread of her skirt where it fanned out on the bed, pressing it into the coverlet, the embroidered blue flowers silky bumps against the pads of his fingers.

'If you are so bent on blackening my eye, go ahead. I won't retaliate.'

Lily Wallace's eyes narrowed, assessing, and he wondered if she might actually try to meet his dare. Her gaze scanned his face, as if she was searching for the right spot to place the invited blow. He should have been amused, but instead he felt a peculiar rise of heat follow the path of her inspection, pinching at his skin, and with a sense of shock he realised he was blushing. It had nothing to do with embarrassment and everything with a spike of undiluted lust thrusting through his body. Until now the heat of attraction had been speculative, familiar, unthreatening. In an instant it flared beyond that, like brushfire after a drought, unexpected and cataclysmic. It took every ounce of his self-control not to draw back from the fire, to keep his breathing even. It cost him, though, both his body and his vanity suffering—he should be well past the age for such conflagrations.

'I would never be so uncouth as to strike a man while I am a guest under his roof,' she said, but her eyes did slide away from his, her first sign of disquiet. It should have gratified him, but it just added to this unexpected agony. His mind reached for the lifeline of anger at her words.

'This isn't my roof, thank God. Ravenscar Hall is no longer entailed and I am certain old Jezebel has enlightened you that she would rather see it razed to the ground than left to the profligate Rakehell Raven.'

There was no amusement in her eyes now, but the emotions in them were anything but gratifying—he needed neither contrition nor pity, certainly not from someone like her. She turned to slip off the bed and for a moment her skirt caught beneath his fingers, riding up her legs, exposing the sleek line of her calf and the shadowed indentation of her ankle before escaping him.

Just like Nicky's headache, his skin felt far too small on him. The absurdity of reacting to the glimmer of a smile and the glimpse of a woman's ankle as if he had never seen an inch of female flesh in his life when just a few nights ago he had seen in full naked glory the whole extent of another woman's anatomy was not as obvious to his body as to his mind. He tried to look away but didn't, watching as she extended her leg to put on her slipper, like a dancer. What would she be like to dance with, this strange girl? In some dark room, music entering from outside so he could be alone with her and explore those curves under the expensive fabrics, test their softness, whether he could make the unshakeable Miss Lily Wallace quiver...

'We can continue reading this later, Nicky. Enjoy your time with your uncle.' Her gaze lifted to his from the preoccupation of putting on her slippers. For a moment she stood there and then turned and left, closing the door quietly behind her.

Then it was just the old nursery room that had been Cat's until her marriage, with her books and now Nicky's dolls on the shelves. The last time he had been here had been twelve years ago, the very last day he had set foot in the Hall until today. It had hardly changed, but he had. It was important to remember that.

He gathered himself and smiled at Nicky. She and Cat and his friends and his work were all that mattered in his life. In a few moments he would leave this house and hopefully never set foot in it again at the very least until the witch was dead and buried.

Chapter Four

Alan recognised his grandmother's old landaulet coming up the drive of the Carr property in Saltford before he even saw the occupants and braced himself. Having to face the old witch twice in a week after not seeing her for over a dozen years was surely a punishment not merited by any of his sins, at least not any recent ones. What on earth would she be doing coming to see an empty property up for sale a good forty minutes from the Hall?

The open landaulet drew abreast, revealing its occupants, but his tension only took a different turn. The fact that it wasn't his grandmother, but Miss Wallace seated beside Mr Prosper and an older woman who was clearly her maid, was just as unwelcome, but for very different reasons. By the hunted expression on the solicitor's face he shared Alan's discomfort at this development.

'I do apologise for my tardiness, my lord.'

'That is quite my fault,' Miss Wallace interceded. 'Since I not only insisted on taking up Mr Prosper in the landaulet when we drove from his offices to Hollywell, but then kept him overlong on my business there, I felt it only proper to ensure he arrive here as swiftly as possible rather than wait for his clerk to arrange for a gig to convey him here from the Ship. So I offered to see him here myself while his clerk arranges to bring the gig.'

'You are too kind, but there really was no need for you to put yourself out, Miss Wallace,' Mr Prosper replied, removing his hat to mop his brow despite the cold wind blowing. 'My clerk will be here presently with the gig, so you needn't linger. I assure you I will see to your requests for Hollywell with all promptness.'

Completely ignoring this polite attempt to send her on her way, Miss Wallace extended her hand and poor Mr Prosper had no choice but to help her descend.

Alan doubted Miss Wallace had been motivated by kindness. Curiosity was probably nearer the mark. But there was something in the smile she flashed him that put him on alert. Mischief and even anger, which surprised him. She hadn't struck him as resentful and, if anything, she might be considered the victor in their two previous encounters. His treacherous body was certainly declaring its utmost willingness to surrender if that would get him past her battlements. It was a sore pity she wasn't already married and disillusioned with wedded bliss. He would have enjoyed broadening her horizons, and his.

Other than the martial flash in her gold-flecked eyes she exemplified the perfect society miss. She was dressed in a very elegant forest-green pelisse with dark-gold military facings and a deceptively simple bonnet with matching ribbons. It enhanced her warm colouring and was far too elegant for the Somerset countryside. In fact, she looked more elegant than most fashionable women he knew in London. With her money and sense of style, she would do very well once she was introduced to London society. Though she would probably ruin it the moment she opened her mouth. London was not very forgiving towards pert young women, heiresses or not, especially if their background was anything but conventional.

On the surface she would make Philip Marston a perfect wife, but the more he saw of her the more he doubted whether Philip understood what he was taking on. In fact, if he had had to guess, he would have thought Philip would choose someone more like his own daughter—classically beautiful, well mannered, wealthy and biddable. Of those criteria Lily Wallace fulfilled only the requirement of wealth.

Not that it was any of his concern. His only concern at the moment was finding a new venue for Hope House, fast, and returning to London. However pleasant it was to watch the outline of her legs against her elegant skirts as she descended from the landaulet, there was nothing to be gained flirting with an heiress who was tangled up with his grandmother and the possible matrimonial target of one of his business partners, no matter how outré and intriguing. She might be different from the usual run of women he enjoyed, but then so would the inmates of bedlam be different. Boredom in the bedroom was no excuse for putting his head into the lion's mouth...or rather the lioness's.

She approached him and her smile widened. It wasn't a welcoming smile and he instinctively reacted to it with a contrary spurt of determination. His initial look around the grounds of this property and others in the environs had only reinforced his conviction that Saltford would not do and that Hollywell House was still the perfect choice for a new Hope House. The odds were long and getting longer, but he wasn't ready to admit defeat quite yet.

'Lord Ravenscar.' Even those two words were a challenge.

'Miss Wallace.'

'I'm surprised at you. Was it *The Mysteries of Udolpho* that gave you the idea?'

He frowned, confused. Was she incapable of a normal conversation?

'I beg your pardon?'

She cocked her head to one side, walking towards the house, and politeness required he keep pace with her.

'You do innocent very well for someone who has very little connection to that concept.'

'I must be very dense, but I have no idea what you are talking about.'

A crease appeared between her brows and she stopped at the foot of the stairs.

'The broken urn?'

'The what? Is this some form of biblical charade?' He had discarded his initial opinion that she was mildly deranged, but he might have to reconsider.

'The creaking door?' she tried, her eyes narrowing.

'Miss Wallace, either you have developed the fever or that rubbish you were reading Nicky is having a dilatory effect on your mind. What the deuce are you talking about?'

'Have you been back to Hollywell House in the past couple of days?'

'No, I have not. Why on earth would I?'

The society smile had completely disappeared and she was frowning as she watched him, as if waiting for him to slip up.

'It appears whoever vandalised the library has been back. That horrid large urn in the hallway was smashed and the effect was embellished with some atmospheric creaking of doors. The latter part might have been accidental, since the latch on one of the doors from the servants' quarters doesn't close properly, but the urn was too heavy to topple over merely because of the wind.'

Alan's fists tightened. The image of her standing in the middle of the mayhem of helmets, breastplates and books returned. With a wary look, Mr Prosper hurried past them up the stairs, a set of keys clinking in his hand. Alan took Miss Wallace's arm and pulled her slightly to one side. Mr Prosper and the house could wait.

'I admit I want Hollywell House, but I don't usually have to resort to such puerile tactics to get what I want and I assure you my taste doesn't run to the Gothic.'

He spoke casually, matching her lightness,

but he felt anything but light-hearted. If she had wreaked havoc to the library the other day and was now breaking urns and hearing noises, she was indeed deranged. If not, someone was actively vandalising the property, which was just as bad.

'I am not fanciful, Lord Ravenscar,' she said coolly. 'When such incidents occur in a house that should be standing empty, I presume someone is up to mischief. I admit I thought that you, rather melodramatically, had decided to add not-so-subtle persuasion to other inducements. If it wasn't you, it was someone else, and not a ghost. But whoever it is, and for whatever reason they may be doing so, it won't work.'

'If you don't know why they are doing it, how do you know it won't work?' he asked, just to annoy her, but his mind was half-focused on other matters. On who indeed might be behind these pranks and on how cold she could look when she chose to; she looked even more the perfect London hostess like that, but then her roguish smile broke through again.

'Must you ruin it by being clever? I had quite set my mind on you being the villain; it would have been so neat. Maybe you still *are* being clever. This could still be some devious machination so you could vanquish the ghost and hope to earn my undying gratitude so I would sell you Hollywell House after all. That would be a plot worthy of Radcliffe.'

'I haven't the imagination or energy for such nonsense,' Alan replied, thoroughly exasperated. Her laughing dismissal of the situation was even more annoying than a fit of hysterics would have been. What was wrong with this woman?

'No, I suppose not. You are not in the least romantic.'

She sounded so dismissive he couldn't resist mounting a defence.

'That is not the general consensus, I assure you.'

'I didn't mean *that* kind of romantic. The *real* kind of romantic.'

'I won't ask for the distinction. I haven't a strong enough stomach.'

'See? That is precisely what I mean. Well, this is most annoying. If you aren't my ghost, then who is?'

She frowned at the ground, scuffing at the gravel with the toe of a fine kid slipper. Why couldn't she act like a normal young woman and be scared? Not that he enjoyed hysterics, but it would be a nice change if she would look at him with something other than disdain or amusement. Those were not the emotions he ordinarily evoked in women. Not that trust or confidence were emotions he tended to evoke in women either, thank the gods, but at the moment he would prefer she not be quite so…unflappable.

'Aren't you in the least bit concerned? At the very least you should avoid going there until the source of this vandalism is uncovered.'

'I have requested that Mr Prosper put it about that the new tenants of the house are moving in, which I hope will discourage any further incidents. Why don't you go a step further and try to convince me that it is after all in my best interest to sell you the property?'

Alan gritted his teeth against the urge to tell her what she was welcome to do with Hollywell.

'I admit I want Hollywell, but I am perfectly capable of separating the two issues. Are you?'

She sighed.

'I don't know what I'm capable of any more. Come, I'm curious to see this house.'

'You aren't invited. Thank you for delivering Mr Prosper, but now you had best return to Lady Jezebel before it begins to rain.'

He wasn't in the least surprised she ignored him and turned towards the stairs.

'You are, without doubt, the most aggravating woman of my acquaintance. Barring my grandmother and that only by a very narrow margin.'

She turned on the top stair, her eyes narrowing into slits of gold, but the tantrum he had almost hoped for didn't materialise. For a moment she didn't answer, just stood there, her eyes on his dreamily, as if lost in an inner conversation. He couldn't remember ever being so disconcerted by a female who was doing absolutely nothing. Young women either fled behind their mama's skirts or used all their wiles to engage his interest, sometimes from behind their mama's skirts. He didn't mind either reaction. He very much minded being scolded, threatened, laughed at or ignored, all of which appeared to be this young woman's repertoire in her dealings with him. If she was doing it on purpose, he might have appreciated her tactics, but though she was clever, she was also peculiarly transparent and it was very clear she was not playing with him, not in that manner at least. Her gaze finally focused and she continued inside.

'I hadn't realised I had such power to provoke you, Lord Ravenscar. I am honoured to receive such an epithet from someone who has undoubtedly met more women than he can properly remember. I believe I read an adage somewhere that notoriety is preferable to obscurity.'

'You misread, then. The phrase is that notoriety should not be mistaken for fame.'

She wrinkled her nose, inspecting the empty drawing room Mr Prosper indicated. They entered and Mr Prosper hovered in the doorway, clearly uncertain whether his role included chaperon services. The maid, surprisingly, merely occupied a chair in the hall and took out a small skein of wool from a bag and began knitting.

'That sounds very stuffy and English. Was it from a morality play, perhaps? One of your grandfather's charming tomes?'

'Greek. Aesop.'

'Ah, that explains it. Wasn't he the one with the tale of the vainglorious Raven?'

'The same. And the crafty fox. How fitting. Your colouring does have a rather…vixenish hue.'

'Thank you. Most often the references are to lionesses, tigresses and other felines. It is a pleasant change to elicit associations to other animals, and a resourceful, intelligent one at that. I dare say given your colouring and name you are only too used to Raven and other fowl references.'

He laughed, crossing the room to where she stood by a window overlooking a scrappy lawn already giving way to the weeds and the weather.

'Especially foul. But I don't mind. Here's another quote for you: *"Censure acquits the Raven but pursues the dove."* So are you certain you wish to be practically alone with me in an empty house? What if I am overpowered by licentious and lustful urges?'

He didn't really expect her to be shocked, nor was she.

'I thought I was a vixen, hardly a dove, but in either case I at least am not so vain as to believe I am capable of evoking overpowering urges in anyone, let alone in someone as jaded as you, and certainly not under the watchful and censorious eyes of Mr Prosper and Greene.'

'You are quite right you are no dove. Doves are soft and padded and coo when petted. What do you do when petted, Lily Wallace?'

Finally a blush. But getting a rise out of her came at a cost of triggering an unwelcome reaction at the thought of petting her. First of peeling away those fashionable layers to the fine cotton muslin underneath. Such expensive fabrics would be near transparent once he stripped away the stays and chemise, a gauzy cobweb of a dress, like wearing the morning mist. Her hair would be a wavy tumble of warmth, a mass of shades, darker than her eyes. She might be no dove, but her body would still be soft...

'Shall we see the other rooms, my lord?' Mr Prosper asked from the doorway.

Alan nodded.

'Yes. Let's start with the bedrooms.'

* * *

Within fifteen minutes of their arrival Alan knew the property wasn't suitable. The only reason he didn't call a halt to their exploration of the old house was Miss Wallace—her curiosity and her attempts to manoeuvre him into disclosing his agenda were too amusing to curtail. Curiosity seemed to work on her in the same way greed worked on some people. In that way she reminded him of his friend Stanton—he could never abandon a problem until he had cracked and subjugated it. But if she was like Stanton, once her curiosity was assuaged, she would be off in search of the next challenge and Alan was rather enjoying her persistence and the effect it had on her natural wariness.

She still didn't trust him an inch, but she was showing a surprising degree of faith in his honour merely by being with him for so long with only a timid solicitor as chaperon. There was an aura of dismissive superiority about her that was worthy of the most spoilt of heiresses and yet she had none of the calm ease of entitlement that women like Penny Marston had. She was no pampered house cat, but a prowling half-wild feline, used to fending for herself. Catherine must have misunderstood—there was no possible way someone like Philip Marston would contemplate marriage with a woman who would challenge his authority at every level, not even for a fortune.

Mr Prosper opened the door into what had probably been an attempt at a library and stood back to allow them to enter. 'This is the last of the rooms,' he announced from the doorway, his eyes darting from them to the darkening window, where the sun was still battling with the clouds lying heavily on the trees. 'We really should leave before it begins to rain in earnest. Shall I find your maid and have the landaulet ready for you, Miss Wallace?'

'Thank you, Mr Prosper, that is very kind.'

Alan waited until the solicitor left the room and went to stand by Lily, where she was inspecting the moulding on the fireplace, her long fingers tracing an elaborate engraving that had long since been worn down to runic incomprehensibility.

'You should have fled while you could, Miss Wallace. I'm afraid your curiosity is about to be repaid with a soaking.'

'I have survived worse.'

'So have I. Even during the last hour.'

She laughed and began pulling on the gloves she had removed while inspecting the carvings.

'What, the house or my presence? Was it so very terrible?'

'It could have been better.'

'How?'

'We could have been alone.'

Finally there was a little surprise and even more wariness. But as he expected, she gathered herself and ploughed forward rather than succumb to the momentary confusion.

'Is Keynsham proving so thin of female company, then, my lord?'

'Not in the least. We are close enough to Bristol to provide for all matter of needs. But variety is the very spice of life and my fare has been somewhat bland recently.'

'Oh, you poor, poor rakehell, are you bored? How simply awful for you.'

Her tone dripped mock-concern, her eyes wide in a wonderful parody of tragic distress, and he tried and failed to restrain his grin. He kept playing into her hands and the worst was he didn't mind it in the least. The only thing he minded was that this flirtation could not be carried to its natural conclusion. Society's mores and rules might be hypocritical, a bore and a nuisance, but up to a point he abided by them simply because it was less of a bother to do so than flout them.

It was rare that his mind parted company with his body so categorically, but as he watched her concentrate on securing the glossy pearl buttons of her glove, her lashes lowered, fanning shadows over the faint dusting of freckles on her cheeks, he felt the distinct separation of those two entities.

She was not the kind of woman he enjoyed and she was not the kind of woman who enjoyed him, but his thumb very much wanted to brush over her long dark lashes and those freckles and down the soft rise of her cheek. He could almost feel it just watching the way those dark spikes, touched with gold at the tips, dipped and rose as she secured her gloves.

The urge became a distinct ache as his gaze descended. Despite her humour, her lips were pressed together, betraying a tension he had sensed from the moment he met her. She might be an indulged heiress, but she was not some frothy confection one could sink a spoon into and taste with impunity. He had never liked syllabub anyway. He preferred spice and this girl was definitely on the spicier end of the female scale. He wondered what she would taste of…if he could coax those tightly held lips into relaxing…

'I counted ten bedrooms and four larger rooms downstairs and two smaller parlours. Smaller than Hollywell House. Does that meet your needs?'

He could almost see her mind working away

at the problem, taking every piece of information he had dangled in front of her and trying to shove it into place to create some conclusive picture. It was so tempting to throw in a few red herrings and watch her grasp at them with that mix of puzzlement, suspicion and determination, like a kitten pursuing a dangled string as if it were a lifeline.

'Do you know what you remind me of?'

Her eyes narrowed.

'I'm not going to like this, am I?'

He laughed.

'Probably not. Forget I said anything. What do you think of the gardens?'

She looked out the window.

'I wouldn't precisely call that a garden. Would you need a garden?'

'A ferret.'

'You need the garden for a ferret?'

'No, you remind me of a ferret.'

He waited for the inevitable outrage to darken her eyes before he continued.

'Not physically, of course, though ferrets can be quite elegant in appearance. It was a reflection on your tenacity and curiosity. Ferrets are also very hard to catch.'

'They also bite. Hard.' Her teeth snapped shut and steam practically rose off her in waves, her fingers unfastening and refastening the last few pearl buttons on her left glove like prayer beads. He removed her hand from the maligned buttons and pressed it between his. It was warm and vibrating with the energy caged inside her, a tingling force.

'I'm surprised any of your buttons survive to the end of the day, the way you worry at them.'

She surprised him again. He had expected her at the very least to pull away and more likely to slap him or resort to the verbal attacks she had engaged in at Hollywell, but instead she smiled and for a moment he had the sensation of the sun thrusting conclusively through the clouds. It certainly had the same effect—a need to narrow his eyes to protect himself.

'They often don't,' she admitted. The tension seeped out of her hand, but she didn't remove it from his grasp. She was doing absolutely nothing, but the sensation of her gloved hand in his was spreading through him like dye in water, swirling and expanding. It hadn't occurred to him his teasing would circle back and take his flank with a full attack of lust. He waited for it to peak and settle into place as all surges of physical attraction did. These pleasant sensations came and went and meant very little in the end. He had outgrown the need to pursue and indulge them, preferring to find physical release with a few very select female friends who knew the rules of the game as well as he and who could be trusted to be discreet and clean and emotionally detached from the act. He had nothing against window shopping, but he no longer bought anything on a whim, certainly nothing as expensive and impractical as a malapert, opinionated heiress.

He dropped her hand and returned to the gargantuan and very ugly fireplace, seeking a mental rope with which to haul himself out of this particular pit, something that would categorically drive her away.

'What do you think? Is it big enough for my harem?'

Lily watched as Lord Ravenscar ran his hand along the dark marble mantel that topped the oversized fireplace, his fingers rising and falling over the moulding. She clasped her own hands together, quashing the tingling heat that lingered from his clasp and made her gloves feel too tight. She had needed just this kind of comment to centre her. It was her fault for initiating the game in the first place. It took her three breaths to find her place again in the order of things. Lily Wallace, heiress. Needs no one and no one tells her what to do. Certainly not a rakehell like Lord Ravenscar.

Almost an hour had passed since they had arrived in Saltford and so far every one of her attempts to uncover his objective had run aground. The only thing she had learned was that he enjoyed dangling decoys and watching her twist to his taunts. She turned resolutely to inspect the fireplace.

'The fireplace? If you like your women short and round, it might fit three.'

He smiled and she felt petty, like a child who was being ignored by her elders and who had just thrown something merely to draw attention to herself.

'Do you like it?'

The change in his tone shoved her further off balance. He had done that before, reach inside her with his voice, set her insides reverberating like the cavern of a bell.

'What?'

'The house, Lily. Do you like it?'

She turned away from the focused force of his eyes and the taunting intimacy in his use of her given name. She was being ridiculous. For the past hour she had trotted after him, provoking and needling, and now that she had his full attention on her, she felt a panicked need to deflect it. She could hardly imagine he was being serious about a harem. He was just poking fun at her thwarted curiosity. But those questions had rumbled, no, purred through the cold room and shot heat through her just as that short clasp of her hand had. She could feel it in her cheeks and in her chest, like brandy swallowed too fast.

Do you like it?

She went over to the window just in time to see the sun lose its battle against the clouds, casting the overgrown lawn into shadow with the suddenness of a dropped blanket. It made the world, the house, the room, smaller. Maybe these peculiar sensations were a sign she, too, was falling ill. It would almost be a relief. No one would expect anything of her if she were ill. She could hide in her room and embrace oblivion, and maybe when she came out the other end of the tunnel, this discomfort would be gone and by some miracle her fate would be decided for her.

'It's not a complicated question, Lily. Do you like the house?'

He was standing directly behind her now.

'No, I don't.'

'Why not?'

She breathed in and answered only the question.

'It feels sullen. Everything is a little too small,

a little too low. I would stifle here. The only thing generous here is the fireplace.'

'You need space.'

Yes, so move away, you're crowding me. She didn't say the words aloud because that would be to pander to his vanity. She frowned up at the clouds. They were gathering in the east. That way was Bristol and ships heading out towards the West Indies and what had once been home but could never be that again.

'Don't you?' she asked.

'I am used to making do with what is at hand.'

'I see. We are back to that. I'm spoilt, I suppose.'

'Most heiresses are. It's not a matter of choice. Or rather it is a matter of too much choice. They can't help themselves from expecting more than they need.'

'How kind of you to be so understanding of my flaws.' Lily thought of the life she had led until her mother's death and wondered what he would have made of their spartan existence on the island or in the mining towns in Brazil. As far as he was concerned, she was the product of the life she had led in Kingston.

He moved to her side, looking out over the grass and weeds as they snapped back and forth in the rising wind. He was so close she felt the fabric of his coat against the sleeve of her pelisse. She wouldn't turn to look because that would give him the satisfaction of knowing how aware she was of him. How many times had she played this game in the drawing rooms and ballrooms of Kingston? She was good at it. It was just another tactical game. His move, hers, his move, hers. In the end she always won because for her it was merely tactics, she had no strategy, nothing she wanted to gain. What she wanted from life had no connection to that game any more than it had to a game of chess. Less. But now that her father was gone she knew those games were over. Now, when Philip Marston returned from Birmingham, she would likely concede and start her new life.

'Since I have so many flaws myself, it would be rather hypocritical to be intolerant of others,' he answered. 'Besides, perfection is vastly over-rated. My closest friends are deeply flawed and much the better for it.'

'I will hazard a wild guess there are no spoilt heiresses among them.'

He laughed and his coat brushed against her arm, raising and lowering the fabric against her arm, and her skin bloomed with goose pimples.

'Not one. One very unspoilt heiress, but she is married to one of my closest friends.'

That was a good excuse to turn towards him and put some distance between them. She was also curious. There was something in his voice. The same tone as he employed with Nicky—intimate and affectionate; a combination that didn't match what she knew of him.

'So you admit the possibility of an unspoilt heiress?'

'There are always exceptions to the rule. In this case Nell wasn't spoilt by being society's darling for years.'

That struck home. She couldn't deny that that was precisely what she had been since her father had brought her to Jamaica after her mother's death when she was fourteen and especially since she had been introduced to Jamaican society four years after that. Not that she had ever believed it meant more than an avid appreciation of her father's fortune.

'Once you start admitting exceptions to rules, you rather undermine the whole point of having them. How do you know I'm not an exception as well?'

'Are you?'

'That is hardly a fair question. Even if we aren't special, we all want to believe we are. Otherwise how could we believe we are worthy of being loved?'

A gallant man would have entered through that wide-open door, but he merely smiled and changed direction.

'I think I've seen enough of this house. We should leave before the weather turns against us completely.'

She didn't move, piqued even though she knew that was precisely what he intended. They were unevenly matched—he was much more experienced in this game, especially since his livelihood probably depended on his performance. She flirted out of boredom and resentment against the constraints society imposed, while he did it for survival. The tales of the Wild Hunt Club that Nicky had delighted in might be grossly exaggerated, but not this man's skill at the game she merely dabbled in. She would hardly sit down with him for a game of cards and put her fortune at risk even if she had control over it, and she should adopt the same caution when it came to the game of flirtation.

It was clear he wasn't really interested in her as an heiress; he would hardly be showing his cards so generously if he was. Well, she wasn't interested in him, not in any way that mattered. She would never marry a man she didn't trust and she would never trust a rake; a fortune-hunting rake famed for his wildness was just adding insult to injury. At least she knew Philip Marston was at his core a man of honour.

But whether it was intelligent or not, the truth was she didn't want to leave yet. Just another sip of champagne before teatime.

'Was your friend who married the heiress part of the Wild Hunt Club as well?'

He leaned against the window frame and crossed his arms.

'Is that nonsense still circulating?'

'Is it nonsense? It was Nicky who told me. Quite proudly, in fact.'

At least she had managed to catch him by surprise.

'Nicky? What on earth would she know about it?'

'You would be surprised what one hears at a girls' school. It's not all Gothic novels and sighs, you know, even though her version of your exploits did sound rather Gothic. Apparently association with you is quite a cachet for her at school.'

'Good God. Does Cat know about this?'

'I don't know, but I presume she does. Your sister may be quiet, but she's no fool. You didn't answer my question.'

'You see, this is precisely what I was talking about. You seem to think you are entitled to answers simply on the strength of asking a question. Life doesn't work that way.'

'I know that. Everything has a price. I can't force you to answer. I am merely inviting you to do so.'

'Inviting. I see. Tell me what Nicky told you—I'm curious what nonsense they are allowing in that very expensive school of hers.'

'Nothing too outrageous. Merely some nonsense that you and your friends always win races because you made a pact with the devil for that privilege. Oh, and that when the three of you ride at night, virtuous women must hide indoors or be swept up in the wild hunt, never to return.'

She didn't know what the amusement in his eyes signified—a male appreciation of his potency or a reaction to the absurdity of the tale?

'Nicky told you this? What nonsense you women subscribe to. I assure you virtuous women are probably the segment of your sex most likely to be safe from the members of the so-called Wild Hunt Club. We prefer responsiveness from the subjects of our midnight raids and virtue is… What is the opposite of an aphrodisiac?'

'Marriage, apparently.'

He burst out laughing.

'Damn, you're wasted as one of that group. You would have made an excellent courtesan.'

He meant to shock her and in a way he did, but it wasn't her virtue that was shocked, but her body.

The thought of being free from all the restraints that held her, body and mind. The possibility of being free to walk up to this man and demand what she wanted...

She shook free of the foreign urge. Because his words also raised the unwelcome memory of that house in Kingston, of the shocked faces of the women who had faced her after her father's death, aware their fate was now in her hands, scared and defensive and even pained. Some of them had truly cared for her father. As far as society was concerned, those women were worse than nothing; they were succubi who destroyed the lives of good men. She hadn't seen that when she stood in that opulent room with its red velvet sofas and lewd paintings. She saw women...some of them younger than she, whose fates had never been their own, at her mercy as they had been at her father's mercy and at the mercy of men like him. As long as they were young and performed their duties, they were adored and then... That night had been the first time she had cried for her parents and especially for herself.

In a less fortunate life she might have had no choice but to become one of those women who had nothing to trade but themselves. Then she, too, would have been at the mercy of men like her father and the members of this Wild Hunt Club, who thought they were somehow redeemed because they didn't pursue virtuous women.

'I don't think so, Lord Ravenscar. No one could ever pay me enough to endure the life those poor women have to endure. Now, as you said before, we should leave before it begins to rain.'

He stopped her by moving to block her path.

'I didn't mean to insult you. Believe it or not, that was a compliment.'

'I do believe it, which is precisely why I find it so offensive that you would assign any positive value to a fate where women have to sell their bodies to survive. It might be a better fate than many women have to face in this world, but it is no compliment. As someone dependent on the frailties of others to make your living, Lord Ravenscar, you should know that better than others.'

There, she had crossed a line and she was glad—finally Rakehell Raven was beginning to show his true colours. The transition from amusement to contrition to fury was as rapid as the explosion of a tropical storm, and the complete collapse of his façade fed her own anger and pain.

'See, it isn't quite so complimentary to be labelled a whore, is it?' she all but spat at him.

'I didn't label you…'

'No, you merely thought it amusing to pay me the *compliment* that I would make a fine doxy. You might not mind the label or the role, but excuse me if I fail to find it entertaining.'

'Not that it is any of your business, but I do not frequent courtesans. I prefer women who enter into arrangements of mutual pleasure of their own accord.'

'Even if I believed you, it only means you would label me somewhere below that breed, so excuse me for not finding your excuses any better than your insults, Mr Rakehell.'

She was too angry to prepare for the move, and once he had grasped her shoulders and pressed her back against the wall, she was damned if she would show fear.

'Careful, Lily Wallace. The fact that you are a woman offers you a certain measure of protection, but no more. Don't push your luck.'

She flattened her palms against his chest and pushed.

'Don't threaten me. I am not gullible enough to be cowed by that Wild Hunt Club nonsense.

You insult me, I'll insult you right back, Alan Piers Cavendish Rothwell.' She tossed back his name at him, in conscious imitation of that moment when Lady Ravenscar had walked into the library at Hollywell. He was not myth. He was just an ill-behaved boy used to people bowing and scraping before his undeniable beauty and charm. Well, she *never* bowed.

She had expected more ranting, not capitulation. She had expected to push him over the edge, but contrarily the fury receded, lightening his eyes from near black to the stormy grey reflecting the building pressure outside the window. They were still heavy with anger and heat, but there was also speculation there. Though he didn't give an inch to the pressure on his chest, the hands that grasped her shoulders softened and shifted—one to cover her own hands where they pushed against him, the other to slide softly down her cheek, leaving a scorched trail as it went before settling on her neck, his thumb just brushing her jawline.

'That was ill done of me. I'm sorry.'

The *bastard*! A sincere apology was the sneakiest, most dastardly tactic of all. It tugged back the tide and left her high and dry and defenceless. If she had held the flanged mace in her hands in that moment, she would have been so tempted to swing and let loose this explosion of fury and confusion. Either that or burst into tears. Something, anything to reflect the extremity of the pressure inside her.

'I'm curious why you flared like that,' he continued, his voice soft, musing. 'That was quite a nerve I touched, wasn't it? What is it, Lily? Is it not the first time someone has called you that?' His eyes were softening as he spoke, releasing his anger like an extended breath. 'No, it's not that, is it? Your impassioned defence indicates all your sympathy appears to be with the women you don't wish to be associated with. Strange.'

She pressed harder, but he didn't move. If anything, he leaned in against her palms, forcing her to feel the hard surface under the superfine linen, his scent closing around her, warm and musky like a tropical evening. The coolness of the wall behind her was no antidote as his heat poured through her, filling her.

'If you want to hit something, go ahead. I think I'll survive.' He didn't remove his hand from her throat, but with his other he curved the fingers of her right hand into her palm and held the fist against his chest.

She never allowed Greene to lace her stays too enthusiastically, but they felt tight now. The invitation to let the pressure inside her loose was so potent she didn't know how she would draw back. She had been so wrong about him. It might not be night-time, but she could feel the pull of this wild hunt. She didn't know what to do with everything inside her; it was all crowding at the door he was forcing open. The only thing holding her back was the conviction that even this was probably a game to him. He was back in control and she was within an inch of losing hers utterly.

'I wish to return to the Hall now.'

His thumb lingered on her chin, rose to skim the line of her lower lip and withdrew. He glanced out the window and exhaled slowly.

'That is probably a good idea. The world has decided to drizzle.'

Chapter Five

Lily wiped the drops from her cloak, but it was a losing battle. She was clearly being doubly punished for her foolishness in forcing her presence on Mr Prosper and Lord Ravenscar. The open landaulet had been a reasonable choice for a quick trip to Keynsham and Hollywell, but less suitable for a longer ride to Saltford in the swiftly shifting autumn weather. Right now the wind was driving rain straight at them and poor Greene was hunched on the seat by her side in mute misery, grumbling under her breath about English climes, English food and English roads.

The coachman glanced back at them, the rain running off the brim of his low-crowned hat.

'There's an inn just over that rise, miss. Small but respectable. Mayhap you should put up there until this blows over or I could go to the Hall and bring the closed coach.'

Greene looked up at that, her face damp and mottled in the cold, and Lily sighed. It was only half an hour further to the Hall, but it was enough for them to be thoroughly soaked.

'Thank you, yes. The coach is a lovely idea.'

The inn was a modest white-and-grey building, but smoke was billowing from the chimney and at the moment that was all Lily cared about. The coachman set up a shout for the landlord and helped them down. Inside the low, narrow entrance the landlord stared at them in some dismay.

'You're more than welcome, miss, but as you can see this is just a country inn and the only private parlour I have has just been...'

'Taken. You are proving exceedingly hard to shake, Miss Wallace.' Lord Ravenscar stood in the doorway at the back of the public room. Even with her cheeks damp from rain, Lily felt the heat rise in them and was thankful for the absence of lighting. Even after her anger and their tense parting, there was no denying the pleasure she felt just at the sight of him.

It had been a very long time since she had felt this kind of fascination and never about a person and she knew that was dangerous. Watching him drive away from Saltford while Mr Prosper had climbed into the gig with his clerk, she had told herself it was all for the best that this was probably the last time she would see this man. She had repeated that uncomforting conviction the whole drive and it just made her pleasure at seeing him again so soon all the more bitter.

'Since the drizzle has become a torrent and there aren't many other inns on this road, it is hardly surprising we sought refuge here, too, my lord. I don't see why my presence here should discommode you.'

'Don't you? Pilcher, bring a warm drink to the parlour for Miss Wallace.'

'There is no need…'

'Don't be a fool. There's a decent fire in the parlour and none out here. Your maid can sit there and glare at me with her basilisk eye. Or if you are so concerned, I will take my ale out here.'

'I didn't mean…'

He stepped back, opened the door and waited, and with a sigh she entered the parlour. It was a cosy little room and the fire was high and welcoming. It was pointless to argue—with him or with herself.

'This is lovely, thank you,' she said, untying her bonnet and cloak. Greene took them and tutted.

'I'll take these to the kitchen and see if we

can brush the rain and mud from them before it settles, Miss Lily.'

Alan watched the door close behind Greene with a twisted smile and motioned Lily to the chair closest to the fire. She sat and extended her gloved hands towards the warmth while he settled on the other chair, folding his arms and stretching his boots out towards the flames.

Seated he appeared even larger than when he had loomed over her. It was ridiculous to be nervous because he was between her and the door, but the room constricted around them to just the small sphere of warmth around the fireplace. She had an outrageous, childish urge to smile at him. Foolishness.

'The maid appears to trust me more than the mistress,' he said after a moment.

'She trusts *me*, at least.'

'I noticed that. You cannot be quite the spoilt brat you appear if you command such loyalty from your groom and maid.'

'My heavens, that was nearly a compliment. Perhaps it is merely that I pay them exorbitantly for their unquestioning fidelity.'

'I can tell the difference.'

'How?'

'Distinguishing between varying shades of loyalty is a skill one develops when one's life depends on it. Where is your bruiser of a groom by the way? Why isn't he driving you?'

'I have sent him on an errand regarding Hollywell. Why, were you hoping for a rematch? Jackson would be happy to oblige. What did you mean about lives depending on knowing true loyalty? Were you referring to the war?'

Just as before he sidestepped her question and returned with one of his own.

'Have you reconsidered selling Hollywell?'

'Will you tell me what you want it for?'

'The ferret is back in force, I see. What difference does it make?'

The door opened and the landlord entered and placed a tray on the table, and the scent of apples and cinnamon filled the air. Lily's mouth watered.

'Miss's maid is helping your groom with your coat, Lord Ravenscar.'

'Thank you, Pilcher.'

Lily picked up her glass and breathed in the scent.

'Cider. I missed this in Brazil.'

He picked up his ale and smiled at her. For once, his smile was neither taunting nor seductive, but it hit her hardest. It felt so right to be sitting there with him. So comfortable and right.

'The simplest pleasures are often the best. Cheers.'

He would know, she reminded herself, struggling to dispel the completely inappropriate fog of wellbeing. He knew all about pleasure. That was all he cared about. His *own* pleasure.

'Will you be visiting Catherine and Nicky again before you leave?'

The cynical gleam returned, both disappointing and reassuring her.

'I'm afraid not. I have some business in the area and then I will be on my way.'

'Nicky will be disappointed. Catherine will, too, though she won't say a word, of course. She never does, but that doesn't mean she doesn't feel it.'

'Are you trying to work on my conscience? It is a futile effort, believe me.'

'I don't waste my time on lost causes. I was merely suggesting you might consider taking her with you to Bristol while you are in the vicinity.

'Why should I take her to Bristol?'

He looked genuinely puzzled, which added fuel to her fire.

'You must know Lady Ravenscar isn't given to entertaining, which means your poor sister spends most of the year cooped up at the Hall with no one to talk to but Lady Ravenscar and

Nicky when she is down from school. She is barely thirty years old and she should not be behaving as if she were seventy. Would it have been so hard to make some time to take her shopping or to an assembly, or are you too busy with your gaming hells and brothels?'

As the words poured out, she knew she was once more crossing a line, that her annoyance was in excess of its stated cause. It wasn't his fault she was marooned at the Hall until she made her decision, that she had no idea what that decision should be, that he kept pushing her out of her hard-earned equilibrium. None of it was his fault and yet it felt like it was. She drew breath, dragging herself back, and looked away from the smoky fury in his eyes.

'I apologise, Lord Ravenscar. It is quite clear you care for your sister and niece and I have no right to interfere in what I don't understand.'

'You're right. You don't.'

She wasn't given to blushing, but she felt the heat of mortification in her cheeks. She probably appeared both childish and shrewish, two attributes she hated. Perhaps he was right that her privileged position as heiress had spoilt her. Usually her sense of humour kept a rein on her temper, but this time she had gone too far.

She waited for the counter-attack, focusing on

the buttons of her gloves, sinking into the familiar ritual of buttoning and unbuttoning them to calm her nervousness. She had never worn gloves on the island and they had been harder to accustom herself to even than corsets. They felt clumsy and unnatural, separating her from the world and hemming her in. She slipped out the buttons one by one, counting out memories for each of them, far-gone memories of the little house in Somerset before their departure to Brazil, then her favourite corners on Isla Padrones, all the people she loved, living and dead, until she was calm and collected again. With each sleek slide of pearl through its loop, her mind settled a little: this one was for her little treehouse the gardener had built for her out of a shipping crate in the mango tree; this was for tickling the manatees with her bare feet when they came to beg in the bay for crusts; this one was for Augustus, who had been her favourite from the island's many half-domesticated dogs; this one was for…

His chair scraped against the floor and she looked up. He hadn't moved, but his gaze was on her hands. For some reason she froze, her fingers still with a pearl button partly unfurled. He had the most amazing lashes, long and definite and the only feminine element in a face that was too virile and male to be truly beautiful. They rose

now as she watched and he was close enough for
her to see a ring of darkened blue, the colour of
night that makes the eyes ache as they search it
for shapes.

'If you're going to take them off, then stop
playing with them and take the damn things off!'

'What?'

He moved with a suddenness that didn't even
give her time to tense, grasping her wrist and
swiftly unhooking the final buttons and tugging
off her glove, tossing it next to his on the table.
His hands were brusque, like an impatient parent,
but she didn't notice that, just the slide and scrape
of his fingers against her wrist as he worked.

When he took her other hand and unhooked
the first button with the same businesslike movement, she turned her arm over and pressed it
down on the table, blocking him. She didn't want
to be treated like an aggravating child.

'I'll do it.'

But he didn't let go, just sat there clasping her
wrist in his hands. She tugged at it, but he tightened his hold. This time she didn't resist when
he turned her hand over, because this time it was
different.

She watched his hands, dazed. Was it possible
that they were even more beautiful than his face?
No, they were too rough-looking to be beauti-

ful, with a series of small white scars along the back of his right hand and one cut still unhealed along the softer skin between his thumb and forefinger. They were the hands of a man who used them for more than gambling and seduction, but they were still mesmerising. They also had to be quite large to make hers look so small by contrast. She didn't have the dainty hands and narrow wrists so admired by men. Her father would make fun of what he called her pianist hands that could span a whole octave when she played on the warped old pianoforte for the islanders. But as Lord Ravenscar's long dark fingers uncovered the pale length of her forearm and the greenish veins at her wrist, she felt fragile, breakable.

He was moving even more slowly now than she had, as if it was a physical effort to continue. Then as the edges of her glove peeled back to reveal the heel of her palm, he raised it and with one finger traced the line between wrist and palm. Her fingers twitched and her body breathed in that faint flush of skin on skin. It lit up the whole right side of her body, ending in a tingle along her cheekbone.

She wanted him to kiss her there. Press that beautiful taunting mouth right there, just as lightly. And then…

'Damn.'

His curse was soft and didn't seem connected to anything, but it rang through her like a stone dropped into a well. His face had an abstracted look as he inspected her hand. It should have sobered her, but it didn't.

She held herself completely still, waiting, but inside her was a rising blaze of a fire that demanded she *do* something. She just had no idea what. He might think her bold, but to do what she wanted to do right now, grab his hand and pull him towards her, make him kiss her, make him peel back much more than her glove, was so outrageous she could hardly believe she was even thinking it. Not thinking it, feeling it, her whole body drawing life at the moment from the contact of his fingers on her wrist. Her legs were clenched, pressing together hard, trying to hold something down.

Maybe she *was* falling ill after all. It must be that. This heat and discomfort and…and *something* made no sense otherwise. This was the fever and it was hitting her hard. She should tell him she needed to get back to the Hall. Soon. Before it became worse.

But she didn't say anything. Not even when his hands started moving again, his thumb sweeping over the skin he exposed, from the line he had traced gently over the hills and valley of her palm and up each finger, curving over its crest and resting at each tip for a moment before continuing to the next. She looked away from the damage he was wreaking, but her eyes caught on his face, intent, calm, utterly focused on what he was doing. Until he looked up.

The dark grey had melted into night and she was just melting. No one had ever looked at her like that, or if they had, she hadn't noticed. No, no one she had ever met *could* look like that. She could give credence to tales of the Wild Hunt, of seductive devils rising from the depths of hell to tempt unwitting maidens who wandered out after dark. Except that it wasn't dark and they were in the private parlour of a small English inn in Somerset in the middle of a rainstorm and she didn't believe in devils any more than she believed in ghosts.

He was just a man.

But she was just a woman.

She hardly noticed her hand stretch under his, her fingers scraping against his palm as it lay lightly on hers, but it had the desired effect. His hand closed on her wrist and he drew her towards him, over the table, his other hand closing on her nape as he stood up, drawing her to her feet, moving towards her.

She opened to the kiss as if it was the most

natural thing in the world. As if she had known this man for years rather than days and this intimacy was part of her own existence, natural, reaching deep inside her to places no one else was allowed.

She didn't know what she had expected, her experience of kissing was just another part of her role as heiress pursued—she had toyed with it and discarded it as interesting but hardly worth the annoyance when kissing turned to pawing. God, had she been wrong. She had had no idea…

She hadn't expected the very contact of his mouth on hers to pour liquid heat through her, to reach even to her toes and fingertips like an ancient spell bringing a statue to life. She needed more; she wrapped her arms around his neck, raising herself on tiptoe, unable to stop her body from pressing against his hard length. A sound burst from deep inside her, a cry of yearning that she had no control over. It was a mistake. He pulled back, his eyes narrowed as if in pain.

'Lily…' It sounded like a protest, but she ignored it. She wouldn't let him stop. She could touch him; her hands realised it before her and were already moving over him, feeling the grain of his skin from the hard angle of his cheekbone to the scrape of stubble on his cheek, then into the warm silk of his hair at his nape, the taut rise of muscle and sinew as he held himself rigid. But when she pressed her mouth to his, sliding against the smooth heat of his lips, he groaned and dug his hand into her hair, angling her head and taking control. No one had ever dared kiss her like this, hard, demanding, his tongue seeking hers, torturing her sensitised lips, nipping at them before suckling them into quivering submission as he moulded her body to his. Her hesitant exploration was submerged in the force of the embrace and she just clung, waiting for disaster or salvation, little whimpers coursing through her without even realising, gathering force.

'Lily...' The single word shivered through her, a whisper of wind high above the storm. He had warned her. She understood the danger of the wild hunt now that it was too late.

She didn't hear the knock and didn't understand why he was suddenly halfway across the room until Greene walked in and laid Lily's cloak over a chair. Without a word he picked up his gloves and hat from the table and left the parlour.

Chapter Six

Alan opened his eyes and stared at the sooty beams.

Had the already cramped rooms at the Ship shrunk overnight?

The dun-coloured walls leaned in, mean and oppressive, and a draught whistled past the warped window frame. No wonder the room was so cold; it felt even icier under the blanket than out of it. He debated staying where he was. What was the point of getting up anyway? The sky outside was still depressingly grey and he would likely only get soaked a third time. Neither he nor Jem had enough clothes with them to spare another dousing like the past couple of days they had spent driving around looking for a new property, none of which had proved any more suitable than the house in Saltford. The only benefit of the massive discomfort had been to distract him, partially, from the persistent and uncomfortable memories of his idiocy at that inn.

Idiocy. The word felt woefully inadequate in the face of the physical torture that careened through his body just at the memory. His mind had never before clung so tenaciously to the sensations of a body pressed against his, to the unique, intoxicating flavour of a woman's mouth and skin. It lingered at the tips of all his nerves and at his core, an aching accusation.

How had he allowed a kiss to so completely escape his control? Her avid response had surprised him and all but knocked him off his feet, but that was no excuse. That was just it; there was no excuse for what he had done.

He turned on his side, trying to stifle his treacherous thoughts and gather the resolution to get out of bed and send for some firewood. His back ached, probably from the sagging bed. His head ached, probably from sheer frustration at being in this cursed corner of the world where everything always went wrong.

But the most abused organ at the moment was his pride and it was about to get worse. After a whole day and a half of marshalling every argument against debasing himself, he knew there was no getting around it—he would have to apologise to that vixen. She might have given his

temper plenty of provocation, but he was responsible for losing it and his pride dictated he swallow it and apologise.

Damn the girl. She would have served him
better if she had swung that mace at him the
day he came across her at Hollywell House so he
could have been knocked out and not fallen into
Jezebel's trap in the first place. Then he would
have taken himself off safely to Bristol and could
have avoided making a thorough fool of himself.

It served him right for teasing her. What the
hell had he been thinking...or rather why the
hell *hadn't* he been thinking? He never should
have succumbed to the informality of her behaviour and engaged in conversations with her that
were as improper as he could imagine with a
gently reared young woman who might one day
become the wife of a business partner, no matter how unconventional. Whatever the merits of
his reputation as a rakehell, not even in his wildest days had he crossed the line with marriage
material, out of pure self-preservation if nothing else, because if there was one price he was
unwilling to pay for his pleasure, it was matrimony. There was a little grey stone by the Hall
to remind him precisely why he would never proceed down that path, no matter what Catherine or
society thought. There were certain mistakes in

life one didn't make twice. Catherine had been too ill to remember, but he could never forget. He had lost his will and his right to a family before it was even a thought in his young mind. There would be no home and no children and that meant he stayed away from virtuous young women. In London he was careful not even to engage them in conversation unless he was safely in the despised but controlled confines of society's playgrounds. However little society trusted him, he trusted it less—it was the hypocritical domain of the likes of his grandmother, and if he gave it a finger, it would snap off his arm, pick the bones clean and beat him over the head with it.

So how the bloody hell had he crossed that acid-etched line with the impertinent heiress? Not just crossed the line, but all but pitched a tent on the other side. He had taunted her, insulted her, kissed her and was well on the way to doing worse if her maid hadn't appeared in time.

He groaned and shoved back the blanket, shivering as he tugged on the bell and went to put on his dressing gown. His head felt heavy and he wondered if the ale he had drunk last night had been bad. It hadn't tasted off, but then the Ship wasn't the type of hostelry he was used to any more and anything was possible. It was too close to Bristol to cater to serious travellers and both the bedrooms and the fare were mediocre at best. He smiled at the thought—he had accused the heiress of being spoilt, but he himself was becoming quite spoilt. Either that or he was getting old. A few years ago he wouldn't have thought twice about staying in a much less commodious inn and a few years before that he had spent more nights than not sleeping on the rocky ground in Spain with nothing more than a scratchy, filthy blanket as cover and a knapsack as a pillow, hoping to make it through another day without being shot or skewered by a bayonet. Now he felt like a creaking, groaning octogenarian because his bed sagged and the window frames weren't true.

Maybe winning that mill at cards five years ago had done him a serious disservice. At the time he had considered it poetic justice—after all, he spent a pretty penny supplying his mistresses with the best in women's clothing, so perhaps it was fitting he should be making his fortune producing the finest muslin fabrics. Not that it had started out that way. The man who had staked the mill had actually laughed at the loss, admitting it was in such bad repair and so deep in debt he hadn't even been able to sell it.

At the time Alan had been furious and seriously considered tossing the key and deed into the Thames. Instead he had dragged himself up to Birmingham, a decision which had changed his life. In two years he had taken over two other failing mills, introducing light wrought-iron power looms with swift gearing and lighter dressing frames. That had brought him into contact with Marston and together they had invested in additional mills and more interestingly in a large manufactory of their newly patented power looms that were transforming the industry. It might not be good *ton*, but it sure as hell beat depending on his skill with horses and cards to make ends meet after selling out from the army. He had staffed both the mills and manufactories with men who had served under his command and then with more and more of the veterans floating around the country in search of employment. With Stanton and Hunter's help, he had transformed an old manufactory nearby into another Hope House, drawing veterans from all over the Midlands, and now they were doing the same in Bristol, or at least they had been until the building they had leased had caught fire. It had been sheer luck that none of the men and their families had died, but the temporary solutions they had found for them in Bristol were abysmal and made the Ship look like Prinny's Brighton Pavilion by comparison. Many of the veterans were already infirm and ailing. If they weren't going to succumb to inflammation of the lungs or worse, he needed to move them to a safer, healthier and larger home. He was through with people dying on his watch when he could do something about it.

He sat down on the side of the bed, drawing the blanket around his shoulders. He had plenty to do before he left Bristol, but before all else he had to gather the resolve to deliver the dreaded apology. If only he could gather the resolve to stand up.

He straightened at a knock on the door and Jem entered with an armful of firewood.

'Well, the landlord's ill, Captain. This place is going from bad to worse; the sooner we move on, the better.'

Alan watched Jem work at the fire.

'My thoughts exactly. We can stay at the Pelican in Bristol until we're done here.'

Jem glanced over his shoulder, frowning.

'You shipshape, sir? You're sounding rusty. Not like you to sleep in either.'

'I didn't sleep in. I barely slept at all. The damn place is like an icehouse. There's nothing wrong with me a decent room won't cure.'

'Getting soft, are we, Captain?'

'Getting old, Jem. Any chance you could find

some warm water for me to shave? I feel as rusty outside as in.'

'I'll take a toddle downstairs and see if there is anyone here not laid up.' He stopped by the door. 'Why don't you get back into bed, sir? At least until the room warms.'

Alan laughed. 'Good God, Jem. Talk about getting soft. What's got into you?'

Jem's shoulders hitched back.

'Nothing, my lord. You're looking a little grey about the gills, that's all.'

Alan sighed with annoyance but pulled his legs back on to the bed. After all they had been through during the long years of war, worrying about a draught was rather absurd. As was the suggestion that he might be sickening. He couldn't help the involuntary shiver that struck through him at the thought. It didn't matter how many years had passed since his parents' deaths, just being confronted with illness could make his mind dive for cover more effectively than any of the real physical threats he had faced during the wars. Seeing Nicky, flushed and feverish, had choked him, forcing him to adopt his best performance for her and Cat's sake. Cat understood, but she herself had been too ill during those weeks in Edinburgh to remember much of what had happened. He never, never wanted to be in that position again. He hadn't been strong enough then and he had only weakened with the years.

In a few moments he would dress, say his goodbyes to Cat and Nicky, grit his teeth and apologise to the vixen, and leave. Then he would do his best not to venture within a dozen miles of Ravenscar for another decade at least. This corner of England was obviously unhealthy for him in all respects.

Chapter Seven

Lily stared at herself in the silver-veined mirror. Her eyes looked huge and murky, a caricature of one of Nicky's desperate heroines. She was tempted to stick her tongue out at the despondent face before her, but Lady Ravenscar's sermons were clearly having an effect and she merely turned her back on the distorted image. Such a childish gesture would be in keeping with her rather more serious act of running away.

Or was it considered running away when one had already arranged one's return and had covered one's tracks?

She crossed the library to place the ornate wooden box with one of her father's silver-tooled duelling pistols on the desk within easy reach. She had left the other one in the bedroom which Mr Prosper's housekeeper had prepared for Lily's 'guests' due to arrive from Jamaica any day now.

The housekeeper had tentatively offered to find servants to occupy the house, but she had accepted Lily's assurance that her guests were arriving with a full complement of their own.

She felt worst about lying to Jackson and Greene, sending them to see their families while she was supposed to go by post-chaise for a flying visit to an old schoolfriend near Bath. Greene particularly had been offended, but the chance to visit her sister after decades abroad won out over professional pride.

So now Lily had three days of absolute solitude in a clean and fully stocked house before the post-chaise she had hired in Bitton returned to collect her and return her to the Hall. The raging wind and threatening clouds outside only made her feel safer. There was no chance anyone would be wandering about the countryside and wondering about the lights peeping out from the curtains in what was supposed to be an empty house. For the next three days she could be alone, utterly alone, in her house.

She spread her arms wide, closing her eyes to encompass the whole of the house in her mind just as she had tried to encompass their little island as a child. Part of her might fear being condemned to loneliness, but she was familiar with it, even comfortable—it was her sanctuary when the noise of life held her back from thinking clearly. Right now she needed that clarity more than ever—she was about to make the most momentous decision of her life. That was why she needed to come to Hollywell—she had a childish conviction that if she could only be utterly alone in a space that was hers and only hers, untainted by memory or disillusion, she would know what she should do about Mr Marston's proposal.

Well, not quite untainted. Just standing in the library made it very clear it was now distinctly tainted with the image of a very large, handsome and unrepentant rake, blast the man.

She lit a wax candle from the flames of the fireplace and placed the candleholder on the big oak desk, running her fingers along its age-softened edge. Albert Curtis had probably written his sermons here and dreamed of the day he would leave it all behind and travel to the mission in Africa. What a pity he had not done so sooner. Another reminder how important it was to go after one's dreams while one could. Aside from the recent rake-related dreams, that is. Those would descend all too swiftly into nightmares.

She just didn't trust the kind of love her mother had abandoned her soul and pride for—in fact, she had developed a serious aversion to her mother's radiant joy when her father arrived on the island, as well as to her father's boyish excitement whenever he was newly on the hunt. Love between men and women, from what she had seen of it, was often either embarrassing, debilitating or downright damaging.

She wanted something better around which to construct the rest of her life. Something meaningful. She knew what her answer should be. When Philip Marston returned from Birmingham, she should say yes and start down the path to her dream of a family. She might have abandoned her young hopes of finding love, but she still yearned to have children. There was abundant love in her waiting to be shared and she wanted lots of children so they would have each other if something happened to her, or just so they would have each other to play with, to read to…

She tried to cling to the images that had accompanied her back to England, but with each passing day her fear was growing that in a marriage with Philip she would just exchange one prison for another. Even the promise of children was no longer enough to calm this fear. She knew what had shifted her from her path.

Admit it, Lily, for once, you are like all those other silly misses—fascinated by a handsome face and a sullied reputation, and piqued that a notorious fortune hunter didn't immediately start chasing you. You have become a thoroughly spoilt brat, just as he said. Well, you have come by your just deserts! He made a fool of you. No, you made a fool of yourself.

She squeezed her eyes shut against the memories that surged upwards again—of his hands holding hers, peeling back the gloves, touching her, his mouth on hers, warm and demanding, setting her alight…

It was like walking around with a bee sting embedded in her skin, knowing it needed to be removed, but afraid to pick at it for fear it would hurt as much in the removal, and all along it seeped venom into her blood, leaving her as feverish as poor Nicky.

It was just a kiss, for heaven's sake! She had been kissed before. That was one of the few benefits of being an heiress—she could flirt with relative impunity. He was an impressively handsome man and clearly well-trained, so why not enjoy a little light entertainment while she was immured here? That was all it was. She was confused only because he was so much more skilled than her past flirts. By a long stretch. She should have given credit to the tales indicating the notorious Rakehell Raven was in a different league from the men she had encountered in Kingston. Older, harder, more experienced and much, much more cynical. It was a salutary lesson not to rest on her laurels. Well, she was warned now. If she saw him again, which she doubted, she would avoid him. She had had her kiss. To invite anything else would be to invite trouble indeed. She might be arrogant as he had accused her, but she was no fool.

A thud echoed through the room and she dropped her book and jumped to her feet. It had been too close for thunder. Someone at the front door? The ghost again? No. She doubted ghosts wore boots. As footsteps approached the library, she wrested the mace from its steely grip and moved towards the desk where her father's pistol was waiting in its box.

'Not that again,' Ravenscar said drily as he opened the door and saw her.

She dropped the mace.

'Not you again,' she replied, her heartbeat thudding painfully in her ears. Fear, anger, relief and unwelcome heat were as tangled as the branches outside were by the storm. She could deny wanting to see him again until the stars stopped shining, but she couldn't lie about the excitement that lit her from within.

He shook the rain from his hat and placed it on the side table. He was dressed for riding and his caped greatcoat and boots were glistening with rain.

'I was riding through the field towards the Hall to say goodbye to Cat and Nicky and I saw the light in the library window. I thought your vandal was here. You should return to the Hall before this storm reaches its full potential. I didn't see a conveyance in the courtyard. Did your pugilistic groom take the horses to the stable? Shall I fetch him?'

His voice was stiff and measured. He was clearly unpleased to see her and against her better judgement it stung. He had also ruined her plans. There was no possible way he would not tell at least Catherine she was at Hollywell.

'Jackson has gone to visit his family. I will return to the Hall when I am through here.'

She expected incredulity or annoyance, but he merely moved into the room and sat down in the chair closest to the door. With the clouds still low, there wasn't much light in the room and it took her a moment to focus away from her discomfort and realise that he was behaving quite strangely. He might be a rake, but he was, up to a point, a gentleman. Common courtesy required that he not sit while she remained standing and the insult was pointed. She gritted her teeth.

'You may continue on your way to the Hall. I shall find my way back. Unless you are angling for another chance to convince me to sell Hollywell.'

He leaned his head back for a moment on the chair.

'No. I realise trying to convince you is a lost cause. But I still must apologise for my behaviour at the inn. It was unforgivable.'

His tone was at variance with his words. It was rough and dismissive and made a mockery of his apology.

'Please don't bother. I'm aware the first offence was mine, but there was no need for you to be so insulting.'

'Was that what I was? Some women might have considered it a compliment.'

'Some women might find you attractive,' she retorted, but she derived no satisfaction from the frown that followed her childish and mendacious dart.

'You didn't resist much at the time.'

'I'm impressed you recall one incident among so many, Lord Ravenscar. As for me, I see nothing wrong in gathering some new experiences here in England. It has been quite flat, isolated as we are at the Hall with only your relations to entertain me. So thank you for alleviating my tedium.'

There, that was a masterly exhibit of insouciance. She was quite proud of herself. Even when he shoved to his feet, a frowning menace, she held her ground and waited. But he just stood there for a moment, his hand on the back of the chair, and both her shame and pique began to fade. He looked different from two days ago. His face was pale and as her eyes ran over him she realised he was wavering slightly and the arm braced on the chair was gripping it too tightly. It reminded her of her father on the mornings after he had been out until the early hours of the morning, she realised with a spurt of outrage and resentment. No doubt he had been enjoying himself thoroughly at some tavern where men of his ilk went gambling and brawling or whatever it was men did with such abandon and which women were supposed to know nothing about. Well, when they showed up like this, how on earth were women not supposed to venture a very good guess?

'You are looking a little worse for wear, my lord. You might need some coffee.' Her voice dripped contempt and he directed her a look out

of half-closed eyes that was a combination of resentment and disgust.

'I need you to see reason and agree to sell Hollywell. Trust me, you don't want to live this close
to Old Jezebel. Besides, if you plan to marry
Marston, you will live with him and this place
will sit idle.'

She stared at him. How could he know that?
Had Catherine told him? It wasn't much of a be-
trayal, but it hurt. She had begun to feel she had
a friend in Catherine, but why should she expect
her to be loyal to her above her own brother?
They were family, after all, and she was nothing.

'What if I don't? What if I decide to live here
on my own? What if all I need is Hollywell?'

He didn't seem to register the childishness of
her protest as he rubbed at a point in the centre
of his forehead and frowned at her.

'You would live here alone?'

She turned away to look out at the lawn slop-
ing down towards the swaying trees and she followed his gaze. She could imagine sitting right
here with a book and a cup of tea. Would it be
so terrible to give up her dreams of a family?

'No. Probably not. I want children and I am
well aware of the cost gossip could have on their
future were I to choose to flout convention.'

Why on earth was she telling this man all this?

It was none of his business and it was a rather pathetic attempt on her part to prove she wasn't merely a selfish and pampered heiress as he had accused her. As if someone like him had any right to pass judgement. A more self-indulgent...

If she had expected her honesty would soften him, she was wrong. His face became even stonier.

'Of course, what woman doesn't dream of her perfect little home and hearth, surrounded by rosy-cheeked bairns. So we are back to Marston. He has enough houses already. He doesn't need Hollywell. We do.'

'Is that how you make ends meet? Help people find things?'

'No, as a gambler I make ends meet by helping people lose things. I'm surprised Jezebel hasn't made you a present of all my sins yet.'

'I must have become bored and stopped paying attention halfway through the list.'

He laughed and pressed the heels of his hands to his eyes in a strangely childish gesture. He really didn't look well, she realised. He was in no state to fence with her.

'You should probably return to Keynsham and sleep it off.'

He didn't answer immediately, but when he

pushed away from the chair, she watched in shock as his face turned an ashy grey under his tan.

'Damn…' he muttered and leaned back on the chair.

She moved towards him and instinctively reached out to touch his cheek before she even realised what she was doing.

'You're not drunk; you are ill!'

He recoiled from her touch as if she had slapped him.

'No, I'm not. Just tired.'

Even his voice was turning ragged. He cleared his throat and looked towards the door, his eyes half-closed, as if assessing the distance needing to be covered.

'We should go.'

For once, she didn't argue. He walked with the concentration of the very drunk, and if she hadn't known better, she would have believed he was indeed tipsy.

'Is your curricle outside?' she asked as they reached the library door and he paused, reaching out to lean his hand on the door jamb.

'No. My groom took it to Bristol. You wait here while I ride to the Hall and have them send a carriage for you.'

She gaped at him. He didn't look like he would make it from the library to the front door.

'You can't ride all the way back, you're ill. We'll do the opposite—you wait here and I will send someone from the Hall...'

'Don't be silly.' The word faded and he half-turned, leaning his back against the wall. The remainders of colour drained from his face and he watched her with a strange fascination, as if she was transforming before his very eyes. 'I might just need...to sit down for a moment...'

He was a great deal heavier than she was prepared for, but she put her shoulder into it and managed to half-coax, half-propel him towards a backless ottoman sofa which was almost long enough for his tall frame.

'My head...it's breaking...' he groaned as he sank down and then slid on to the cushioned armrest.

'It's too hard for that,' she murmured, touching her fingers to his forehead again. If anything, he felt hotter and his dark hair was clinging to the perspiration that was forming there. She must have been very unperceptive not to have realised immediately something was wrong with him. She had become so defensive around him she was losing her perspective. 'You have the fever. I will bring a pillow and some blankets.'

His eyes opened, a flickering, intense look that stopped her.

'No, I don't!'

The words were slurred, but the denial was very clear.

'I'm afraid saying it isn't so won't make any odds in this case, Lord Ravenscar. You most definitely have the fever. Doctor Scovell told us there have even been several fatalities in the past weeks, and if you don't want to put a premature end to your hedonistic existence, I suggest you rest here until I find some way of conveying you to the…to town.'

She corrected herself quickly. She was talking too much, she knew, a cover as much to mask her own fear as to forestall any resistance on his part. He should not be riding in this state and in this weather; he would probably fall off his horse and die of exposure if he didn't drown outright in the rain and mud-filled ditches.

'No…' He shifted, trying to lever himself up. 'I won't go…'

He was no fool; he had probably guessed her intention. She pressed her hands against his shoulders, holding him down more easily than she had expected.

'Fine, don't go. Stay here. I'll fetch blankets.'

He sank back and she could see he was beginning to shiver. This meant the fever had just begun to climb and she felt a spurt of alarm.

He was so hot already, hotter than even Lady Ravenscar and Catherine had been when they had fallen ill.

'Can't go alone...' he mumbled. 'The ghosts...'

'They had best not tangle with me right now, I'm in no mood for hauntings. I will return as quickly as I am able, but you must stay right here. If you move, I will be annoyed.'

She couldn't make out his response, but it didn't sound complimentary.

It took her just moments to bring some blankets and a pillow from the rooms upstairs, and though he hadn't moved from the sofa, the change was once again alarming. He was still pale under his tan, but his sharp-cut cheekbones were stained with colour, his eyes pressed shut as if in pain and the shaking was getting worse. He said something unintelligible when she raised his head to place the pillow under it, but he just lay there as she unfastened the buttons of his greatcoat and draped the blankets over him.

When she was done, she pressed the back of her hand to his burning cheek, trying not to be distracted by the contrast between the silky skin and the scrape of dark stubble. She had never seen anyone succumb so violently and so quickly. He must have been ill a day already. Anyone less stubborn would have had the sense to keep to his bed today. What was wrong with men?

'Oh, God, my head.' The words, hoarse and half-swallowed, dragged her out of the strange fog of fear that had begun to take hold of her. He shifted, his own hand falling from the sofa, and she picked it up in hers. It was as hot, but very dry, like paper just before it burst into flame. His eyes opened, dark and glittering, and she was caught like an animal in a predator's glare.

His hand tightened on hers with surprising force.

'Don't leave!'

There was outright panic in his eyes. They were dilated, the fever darkening them to black. It was clear he was caught in some delirious thought of his own, but she answered him as if he was completely rational.

'I won't. I promise.'

'Promise…'

'I promise,' she repeated, and he closed his eyes, but his hand clung to hers, hot and dry, twitching slightly.

Even as the words left her lips, she knew they were a mistake. The storm raging outside had come as quickly as his fever, but it did not look like it was going to lighten, which meant the fields between Hollywell and the Hall would soon be waterlogged and impassable on foot, so if she was going to bring help, she should leave soon. But the promise had a superstitious power, as if by breaking it, even for a good purpose, she would be putting him in grave risk. It would be like the night she had sat with the housekeeper's tiny new baby, Bento, while her mother had tended to poor Marta as she lay bleeding after a difficult and far too early birth. She had been so thirsty and had left for just a moment to fill the pitcher of boiled lemon water. Her mother had told her the baby had been born much too early and would have died whether she had been there or not, but her ten-year-old mind had rejected that palliative. She had been tired and thirsty and she had left her charge and death had stolen him in her absence. She knew her mother was right, that to believe otherwise was hubris, a belief in her own power and importance, but ever since then she had been very careful not to promise anything she wasn't certain she could fulfil.

So the moment she spoke the words she felt the old childish weight of fear and oppression. She could not leave him. If she did, she might come back and find him too still, too quiet, the heat of fever seeping out like water from a cracked vessel, unstoppable. All her logic, that she should fetch help, that she should not be here alone with him in the descending gloom of evening, was useless in the face of her fear of the consequences of going back on her word.

A flash of lightning turned the world to black and white for a second and his eyes opened.

'Thunder…'

'That was close. Any second now…' The crash drowned out her words, but he shook his head.

'My horse…outside…doesn't like thunder.'

He struggled to rise, but she pressed him back again.

'I'll see to him. I will be right back.'

'No, you can't ride him.'

'I won't, I promise, just lead him to the stables. Just until you are recovered.'

His eyes closed and she had no idea if he even heard her.

She hurried over to the desk and after some rummaging found what she needed. When she was done, she rushed outside, wondering where he had left his horse, but luckily it was tied by the front door and was grazing at the weeds poking along through the edge of the gravel, completely ignoring the lashing wind and rain. She stared at the animal with some dismay. It was an enormous black gelding with a long silky mane and tail which glistened in the fading light. She took a step forward and it raised its head and turned to stare at her with a look that was distinctly menacing, as if daring her to approach.

Blast the man, trust him to bring a horse as ill-tempered as he.

'There, boy,' she cooed as she approached. He sidled, watching her with his head lowered and his ears tucked back. She was not deceived; this was not a submissive gesture. Still, she moved forward with a confidence that was utterly feigned and managed to tuck a note into the belt of the saddle, where it might escape the rain. Then she untied his reins, throwing them over his neck before he could react. For a moment his liquid eyes focused on her as if debating squashing her between his enormous body and the stone column, but then he merely danced sideways, becoming aware of his freedom.

'That's right, off you go!'

The gelding bent to nip at the weeds again and with a growl of exasperation she waved her hands in the air.

'Shoo! Off you go!'

He trotted for a few steps and recklessly she moved towards him, her hands still waving like a demented houri.

'Oh, for heaven's sake. Faster!' she yelled at him and was supported by a crack of lightning and thunder, almost simultaneous. Finally the stallion sped into a canter down the drive, kicking up gravel.

She pushed her dripping hair out of her eyes and watched him disappear, wondering if he would ever be found, and if so, would anyone notice the paper tucked into the saddle or whether they would merely steal this clearly valuable horse. If so, Alan, if he recovered, would have her head. She half-smiled at the fury he would probably unleash on her anyway at putting his beautiful horse at risk, but that was his own fault. He never should have ventured outdoors if he felt unwell. Any sane person would have known their limits.

Back in the library she relaxed slightly. He was still breathing and still on the sofa, but each breath seemed to be an act of will, dredged up out of a great depth. She placed her hand on his forehead and he mumbled something, twisting away. She couldn't make out the words, but it sounded rude. She was tempted to respond by telling him what she had done with his precious brute of a horse, but that would probably drag him out of his stupor and make him do something foolish, so she merely sat down by his side and took his hand. The clouds were so thick they had turned afternoon into evening, leaching the colour from the room. This was her fault. She must have been mad to conceive of such a scheme. The day her father had caught her trying to board the ship to England he had told her running away never solved anything. He should have added it only complicated matters.

'You're a stubborn, stubborn fool,' she said aloud, as much to herself as to him, and his hand twitched, closing painfully around hers. She waited for it to ease again and rubbed it gently. Someone would find his horse and perhaps even the note. She just had to ensure he was comfortable and safe until then.

She didn't try to detach her hand again, just sat there and looked. Would it be the same no matter how many times she saw him? This sense of amazement and revelation? The way her body shifted from a medium of mundane existence to an entity with its own demands. Worst of all was the sense of rightness, of coming home.

Absurd.

Undeniable.

Even at his worst, he was so painfully handsome she wondered why she hadn't realised it the moment he strode into the Hollywell library. Yes, she had noticed he was handsome, but not that it would be hard to look away. Harder not to reach out and touch.

She curled her fingers into her palm.

Be sensible. Remember his anger at the inn.

Remember your own anger and contempt for what he symbolises. No, for what he *is*. Don't put any distance between him and his actions, that way weakness lies. That way you start forgiving and explaining away and feeling things that shouldn't be allowed, like sympathy and concern and a ridiculous conviction that you know him.

But she felt it anyway, a spreading of him into her, a knowledge of him. It might be utterly false, but it was so strong she couldn't turn it into a lie until it was proved so. Conclusively. She needed him to mend so he could become himself again, between that rakish charm and resentful anger. Maybe then she could defend herself better because now she had no defence against these feelings except fear.

She eased her hand away, resisting the temptation to touch his face, and stood up. His arm swept out and bumped into her skirts and caught at them feebly. She stood looking down at him for a moment and sat down again, untangling his hand from the muslin skirt with its embroidered flowers and tucking it between hers again. The fire was strong enough for the moment. She would tend to it in a little while.

She looked at the comfortable bed awaiting her and sighed. After two hours it was unlikely rescue would arrive before the morrow and she had best take what she needed to spend the night in the library. In between bathing his forehead with a damp cloth to calm his fevered mutterings, she had prepared herself tea on the hob over the library fireplace and brought a basket of bread and cheese from the stores Mr Prosper's housekeeper had stocked in the pantry. She rolled up another blanket and pillow, her toothbrush and tooth powder, and resigned herself to a very uncomfortable night on the floor.

Halfway down the corridor to the stairway, she stopped abruptly.

That was definitely a thud, not thunder. For a moment she remained frozen, her heart beating hard and fast, wishing she had taken one of her father's pistols with her. The second thud was followed by a faint groan and alarm raced over her skin, sharp and stinging, raising goose pimples as it went. But even as her body went into a shocked crouch, her mind moved forward. Something thudding and groaning in a house whose only other occupant was a very ill and very stubborn man most likely had nothing to do with the supernatural.

She dropped the bedclothes and ran.

He had made it halfway to the front door. Kneeling on the floor and in the gleam of her candle, he looked like a medieval supplicant before an altar. His caped greatcoat was spread around him like a cloak, his dark head bowed, his weight braced on one arm.

'You fool. What on earth are you doing?'

'Keynsham,' he muttered, clearly trying to get back on his feet, but he stopped when she placed her hand on his forehead. He was burning.

'Keynsham? Really? In a storm and on foot?' she asked, fear pouring acid into her voice. 'You want to be stubborn? Then stand up. Now.'

He finally turned to her, his eyes near black, his pupils dilated.

'You…'

His voice was slurred and she couldn't tell if there was annoyance or distaste there.

'Yes, me. You want Hollywell House from me, right?'

His eyelids flickered closed and she pinched his arm and he nodded.

'You…'

'Well, if you want it, I want you to stand up. If you don't, I will crack a candlestick on your stubborn head and drag you back to the library by your heels.'

'Vixen.'

That was clearer. She turned so that she could slide her arm around his back and brace his weight against her shoulder.

'Up with you.'

She managed to get him on his legs but would have fallen if she hadn't braced her own arm against the wall.

'Sorry...' he mumbled. 'Ill...'

Her heart was thudding so hard she thought it might break something inside her. She felt the kind of fear she had once felt when a green water boa had slithered out of the swampy bushes in Brazil less than a yard away from her, enormous, shiny, heading towards her with an intentness in its tiny glinting eyes that still came back to her in dreams almost twenty years later. It was elemental, demanding action. She had never felt this scared about the possibility of someone dying.

She managed to straighten and also push back at her fear. He was just feverish. He wasn't dying. There was no need to become all foolish and soft.

They entered the library, his long lean body hard against her side, the folds of his coat tangling in her legs and nearly tripping her. He sank down on to the sofa, breathing heavily, and she sat down with him for a moment, afraid to let him go. She could feel the tremors rise through his body, like tiny earthquakes, and she could feel him try to stop them, his muscles locking down. Even this he was fighting, she thought in frustration.

'Lie down,' she whispered, and a tremor shook him so hard she locked her arms around him again, afraid he might fall forward. But then it passed and she managed to ease him down.

He sank back into a shaky stupor, occasionally muttering something about someone named Rickie, and sometimes his eyes would flicker open with that same unfocused, haunted look. She began wondering if the clock on the mantelpiece was even working, it moved so slowly, but it was already close on ten o'clock at night, so it must have moved quite a great deal since her arrival. She was fully awake and achy in a way that had nothing to do with illness, and the superstitious fear was back—she had to remain on alert or something terrible would happen.

Was this what Catherine felt sitting by Nicky's sickbed at night, afraid to sleep?

The comparison was ridiculous; this was not her child, not a child at all, but a very large and very aggravating man. Perhaps it was that he was no one's child and someone *should* be sitting here worrying. If he had been her child, would it have been like this? No, she admitted. It would be different. She would not still be scalded all down her side where his body had pressed the length of hers. She would not have to keep her hands curled so as not to be tempted to touch.

Her fingers ached with the need to trace the tense grooves by his mouth, to ease the frown forming two sharp lines between his black-winged brows and to test the silkiness of his black hair. And definitely not to press her lips to his. They looked hot, too; tense, just a little parted.

She surrendered to the urge to touch, her fingers seeking the vulnerable hollow by his temple, where the skin was soft, as velvety as the inside of a hibiscus leaf, following it to where it thinned over the ridge of bone. She loved his cheekbones, they were everything that was right and wrong with him. Sharp cut, uncompromising until they gave way to this softness which was always a little in the shadow. Then there were the lines on either side of his mouth, two gauges of his mood. Even when he wasn't smiling, there was usually still a little curve in them, a curiosity or lingering warmth. But she had seen them as straight as a hanging blade when he had been angry at her.

She smoothed her fingers over one—it wasn't like that now; it was shifting, restless. Perhaps he was dreaming. She rested her fingers lightly on his mouth. His breath was the shallow swift breath of a fever, a tangible effort that fanned over her fingertips. She sank into that simple sensation—her skin on his, his breath alternately warming and cooling the spaces between her fingers. She wasn't brave enough to do it, but she imagined this against her own mouth, that hot firm surface moving against her lips like they had in the inn. That kiss had been a curse, a snatching of her soul and will—right now she could not imagine anyone kissing her again but him. Her lips were half-burned with the need to recapture that embrace; they felt thicker, stinging a little as if she, too, was fevered and dry.

He isn't even doing anything, you foolish girl. He is ill and you are not only doing something improper, it is unfair to him. You wouldn't want someone to kiss you while you slept, no matter what the silly fairy tales said about redemptive powers.

I wouldn't mind if it was him, she replied. I would only mind if I didn't wake.

Well, he isn't you and he most likely would mind.

She removed her fingers, curling them in.

'I'm sorry,' she murmured, and he opened his eyes, a sharp silvery grey, his pupils constricted, faraway. She kept still, waiting for him to close his eyes again as he had each time these brief moments of waking had occurred so far, but he just watched her, his pupils dilating.

'What for?' His voice was hardly more than

a rasp of cloth on cloth, but he sounded fully rational, even curious.

She gave a little laugh. Trust him to become rational at the worst possible moment and ask the worst possible question. At least she had resisted the urge to kiss him. That might have been difficult to explain.

'Go back to sleep.'

'Why? Where am I?'

His eyes swept the room but returned to hers, now with another level of realisation.

'Hollywell. I forgot. Hell.'

Each word was dragged upwards, but fading. Another of the tremors that had scared her shook him.

'Everything hurts… Hate this.'

She so desperately wanted to reassure him, promise him he was going to be well, but he wouldn't believe her and she was afraid the words themselves would have a runic force, twisting fate to prove her wrong. She dipped the cloth in the bowl of water and wrung it.

'Close your eyes.'

That was a mistake. He had been fading, but her words changed the rhythm of his breathing, the struggle showing as clear as storm clouds in his eyes.

'No. That's how… No. Where's Cat?' His words were slurred, but the intensity was unmistakable.

'Catherine isn't ill. She is with Nicky, who has recovered enough to start making demands of everyone and everything. It's the truth, I prom… It's the truth, Alan. Now close your eyes and we shall see if we can lower your fever so you can return to running away.'

'Vixen.' But he closed his eyes and she focused on touching his face only with the damp cloth.

'Ferret, vixen… What next? Mole? Field mouse? Slug?'

The lines on the side of his mouth curved a little, then flattened.

'Sorry.'

'Don't apologise. I told you, I like your choices of fauna. Vixens and ferrets are very resourceful; they must depend on their wits rather than brute strength. Of course, you would say I need depend on neither because I am an heiress.'

Again his smile flickered, but then he was gone and she was alone with herself again.

Chapter Eight

It was white, bright and yellow at the edges, very white at the centre. He closed his eyes again and turned away, but he was so stiff his head hardly moved. Not just his head was stuck, nothing seemed to move. Was he tied down? Yes, here it was, something pressing his head into the earth. God, they were burying him! No, it was softer, just a light touch, but very hot, or perhaps that was him because he felt hot all over and in pain. Now he could feel that all over, too.

Oh, hell, he remembered.

I'm ill. I hate this.

He turned back to find that touch and there it was, soft, light, cool, just skimming his forehead and down to his cheek. He could feel his stubble catch at the caress and wished she would continue to his mouth so he could taste her. Perhaps this was still part of the jumble of dreams hovering around the edges of his mind, billowy white clouds on the horizon.

Then the hand was gone.

'Can you hear me? You should try to drink something. Do you think you could try?'

'I'm never ill.' Was that his voice? Pathetic.

'So you already told me. Twice. Well, now you are.'

'Shouldn't be here. You'll be ill.' He sounded drunk, even to himself.

'If I am going to be ill, I will be ill and finally someone will nurse *me*. Now stop arguing about everything. This is becoming very repetitive. You are ill, you aren't going to Keynsham and you have no choice about who is going to nurse you because there is no one else here.'

He forced his eyes open at that.

'Hollywell. I saw the light in the library.'

She put down the cloth she had been bathing his face with.

'I thought you were the ghost thumping around when you came in.'

He watched the corner of her smile until his eyes grew heavy again.

'You should've run. Ghosts… Dangerous…'

She laughed at that, a warm sound that pressed back at the core of pain. Even in the murk of thudding misery, some part of him was carving out spaces of awareness. One was engaged in following the movements of the cloth and her fingers over his burning face. Another was an echo chamber for her sounds—her voice, moving between brusque and soothing, the rustle and shift of her clothes. Each space expanded and took centre stage in turn, like moving from stall to stall at a village fair. Now it was her laugh, an infectious tumble of sound, at his reply.

'Too true. Now it's time to be quiet. You must sleep...'

'No!'

Not sleep. He forced his eyes open even though the light burned, adding to the ache that was weighing him down.

She wasn't smiling now, the auburn brows were tugged together, separated by only two deep furrows, and the honeyed eyes were worried.

'You *must* sleep. The more you fight, the weaker you make yourself. This isn't a case for brute force.' Her voice had changed, lowered, or he was fading again. He didn't want to go yet. He might not come back from the darkness this time.

'Lily... Don't go.' He hadn't meant to say that, perhaps he hadn't.

He couldn't keep his eyes open, they burned so much. Everything was burning, pounding, like the siege in Ciudad Rodrigo, where they had been sent in to help hold off the French until the English and Portuguese could complete the Torres Vedras forts. They should have been just the advance force for Craufurd and the Light Brigade, but they and the Spanish had waited in vain, week after week of French cannonballs slamming against ancient rock, each strike jarring them to their teeth, covering them with dust and raising the stench of rotting bodies from the earth.

In the end the Spanish Commander, Herrasti, had warned them he was going to surrender, giving them a night to make their escape through French lines. His men had been exhausted, drained of will. They had begged to be left to sleep and he had shouted at them, 'If you sleep, you'll wake up in a French prison or not wake up at all...'

Her hand was leagues cooler than his, closing around his aching fingers. He had no skin, no muscle left, just bones, knuckles hard and white pressed together in her hand, as smooth as satin, sliding over his.

'Not tonight.' Her voice had dipped low, into the water. 'No dying tonight. The grim reaper will have to grapple with me and I don't fancy his odds at the moment. So sleep.'

He didn't trust her, but there was nothing he could do. Her voice was sinking him lower and lower, disintegrating him. All he had left was the slide of her thumb over the back of his hand and then that was gone as well. With his last breath, he clung to the lifeline.

'Lily, stay...'

He must have slept, because this time when he woke again, he was thirsty.

He knew that feeling too well from the war. It wasn't like hunger. Hunger was easy; you felt it in your gut. Thirst often started nameless, a need that shifted around the body, searching for something to lean on, aggravating the nerves as it went. He groped after it and an image rose—as sharp as if he was there—Rickie was seated on a small rug by the kitchen hearth, the warmest place in their house in Edinburgh, with one of the neighbours' kittens a ball of fur in his small lap. That much might have been a real memory, but in this image seated on the floor by his side and leaning against the rough stone wall with a book in her lap was Lily.

He must be ill, the vision had all the power of a hallucination, subverting reality and memory. It wasn't even based on a real memory. Neither of his parents had read books to them and had certainly been too proper to sit by the kitchen hearth, and though he and Cat had read a great deal, it had been a solitary occupation. Perhaps he had read to Rickie, but he couldn't remember. He remembered them playing with a ball he fashioned from strips of rags stuffed into a sock Cat knitted. Cards. He had learned some tricks in the market near his school and Rickie loved watching him practise, his frail little hands trying and failing to mimic his movements.

He pressed his palm against the ache in his forehead, dragging his thoughts to the surface—he wasn't in Edinburgh. He couldn't be. So where the hell was he?

His body reviewed its position and reported. This bed was even more uncomfortable than his bed at the Ship. Not a bed, a sofa? The wooden scrolling was digging into his shoulder and the side of his leg, and it was much too short. And there was something on his chest. No, someone.

That and the thirst finally brought him to the surface and he forced open his eyes.

Her hair had tumbled from its pins and lay over her shoulder, a cinnamon brown in the gloomy room. She was seated on the floor, her head leaning against his chest, and he couldn't see much of her face, just the curve of her cheek, the auburn upward brush of her eyebrow and those long gold-tipped eyelashes spearing her faint freckles. His brief spasm of concern faded and he didn't move. She was merely asleep. Whether this was real or merely a fever-induced hallucination, it was surprisingly pleasant and he didn't want to disturb it.

What the hell was he doing in Albert's library with Lily Wallace, sleeping?

Then his memory reasserted itself. The light in the window. Lily. His head. Oh, hell.

He looked carefully towards the window. The storm was still raging, but it wasn't dark, which meant he could not have been unconscious for too long. He had to leave before anyone found them like this.

If he could only find a way to make his body do what he wanted.

He struggled to pull himself into a sitting position while trying not to wake Lily. It wasn't her weight on his chest that defeated him, but his muscles which were transformed into aching stalks of damp straw. How the hell was sitting so difficult? He had been sitting since he was a baby. One didn't forget how to do it, did they?

He only succeeded in shifting Lily and she woke into an alertness worthy of his best soldiers.

'You're awake. Ow!' She rose on to her knees, then squeaked and fell back on to her behind.

Fear drove him into a half-sitting position after all.

'What is wrong? Are you hurt?'

It was humiliating. His voice was weaker than his muscles.

'My legs are all pins and needles,' she replied, rubbing at her thigh. The cheek that had rested against him was red and marked from the folds of his coat and even in his pathetic state he almost acted on the urge to press his mouth to those marks and coax her skin smooth again. He closed his eyes. Not appropriate thoughts under any circumstances; right now they were as near disastrous as possible. He had to rise, get on his horse and continue to the Hall. She must return there as soon as possible. Had he been hallucinating or did she actually say she was there alone? He must have been. She could not be that mad.

Whatever the case, he had to leave. If she really was there alone, he would ride to the Hall and have Catherine send the carriage for her right away. There was no other choice. If only he could stay on his horse long enough to make it there. That was debatable. Right now the act of standing up felt beyond him.

Mostly he was thirsty.

'I need to reach the Hall. Have them send a carriage for you. It will be dark soon.'

She had made it to her knees, but at that she stopped.

'Not for a while. It is not yet one o'clock.'

'One…' He frowned, glancing at the windows again. It looked like they were underwater and sounded like they were surrounded by drums, but it was grey, not black. 'It can't be one o'clock at night. It is still light. The clock must be wrong.'

She stood, testing her weight on one leg and wincing.

'One in the afternoon. You slept for quite a while. When you weren't trying to escape. You still sound terrible and you must drink something. I will fetch some water for a new kettle of tea. Please don't wander off, you will only fall down again and my back is aching with dragging you back here.'

Alan didn't respond. Perhaps he still was feverish, because none of what she said made sense other than the point about tea. He let his eyes drift shut. Perhaps next time he opened them the world would be cognisable.

'Here.'

He must have slept again, because she could not have brewed tea so swiftly. The smell was unmistakable and wonderful and his mouth tried to water and failed. When he succeeded in sitting up enough to take the cup, the first sip of the hot, sweet liquid was like a benediction. It filled him, shaped him from the inside, and for a moment it drained away the pain and confusion.

They didn't speak as they drank and she kept her own gaze on her cup. Her cheek had regained its customary soft lustre with its faint dusting of freckles and he wished she still bore the signs which had been proof she had been that close. She had also collected her hair into a knot low on her nape and other than her crumpled skirts she looked cool and collected once more. Which made no sense if what she had just said was true. None of this made sense. It could not possibly be that he was alone with Lily Wallace at Hollywell almost a full day after spotting the light in the window, could it?

'More tea?' she asked politely as she placed her cup on a small table she had drawn up by the sofa.

'Not yet. First... What on earth are you doing here?'

'Running away.'

'Running... Why? From whom?'

'Just for a few days. I needed to think. I didn't expect guests.' Her mouth rose at the corners, but she still didn't meet his eyes and he realised she was nervous. As well she should be. Bloody hell, they were in trouble.

'I am trying to understand. Where does Lady Jezebel think you are?'

'In Bath. She thinks I departed for a few days with Jackson and my maid to visit a friend who lives in Bath.'

'Your maid and groom are here as well?'

'No. I left them waiting for the London coach on their way to visit their families. Then I directed the post-chaise to take me here.'

'But…why?'

'I told you. I needed to be alone. Utterly alone. Someplace of my own so I could think. I asked Mr Prosper to stock Hollywell for guests a couple days ago so that I would have everything I needed.'

She finally looked up, her eyes dark and pleading.

'This might be the last time I will have to really be alone, before… I thought I would be able to think things through in peace here. It's so quiet.'

'You're mad. You can't just… It just isn't done, Lily!'

She shrugged. 'You sound like your grandmother. Of course it isn't done and yet I have done it. Here I am. I never expected anyone to come by, certainly not in this weather. Last I looked this morning the drive looks like a tributary of the Amazon.'

He pushed himself further upright. 'My horse. I must…'

'He ran away,' she said hurriedly, raising her hands as if to press him back, but he pushed into a sitting position and leaned his head in his hands, trying to think.

He had been alone with her at Hollywell for a full day. The fact that no one knew this yet made no difference. Her rashness and his fever had just sealed their fate.

'You have to return to the Hall. Now.'

'No, I cannot. Everyone thinks I went to Bath. What on earth would I say if I suddenly appeared the following day, as muddy and wet as a bog monster and without my luggage? As soon as the rain stops and you are well enough to leave, you can walk to Keynsham. I will stay here until the post-chaise I hired returns for me in two days' time. You see, I have thought it all through.'

He didn't raise his head. He hadn't felt so bruised since the forced march out of Portugal under Moore. She wasn't mad, yet she was if she thought it was that simple.

'You aren't well enough to walk to Keynsham yet,' she continued, infuriatingly matter of fact. 'But you cannot spend another night here on the sofa. Do you think you can manage the stairs? The bedrooms have been aired.'

The bedrooms have been aired.

Lily. You're mad.

He didn't say it. Partially because he knew that under her cheerful bravado she must be as aware as he of the consequences awaiting them and partially because he couldn't help the anticipation that was building as his mind and body absorbed this new reality.

He was about to break another vow. It was becoming a habit.

Compromised by an heiress.

Marriage.

Hunter and Stanton would split with laughter.

'Very well. Upstairs.'

It wasn't as bad as he anticipated. Halfway up the stairs his legs began to remember their function and he could have made do with leaning on the banister, but he kept his arm around her for the pure pleasure of it. This indulgence almost cost him his balance halfway down the corridor when Lily suddenly shuddered and leapt to one side.

'Lily! What's wrong?' He managed to stop from keeling over by propping himself against the wall and he pulled her against him in one movement.

'I stepped on something. It was soft and… Oh, no, it's a mouse. I killed it.'

He found what she was staring at in the faint light of the tapers she had lit along the corridor to light their way. A tiny grey bundle in the centre of the carpet. His head was pounding and his body felt it was a hundred years old, but he couldn't help it, he started laughing, then winced as she jabbed him with her elbow.

'Oh, you heartless brute. It isn't funny!'

'I'm not… I'm not laughing at that. I don't know why I'm laughing. But you can relax that conscience, sweetheart. It wasn't a vixen that did your grey friend in, but a cat. Those are claw marks.'

He felt her shudder again as she looked and then glanced away and he pulled her more firmly against him. What a strange little thing she was. To brave being alone in a haunted house and caring for a felled rake, but then to come apart at the seams over a mangled rodent.

'I forgot all about it, but Albert had a cat, a very unfriendly ginger tabby who was always disappearing behind furniture and making a general nuisance of himself. I thought someone would have taken it, but perhaps not. It might explain your broken urn if he's been chasing mice around an empty house. Come, let's leave the little fellow for now. There's nothing you can do for him.'

'I hate leaving him there.'

'I'll toss him out the window, then.'

'No…leave him. The tabby is probably hungry. I'll try not to think about it.'

He kept a firm hold on his smile until she had deposited him on the side of the bed with all the concentration of a three-year-old carrying a full glass of water.

'You should lie down.'

So should you, right here with me.

He didn't say the words, but as they surfaced in his mind he vaguely remembered asking her not to leave when the fever had been high, clinging to her hand like a child. She must think him pathetic. Even if she did lie down with him, he was in no shape yet to do anything about it. Yet.

In the light of the single candle she looked younger, unusually awkward as she stood watching him. Was she waiting for him to fall over again? What a blow to his vanity. Here he was worried about the consequences of compromising her when she probably thought him an object of pity. But whatever either of them thought, they would likely only leave this house categorically betrothed. Did she realise that? For someone so sophisticated she could be incredibly naïve. If he said anything, she would likely run away again, storm notwithstanding.

Would it be so terrible to marry her?

It might be. He remembered most of the things she had said to him and this particular comment lingered. She had been clear about what she wanted from life—a home. Children.

It was his turn to shudder and he finally gave in and lay down, closing his eyes. The darkness was filling him again, but of a different kind. Right now he would welcome unconsciousness, anything but the great yawning pit of that winter almost two decades ago. Not even the snow had held off the stench of the bodies. He had smelled death so often during the war, rank and tangy in the Spanish sun, laced with the sting of lye. But that was nothing next to the memory of the subterranean, putrid scent of the snow-dusted bodies outside their home that winter as he tried to stave off death inside. He had failed, they had died and that was that. He wouldn't willingly go there again. He had made a promise to himself.

Except that now he might have no choice. He played by the rules, and though he had never meant to break them, they were as shattered as Albert's ugly old urn.

He would marry her.

Her scent, roses and something else, told him she was closer. Then he felt the weight of a blanket on him. He wanted to pull her to him. If his fate was sealed, he might as well enjoy it, but he kept his eyes shut. She would probably box his ears and they were already ringing. Perhaps it was best not to put fantasy to the test in his present state.

'Would you like me to read to you?'

That was neutral. He opened his eyes.

'Mysteries of Udolpho?'

'Goodness, no. There are the books in the library downstairs and I brought a few with me as well. I shall fetch some. It might help you sleep.'

She nodded briskly and left the room before he could stop her. He closed his eyes again and his body seemed to sink deeper into the bed like a hot air balloon emptying of air. He had truly forgotten how miserable it was to be ill, if he had ever known. He should try to remember this feeling so he could have a little more patience when next he came across someone in this state. He didn't know if it was better or worse having someone like her as a nurse.

Someone like her. He couldn't imagine anyone quite like her. She was like one of those strange beasts occasionally paraded at Astley's or some village freak. He never knew what she would do next.

He knew what he would like her to do next and it didn't involve books, but now that he was coherent again it was unlikely she would touch him. At least until, or if, she married him. He didn't remember much of the fever, but the physical imprint of her body on his lingered. The soft pressure of her lush breasts against him as she had helped him on to the sofa…

He turned on his side, his body thudding with heat that had nothing to do with fever. He didn't know whether to hope she returned or not, but then the door opened and she came in with a hesitant smile.

'I've brought a choice.'

'As long as there are none of my grandfather's sermons among them,' he managed, levering himself back into a sitting position, too weak to look away from the line of her thigh as she pulled over the chair by the dresser and sat. His hands prickled with the need to feel that line. All he had to do was extend his arm. First above the dress and then, slowly, below.

He watched the uptilt of her chin, the line of light and shadow down her throat and down further towards her fashionable bodice. She had changed out of her rumpled gown of the previous day and even without her maid she looked cool and elegant. At least in that respect she was like her namesake, though the colouring was far too fiery. But then, Lily could be short for Lilith. It suited her, that ambiguous female who sought life and knowledge with her arms open and was condemned for her audacity. This Lily probably would have an opinion about her, too. He could well imagine it. He would save that conversation for later.

'You choose,' he said lazily. The crease between her brows deepened as she looked down at the three books, then she gave a little laugh and opened one of them, tucking her feet under her on the chair as she had on Nicky's bed, the unconscious intimacy another slap to his restraint.

'Here—*Nightmare Abbey.*'

'That sounds worse than *Udolpho.*'

'It's by Thomas Love Peacock and it's *meant* to sound worse. He makes fun of all those novels, not to mention quite a bit of fun of Shelley and of Goethe's *Werther* and of transcendental philosophy. I thought of him because Mr Glowry's butler is named Raven and the only ghost is a somnambulist steward named Crow.'

'Too much fowl.'

'Bear with me, I will read just enough to put you to sleep. *"Nightmare Abbey, a venerable family mansion in a highly picturesque state of semi-dilapidation...'*

Alan leaned back against the headboard and closed his eyes, more to block out the sight of her than out of any weariness. It didn't do much good because her voice was just as seductive.

'*"Mr Glowry used to say that his house was no better than a spacious kennel, for everyone in it led the life of a dog..."* I wonder if he would have found Ravenscar Hall an improvement on his Abbey? Sorry, where was I...? Ah. *"...disappointed in love and friendship..."'* she continued.

Her reading certainly missed the mark, if the mark was to put him to sleep. The only salvation came from the fact that the tale was actually amusing—especially when she acted out the voices of the Glowrys and the other characters.

When it came to a discussion comparing women to musical dolls and lottery draws, he opened his eyes to watch her face.

'*"It is only after marriage that they show their true qualities. Marriage is, therefore, a lottery, and the less choice and selection a man bestows upon his ticket the better..."'* She grinned and lowered the book for a moment. 'I thought you might appreciate how closely your ideas match with Mr Glowry's.'

He covered his eyes again against her elfin smile.

'You wrong me. Keep reading. But could you skim over that fool Scythorp's impassioned proclamations? If I were there, I would probably push him out of his tower rather than listen to another anguished diatribe.'

'I told you—you aren't in the least romantic. Now, stop interrupting. This is supposed to put you to sleep.'

He almost pointed out that not even the driest legal document, if read in her husky, humorous voice, was likely to put him to sleep.

He was still far too wide awake when she closed the book.

'That is enough for now. Did you like it thus far?'

'Better than I would one of Nicky's. I never understood why those novels are so successful.'

She touched the edge of the book with its worn spine and corners.

'Because they are about loneliness, our greatest fear.'

'I thought death was our greatest fear.'

'I think loneliness is worse.'

Loneliness. At least that was a topic he understood. It wasn't a word he would associate with someone as outwardly confident as she appeared, but then he didn't know her, not really. There was a whole history in those five words and they just made what had to happen all the worse. There was no possible way he could provide her with what she needed in life.

Even knowing the disaster that was looming, it was hard to regret this twist in his fate—he had never thought he would be weak enough to allow physical passion to overcome caution, but there was no point in denying the physical pull she had on him was trumping all good sense. Even as weak as he still was, he was so tempted to touch her; he was even envious of the book warming itself in her lap. He looked away, groping for an anchor.

'Cat mentioned you lived on an island in Brazil before you lived in Jamaica. Were you lonely there?'

She shrugged.

'I was, a little. I missed my father because he remained on the mainland, at the mines. I don't think my mother was lonely. Once, she told me she and my father were far happier together since she had come to the island. Every year she went with my father to Kingston, but she was always so happy to return. I thought it was because she didn't like seeing or hearing about his mistresses, but I think she felt safe on the island and she loved the excitement of waiting for him, running down to the docks when they came to tell us his ship was entering the bay. I had this little house…well, a crate on the mango tree in our garden, and I could see down the path towards the port and I would watch her run. She was like a little girl. Towards the end I hated watching her when he came.'

'Didn't you run when his ship arrived?'

'No. I could never compete with her enthusiasm, so I never tried.'

'You are too smart for your own good, Lily Wallace.'

'So we are back to the crafty vixen.' She shifted, pressing the book between her palms, her mouth flattening into a tense line.

'I didn't mean it like that. I meant that being lonely and being intelligent is a brutal combination. Hell, don't cry, I didn't mean…'

She rubbed her eyes.

'I'm not crying, I am merely tired. You made me think of them.'

'I'm sorry.'

'Don't be, I wasn't unhappy. I did have friends even if they weren't my age and then there was Rupert.'

'Rupert?'

The tension faded as she smiled at the memory. That was a new expression, too. Wistful, the faint echo of a child's joyous smile.

'I might not have run when my father's ship arrived, but I did run down to the bay when I saw Rupert from the mango tree. We would swim together and I would imagine we were an enchanted prince and princess banished to the islands, and when the spell would be lifted, we would be swept back to our kingdom and live happily ever after. There, now you may laugh at me.'

Her eyes focused again, challenging him, but the image lingered. He could see her as a little girl, tumbled red-brown hair and more freckles than she had now. The light filling her the moment she saw her friend.

He wasn't in the least amused, but he did his best to push back at the irrational jab of jealousy. She had been a child, so what if she had run to greet some boy. It was ancient history and none of his concern.

'Well, I hate to drag you out of your fairy tale, but I'm afraid no one is going to lift this particular spell. It is time we put it on the table, isn't it?'

'Put...' The last of the light faded and the society miss was back, cool and calm.

'There is no getting around it, Lily.'

She shook her head. 'No one knows you are here…'

'I *am* here. Alone with you. I won't even start on the sheer and utter madness of what you did… coming here in the first place to an empty house, on your own, lying to everyone…' He shoved off the bed, ignoring the resistance in his muscles. 'You aren't ten years old, Lily. If you throw a tantrum, because that is all this was, then you risk the consequences. You are luckier than you deserve that it was I who came by and not who-ever had vandalised the library. My God, do you realise what a risk you took? For what? Just to be alone? Is your clever little mind even capable of encompassing what might have happened to you? Hell, what *has* happened to you and not just to you. You don't live on an island any longer, Lily, and you can't buy your way out of trouble. When I walk out of here tomorrow, if I don't get struck by lightning, which at the moment is not an option to be despised, we will have spent two days alone together and whether I was at death's door for that time or indulging in an orgy makes no odds. I may be a rake, as you delight in point-ing out, but I play by the rules. We are now be-trothed. It is as simple as that.'

Simple.

Lily stood as well, her cheeks pinched with

cold. He had lulled her for a moment with that humourous charm and, worse, that compassion which appeared so real. It might even have been real, but so was this. She had seen him angry before, but not as coldly implacable as an envoy from Hades. He would not negotiate; he would take.

She could not even hide behind the defences of her own mind. What *had* she been thinking? What madness had taken her? She had planned it, sending Greene and Jackson away and hiring the post-chaise and spreading lies, but it wasn't very different from those blind urges that had sent her running from the new house in Kingston ten years ago. A childish denial of her fate. Even then she had known it was futile. She had never been surprised her father found her or that someone delivered her home. She had expected to fail. This time was no different. She had known all along that at the end of her three days of rebellion the post-chaise would bring her back to the Hall, in time for Philip Marston's return, her engagement, marriage, life. Perhaps her fascination with Alan was no more than another rebellion against that fate.

Except that she was now betrothed to him. To Lord Ravenscar, rakehell.

She had never planned this. She should not want this. She should resist it with every fibre of her being. Because unlike Philip he was dangerous to her. It wasn't merely that he would never be faithful to her, she had no reason to believe that Philip would be, but with Philip she could accept it as long as she had what she wanted—a modicum of independence and a home that was hers. Children. A family. If she married Alan, she would want more. He had given her a taste of something she hadn't known mattered—passion, honesty. He might be a rake, but he was one of the most honest men she had met and it released something in her, like the moment Greene released the laces of her stays.

She looked at the chiselled, uncompromising face. He would face his fate just as he would have faced a firing squad in time of war. Angry, but accepting. She must face hers—she was about to become her mother. In love with an unrepentant rake.

Or she could save them both—she could marry Philip. She would have to tell him everything, of course, and let him choose. But first *she* would have to choose.

She closed her eyes briefly.

'You should rest. We will discuss this tomorrow.'

He caught her hand.

'It is best to accept the inevitable, Lily. Dreaming about some boy you loved years ago is all well and good between the pages of a novel, but this is our reality now.'

The absurdity of that idea raised her for a moment above the swell of misery that had been roiling in her.

'He's not a boy. Rupert is a manatee.'

'A...what?'

'A manatee. Sometimes they are called sea cows. They are very big and fat and grey and quite friendly. There were several manatees that lived in the mangrove bay on the island and I used to swim with them as a child.'

'A manatee.'

'They are very gentle and they like being fed. I told you, I didn't have many friends on the island, so I named them and made believe they were really enchanted princes and princesses who had been turned into manatees and one day their parents would come and find them and remove the spell, but meanwhile they were my friends. Rupert in particular.'

He let out his breath.

'I still have a hard time realising how lonely you must have been.'

Not as lonely as I feel right now and that's your fault.

'Children often create imaginary friends.'

'Would it cost you so much to admit that you were lonely?'

'Didn't you yourself say something to your grandmother about practising what you preach?'

His smile was wry as he released her hand to trace the line of her jaw with his fingers, from ear to chin, lingering there, coaxing her face towards him. It wasn't fair of him, touching her like that. So soft it made her ache for more.

'Life with you is unlikely to be boring, Lily Wallace.'

She finally managed to stand and move to the door.

'Your compliments leave a great deal to be desired, Lord Ravenscar.'

He stood up.

'I always preferred actions to words. Shall I show you precisely how flattering I can be? Or would you prefer to leave before I am tempted to show you a very effective antidote to loneliness?'

She searched desperately for some clever retort that would prove how unaffected she was, but when he took a step towards her, she hurried out and closed the door.

Chapter Nine

❧❧❧❧

At least this time she wasn't asleep when the noises began.

She should have been after the events of the past day, but she remained frustratingly awake, thoughts and images darting around her mind like a school of colourful fish in the bay.

She had remained resolutely in her room after their confrontation, almost expecting him to barge in and continue their confrontation, or worse...hoping he would. But nothing interrupted her futile attempts to read and resolutely reread the same pages of her book but the flashes of lightning and barking crashes of thunder. Perhaps the tropical storms of the Caribbean had followed her to England except that she was cold despite the fire, inside and out.

The sound was so soft at first, a faint scratching and clicking. It might have been a branch tapping at her window, the wind outside was high enough, whooping and hissing, except that there were no trees near any of Hollywell's windows and the sounds hadn't come from outside.

Could it be the tabby cat, come to collect its kill? Grateful for an excuse to act, she slipped out of bed and picked up the candlestick when the sound came again. A scratching and something else, just by her door. Breathing? She had no idea, but she knew it wasn't Alan. And not a cat either. Then it was gone and she let her breath out but didn't move, every cell focused, waiting.

Don't be ridiculous, Lily Wallace. Remember what you told Alan…if there are sounds, they have a perfectly rational, earthly cause. Either go see if there is anything there or ignore it and read your book.

Oh, blast it.

She tiptoed to the door and raised the candlestick ahead of her, trying to see into the gloom of the corridor. Perhaps it was Alan after all. Could he possibly be wandering about at night again? He was no longer ill enough to justify such stupidity, was he? Perhaps it was the cat. Now that she had been looking, she had seen the wet marks of its paws in the kitchens. No doubt somewhere there was a window or door that wasn't quite secure, but she had not yet found it.

She froze—there it was again, closer. Scratching and snuffling. She wanted to draw back, close the door, lock it. Several doors down she saw a line of faint golden light under Alan's door. He *was* awake. Was he ill again? She had thought he was better, but hadn't Mr Curtis been well enough to go to church and then he had dropped dead? Perhaps Alan was even now lying on the floor of his room, dying... She hurried forward and her hand was already raised to knock on his door when she saw it. Just a flicker out of the corner of her eye and she turned, raising her candle.

'Oh, God.'

She dropped the candlestick and it hit the carpet with a thump. The world went black and her imagination wild. She closed her eyes against what she had seen and groped desperately in the dark for the knob. The door opened abruptly and she propelled herself inside and slammed against something hard.

'Lily. Good God, what is it?' Alan's arms went around her.

Alan. Oh, thank God, Alan. She turned to him, practically burrowing into his side, her hands fisting on the warm fabric of his shirt.

'There's something there in the corridor. I saw it. It's not human. Alan, no...' She tightened her hold on his shirt as he started towards the door, but he merely tucked her against his other side and stepped into the doorway and stopped. He started shaking against her and instinctively her arms went around him in case he was about to collapse. His arms tightened around her as well, drawing her back into the room and closing the door, his mouth brushing her hair.

'I warned you about those novels, didn't I?'

He was laughing! She tilted her head back, between horror and outrage.

'I'm serious, there is something out there. I am not delusional, Alan!'

'It's not out there any more; it's in here now. Hello, Grim, old boy. No one told me you were still alive. How on earth did you get into Hollywell? Looking for the tabby? This place is a menagerie.'

His voice was so uncharacteristically gentle, especially after the acrimony earlier that evening, that she instinctively relaxed, but a huffing breath against her leg made her tighten her hold on Alan. She looked down into liquid eyes, filmy with age, of a tall black-as-pitch dog leaning its rain-dampened head lovingly against Alan's thigh as Alan's free hand stroked him.

'Where did he come from?' she whispered, reaching out to touch the dog's ear.

'I don't know. Haven't you ever seen him around before?'

'No. How did he enter?'

'Probably the same way the tabby did. You need to have the windows and doors checked. Or perhaps he's a ghost,' Alan suggested. 'He likes that, don't stop.'

She pulled the ear gently between her fingers, sinking into the rhythm to calm her shaking.

'You know him? What did you call him?'

'Grim. He used to be my dog. I found him when he was a pup with his leg caught in a rabbit trap a year or so before I left Ravenscar, but I couldn't keep him at the Hall because my grandfather hated animals, so Jasper and Mary kept him for me. Albert didn't mention him when I saw him last month, so I presumed he had died years ago. Where have you been, boy?'

'Could he possibly have come looking for you?'

'It's possible. He always had a keen sense of smell; he knew when I was returning from school and would meet me halfway from the coach in Keynsham. Make your apologies to the lady, Grim. You scared this fearless Amazon as white as her nightdress.'

'He did not!' She began pulling away, but his arms tightened on her and only then did she realise he had been stroking her back as well as the dog. It had been so natural and right she hadn't noticed except now to miss it.

'Whiter,' he murmured. 'That muslin is a delicious shade of rich cream. Now we just need some peaches and strawberries to dip in it... That's better. You were looking a little ghost-like yourself for a moment. Did he wake you?'

She looked back down into the adoring eyes of the aged dog, escaping from the less adoring but far more unsettling eyes of his erstwhile master. But she made no effort to move away from the heat of his body.

'I couldn't sleep and then I heard something...'

'Lily, you can't charge after ghosts in the middle of the night. It's dangerous. You are too brave for your own good.'

'I'm not, I was absolutely terrified. My mind just froze.'

He pulled her against him and she pressed her cheek into the warmth of his shoulder. In a moment she would go.

'Fear is natural and healthy, Lily. It means you have something to lose. If you weren't scared, I'd be worried about you. Whenever any of my soldiers really turned their back on fear, I knew they were in trouble. Sometimes we have to put it aside, but never put it away. You should be a little more forgiving towards yourself.'

His voice flowed over her hair, warm and soothing and his hand was caressing again. Smooth and gentle, his fingers shaping and re-shaping the curve of her waist and hip. Each motion sent a shiver of heat through her abdomen, gathering between her thighs and tingling over her chest.

She drew back, remembering his cold anger from before.

'That is rather in conflict with your comments earlier this evening. I thought I was being too forgiving towards myself.'

He considered her, but the coldness she had expected didn't return.

'Perhaps both. In any case, next time you hear a bump in the night, set the bells pealing, but stay in your room. Haven't any of those novels taught you anything?'

His voice was sinking, hoarse now, a warning in itself. She tried to pull herself back behind her usual defences.

'Just that fiction is more exciting than fact.'

'That won't do. That is practically an invitation to prove you wrong.'

The wicked amusement was back, a clear invitation to match his light-hearted flirt, but it had the opposite effect on her. The absence of his cold anger was such a relief she felt ten times a fool at how willing she was to lose herself at the first sign of warmth from him.

'I am sorry I bothered you. You should be resting. You may think you are recovered, but you aren't yet.'

'Ah, the scold is back. I was wondering how long before you tried to reassert your authority. I am much better, thanks to your nursing skills. I just need a bath and a shave and I shall be human again.'

She knew what he was doing. These were Wellington's tactics—lure the enemy forward with a view of an innocuous landscape, and when they crested the hill, they would find the British lying in wait and be stormed. She had read about it, she had seen Alan use the precise same tactic on her before and still she was walked straight up that hill. Willingly. She tried to stop short of the crest and retain some dignity.

'You still should be resting. It is fools like you who do the most damage to themselves. Remember that Mr Curtis thought he was well enough to go deliver a sermon.'

'Albert was sixty and had a weak heart. But if you want me in bed, you have only to ask. Or better yet, you could help me. I'm becoming quite fond of leaning on you.'

'Lord Ravenscar…'

'Grim, remind the lady that she has already called me by my given name, on very intimate occasions, and that we are to all intents and purposes betrothed. It is a little late for formality.'

She wanted so desperately to give in, to match the light-hearted acceptance of their fates.

Right now, right here, the choice was clear. She wanted Alan.

He wanted her, too. Even if it was a different kind of need, she could feel it in the heat radiating from his body, in the coaxing pressure of his fingers against her. Mostly she could see it in the depth of his gaze—an avid, dark possessiveness under the enticing smile. He might not want to be forced into matrimony any more than she, but she wasn't the only one in thrall to this desire.

Would it be so terrible? She wasn't her mother. She wouldn't sit on an island and wait for months at a stretch. She would demand much more.

His hand was stroking her back again, lingering on the edges of her hip before moving back up. Each time trailing a little lower until she was anticipating where he would pause and retreat, tingling with both pleasure and rising expectation which each foray. Then it stopped and she could feel her pulse thumping beneath his fingers.

'If I were halfway a gentleman, I would point out that you shouldn't be alone with me in a bedroom. Grim is not an adequate chaperon.'

Even this reminder of the impropriety of being here with him, standing against him as if they were lovers, was a subtle invitation. But it was still a reminder—she could not blame him for still hoping the disaster could yet be averted. He might not believe he had a choice but to offer marriage, but she could still release him from this predicament. Marriage with Philip Marston would extricate them both from their mistakes. Not elegantly, but conclusively.

The problem was that she didn't want to be reminded. If it was up to her to move away from him, she didn't know if she could.

'I was here with you this afternoon,' she pointed out, playing for time. Grim yawned and padded over to the fire and sank down beside it with another luxuriant yawn, watching them.

'I wasn't myself this afternoon.'

'You were surly, critical and annoyed at me. I think that was very much in character.'

His fingers moved again, even more gently this time, the slide of fabric on the swell of her hip was so soft it made no sense for it to send such fire through her veins, gathering in places she hardly ever noticed but now couldn't ignore.

'I was surly, critical and annoyed because I wanted to do this, but could barely stand. I'm feeling much better now. See?'

She did see. Apparently he recovered as swiftly as he fell ill. Even the greyish tinge that had alarmed her yesterday was gone; his skin looked...warm. Tasty. Not peaches and cream, but something earthy, heady, with depth of texture and taste. Chocolate and spices and cognac. A hedonistic feast.

'I'm hungry,' she blurted out, and the laughter died out of his eyes. The heat that had been simmering in them, singeing the surface of her skin, became an instant blaze and then like his avian namesake he swooped.

She had expected the teasing to continue, he had appeared so collected, almost light-hearted, but he had misled her again. There was no teasing this time, no slow seduction. Instead he picked up right where they had left off at the inn, plunging her into the middle of a storm and taking the decision away from her.

She didn't care; this was what she wanted—his hands on her, one curving over her buttocks, pulling her against him, his other on her nape, his fingers splayed, hot and hard, against her tingling scalp. He kissed her as he had that first time in the inn, but this time without anger, just a hunger to match hers, a deep drawing on her soul. He suckled her lower lip into his mouth, tasting and feasting on it as his body moved against hers, holding her hard against his arousal, raising her thigh against his so he could fit himself better against her.

She hadn't even felt him untie her belt, but now both his hands were moving over her hips and thighs, not on her dressing gown but under it, just the near-transparent cotton of her nightgown shifting between his palms and her skin. She wanted it gone, she wanted his hands where they belonged, on her skin, touching her where it ached.

She shuddered, finally reaching up to touch him as he was touching her, sliding her arms around him, her hand deep in his hair, raising herself to meet his kiss, her fingers pressing hard into his nape, holding him there as she tasted the lips she had so guiltily caressed when he was ill. This was what she had wanted to do...and this...

'Lily!' It was a growl, deep and shaken, and then drowned as he took back control, his hands raising her nightgown, his fingers finally finding her flesh. 'Lily...'

She clung to him as his hands mapped the soft

skin of her thighs; each rise and fall was a wave crashing over her, pummelling her from inside, grinding her into a fine dust of sensations. Now her world wasn't expanding any longer, it was imploding, reducing itself to nothing more than the object of his touch and the raging, devouring heat at her centre.

'Alan.' She wrapped her arms around his neck, raising herself to bring her mouth to his, her fingers anchoring in his hair. It was silkier even than it looked, liquid between her fingers, but the muscles of his neck were as hard as rock with tension.

When the resistance broke, it was complete. He dragged her against him, his mouth closing on hers with a feral growl, his hand on her backside pressing her hard against his thighs. She had never felt a man's arousal before, but she instinctively knew what it was, her body awakening further, pressing back, urgent with the need to rise against him, do something to answer the sensitive pulsing at her core.

This is it, she thought. This was what she had been waiting for. This desire was even more potent than her terror had been. This was a doorway to a different kind of fear of destruction. Under the fire he was setting loose, something in her was shifting, opening to a new reality. With just his hands and touch and taste, with the movement of his long lean body against hers, he was showing how constrained she had been until that moment, how much more there was to the world, to him. To herself.

'Show me, Alan...'

Every time she said his name Alan lost his footing. He had resisted every urge to go to her room, apologise for his accusations, because he had been afraid of precisely this happening. He should be thinking of every possible way to avert disaster, but instead he was clinging to a cliff face and desperate to let go, slip into her heat, into the passion that blazed beneath her surface, waiting to be set free. He wanted to be the one to set it free, to strip away her defences, her clothes, everything that kept her from him. To lay her bare to the soul and the skies.

His.

This conviction might be madness, it might pass and fade, but right now it filled the universe.

His.

'Lily.'

He said her name against the kiss-swollen softness of her lips, the authors of the smile that taunted his days and his dreams. He tasted them, slowly, drawing them between his teeth, teasing them with his tongue as her fingers tightened in his hair, her breathing ragged against his, gathering into breathy, devastating moans.

If she could melt like this from a kiss, what would she be like when he touched her? When he slid his fingers along the damp he knew was already gathering, preparing her for him. When he licked his way down her beautiful body, worshipped the breasts that still haunted him ever since they had pressed against him at the inn, high and firm.

God, he wanted to see her, touch her, feast on her. He wanted to watch her explore his body, her own body, touch herself, teach him everything she loved so he could take her to heaven. If she let him, he would show her what she was capable of...set free; she would love like a goddess, like the elements, wild and untamed. She would consume him.

'Lily...you're killing me,' he growled, but she just moaned his name again, moving against him restlessly, sending a cascading shudder through his body, pooling in his groin with an aching agony that was so powerful he froze, frightened at the foreign intensity of his need. How could she always take him so far so fast?

He captured her face in his hands, staring down into her eyes. Her pupils were pinpricks encased in golden pools, molten and full of need. If he chose, he could take her now. They had to wed anyway. What difference did it make if he took her now or waited until the formal vows sealed their fates? At least that would put a categorical seal on this fiasco. He would press her down on the bed and seduce her until she begged him for release, and when he had given her a taste of pleasure, he would sink into her, lose himself in her…

Risk leaving her with child.

He dragged his hands away from her. Never, never in his life had he risked that. He must still be ill to even have considered…

'Enough. Lily. We must stop.'

Her hands still reached out to him, her mouth shaped the last word, her eyelids sank and rose, very slowly.

He gritted his teeth and took another step back.

'Go to your room. We will talk tomorrow.'

'Talk…'

'Tomorrow. Right now you need to leave. Now.'

He saw the vixen surface with a mix of regret and relief. Her eyes hardened from honey to agate, her mouth flattened with tension and rejection. Then even those emotions were swept away under the socialite's façade, only the burn of colour on her cheeks proving this had been deadly serious. He wanted to soothe her, ease her out of it, but he was dangling from the finest thread and the charm that served him so well with other women was beyond him.

He didn't want to charm her, he wanted to possess her.

He nearly weakened, his hands rising of their own accord, when her chin went up and she shrugged. Her lips parted, but whatever response she had been contemplating foundered and she merely shrugged again and left, not bothering to close the door.

Grim whined and came to lean against him as he sat down on the bed. The fire was fading. He should either stoke it or get into bed. He had thought he was recovered, but he preferred to believe he was still unwell rather than credit Lily with this hot, shaky sensation. He should have walked out the door the moment he had woken from his fever, as weak as a kitten or not. He should have known... He *had* known she was nothing but trouble. From that first moment in the Hollywell library. What kind of woman wields a damn mace anyway? Any but the world's greatest fool would have known.

Grim rested his muzzle on Alan's thigh, closing his eyes. Alan stroked his head instinctively. Had it really been over a dozen years since he had seen this dog? It was amazing he was still alive.

He probably wouldn't live much longer.

'My poor Grim, I abandoned you, didn't I?'

Grim yawned and padded over to curl into a crescent by the orange remains of the fire. Alan had forgotten Grim would lie down like that by the library fire while he sat with Jasper and Mary. He sank his head in his hands, his elbows on his knees, listening to the dog's huffing breath. He had forgotten how comforting it had been to listen to Grim's breathing in the same room with him when he came to Hollywell to escape the cold hostility of the Hall or when he went to sit by Rickie's grave.

Chapter Ten

Lily stared out the library window at the scrubbed blue skies of a perfect autumn morning. The only reminder of the storm was the dance of wind in the trees. At least this meant Alan wouldn't be soaked to the skin if he walked to Keynsham. She should be grateful, but she wasn't. Why couldn't the roads and fields be flooded, or better yet, an early snowstorm descend upon them and give them one more day…?

She didn't want this time with him to end. She wanted to wrap herself around him, keep him here with her. These feelings were unstoppable, unbearable, and she didn't know what to do. She knew it wasn't the same for him. Otherwise he could not have been in control so quickly after she had all but melted into a puddle at his feet. He wanted to bed her, but he had probably wanted to bed dozens of women and it had meant nothing in the end. For her this was becoming everything.

The squeal was so high-pitched her mind immediately rejected the possibility that this was a trick of the wind. She hurried into the hallway in time to see a ginger streak coming down the stairs, Grim in pursuit. The ginger tabby paid no attention to Lily, its tail high and just curved at the tip as it skidded into the library, its solid body thumping against the doorway. Grim wasn't as swift, but he was large and his lean body drank up the distance in pursuit. His size was an impediment, though, and she spread her legs and planted herself in the library door.

'That's enough, you two!'

Grim's paws scrabbled on the wooden hallway floor as he curved to avoid collision. Behind her she could see the tabby had jumped on to the bookcase in the middle of the room, flanked by the suits of armour and glaring at Lily as if she had spoilt his fun.

Grim growled at the tabby and looked up at Lily, clearly waiting for permission to continue.

Curious, Lily stood back and Grim gathered his old body and proceeded according to plan.

This time only one suit of armour suffered damage. Grim's leap for the tabby did set the bookcase rocking, but the tabby leapt, landing gracefully on the helmet until it toppled to the ground, taking one of the shoulder plates with it in a muted clang. The tabby skidded past Lily's legs again, but Grim stood there, panting and content, clearly waiting to be adulated. Lily relented and scratched his head.

'I see this is a habit. Perhaps I should be grateful you two haven't wreaked worse damage.'

'So you have identified the vandals?'

Alan stood in the doorway, surveying the beheaded knight, and Grim padded over to him, his nails clicking on the wood and his filmy eyes glistening with sheepish pride. 'I found Grim's point of infiltration. It was a door to the garden from one of the small back parlours in the north wing. The catch is faulty.'

He looked much as he had when he arrived two days ago—handsome, forbidding, tense. She didn't speak and he continued.

'Grim can stand guard until I can send someone for you from the Hall. Then later we can sit down and discuss...'

He stopped just as Grim raised his head, nudging Alan's hand. Then she heard it, too. A clatter of wheels.

'Stay here. Don't say a word.'

The door closed behind him before she could respond and she hurried over to press her ear to the wooden surface. She hoped it was the post-chaise, but they weren't due for another day. Could they have mistaken the date?

'Alan Rothwell!'

'Alan! Oh, thank goodness!'

Lady Ravenscar's and Catherine's voices were unmistakable and Lily leaned her forehead on the door. At least that meant he wouldn't have to walk to Keynsham.

'What is the meaning of this?' Lady Ravenscar was demanding, but Lily was surprised to hear her voice shake. 'They found your horse... riderless...and the note. I thought I recognised the hand...but I don't understand!'

'Grandmama!'

Lily heard the clatter, Catherine's cry and Alan's curse and she pulled open the door. It wasn't Alan who had collapsed, but Lady Ravenscar, whose cane had fallen to the ground and who was now supported between Catherine and Alan. Unfortunately Lady Ravenscar hadn't fainted and her gaze locked with Lily's and her voice at least showed she wasn't at death's door.

'I knew it! Lily Wallace!'

Grim padded over and leaned his head against Lily's side in a show of much-needed solidarity as the three Rothwells sent her looks of outrage, shock and impatient annoyance.

She placed her hand on Grim's back.

'Would you care for some tea? I have just put on the kettle.'

Chapter Eleven

'If you please, miss. Lady Ravenscar asked if you will join her when you are ready. In the Rose Room.'

Lily secured the clasp of her mother's gold pendant and shook out the pale blue muslin skirts of her dress. None of her thoughts reflected in her mirror image. She looked calm, even bored, which was nothing less than amazing.

'Is she alone, Sue?'

'No, miss. Lord Ravenscar and Lady Catherine are with her, taking tea.'

That sounded so civilised. She wondered what the servants were making of all this and if they were accepting the fiction spun between the three Rothwells to explain her precipitous return or Alan's presence.

At least the horse had been found by a farmer near Bitton who knew little of the Rothwells and hopefully cared less about the particulars of the peculiar message requesting Lady Ravenscar be alerted that her grandson was ill at Holly-well and could she send a carriage. He had done as requested—driven over through the storm to the Hall, horse in tow and the note in his breast pocket. The only hitch in Lily's plans had been that Partridge, the butler, had seen the note before Lady Ravenscar. But whether the face-saving machinations were effective or not, Lady Ravenscar's words to her at the foot of the stairs upon their return to the Hall had been meant for her ears only and left little to the imagination.

'I will not allow you to add to the damage to my grandson's reputation, Lily Wallace. However, although this is not quite how I would have hoped matters progressed, it might do very well after all. Now, go bathe and dress and come down promptly, we have a great many particulars to see to.' When Lily's foot was already on the first stair, she had added, 'Welcome home.'

Home.

She paused at the door to the Rose Room, grateful Partridge was not hovering about to hurry her along. She gathered herself, took a deep breath and opened the door.

If they had been talking, they fell silent as she entered, the motionless tableau thankfully broken by Grim, who left Alan's side and padded over to her. A thankful burn of moisture in her eyes made her look down as she petted his soft head, grateful that Alan had insisted the old dog accompany them in the carriage, despite Lady Ravenscar's expostulations. She was glad he was here.

Lady Ravenscar spoke first.

'Sit down, Miss Wallace. We have a great deal to discuss. Catherine, perhaps you'd prefer to return to Nicola now.'

After a tense moment Catherine stood and with a glance at her brother she moved towards the door, sending a reassuring smile at Lily that did little to relax Lily's nerves. She resisted reaching out to the other woman as she passed, begging her to stay.

'Sit down, Lily,' Lady Ravenscar repeated, underlining her command with a light tap of her cane on the floor.

Lily did as she was told, readying herself for the attack and wondering what Alan was thinking as he sat down as well. By the look on his face it was best not to know. She reached out to Grim and the dog settled by her side and rested his head on her thigh, waiting to be indulged.

'Well, Lily Wallace, you have gone your length.' There was a peculiar tone to the old woman's words, certainly not the disdain Lily had expected. 'My grandson has accepted his measure of culpability in what has transpired over the past couple of days, but for a change it appears that the bulk of blame lies elsewhere. It makes no odds, of course—the end result is the same. He has also agreed it would be best to proceed as if this courtship, such as it is, took place here at the Hall and with my full approval. To this end he has agreed to remain here at the Hall until we make our announcement. This will quiet any possible whispers regarding your movements these past couple of days. Given Alan's reputation I doubt anyone would be surprised to hear he has secured your favours so swiftly.'

Lily matched the rhythm of her breathing to the stroking of her hand on Grim's head. Slow and steady. The urge to look at Alan overcame caution, but if she expected comfort, there was none. His face was colder even than his grandmother's, distant and watchful. She could almost believe it had nothing to do with him.

'Your mother was a Woodcote and, though not of the first families, your father's birth was unexceptionable and thus no barrier to marriage to a Rothwell. Given my grandson's reputation, I believe we can be grateful he has done so well.

Certainly your lineage can be considered superior to the woman my son married…'

'Careful how you speak of my mother, Lady Jezebel.' Alan's voice was liquid steel and Lady Ravenscar blinked at the unveiled menace.

'I was merely stating that I am not disappointed in your choice, Alan.'

'Unlike my father's, I understand. You keep my mother out of this. She was a better woman than ever you will be.'

Grim's head slid higher on Lily's thigh, his whole body angling away from the antagonism between the two Rothwells.

'She should not have encouraged him to run away from his responsibilities for the dubious fantasy of becoming a doctor. A doctor!'

'She was trying to make him happy. Which was something neither of his parents ever bothered doing!'

'Perhaps if he had applied himself…'

Alan surged to his feet.

'Yes, do remind me on how many levels my father was a disappointment and how far he fell from the stellar example set by his own esteemed papa. It has been quite a few years since I have had to suffer through those charming lectures. Perhaps if your vicious brute of a husband hadn't beaten your son into submission, he might have proven a little less of a disappointment, Jezebel.'

There was a momentary flash of emotion in the old lady's eyes and Lily wanted to step forward and intercede before something bad happened. Though obviously many bad things had already happened.

'Believe me,' he continued, 'if I ever were to discover that I was no longer a disappointment to you, Jezebel, I would take a very hard look to see where I had gone wrong. Now I suggest that, as you yourself said for the sake of this family you appear to suddenly value so highly, you and I find a better way to deal with our mutual dislike until we resolve the issue at hand. That is as much of an olive branch as you are ever likely to get from me, so let me know how you wish to proceed from here.'

He didn't even look at Lily as he stalked out the garden door and she didn't move even after the air stopped shuddering from the slam. Clearly he was mending fast, Lily thought with a twinge of contrary regret.

'That boy! Impossible!'

Lady Ravenscar thumped her cane angrily on the floor, glaring after him.

'Shall I leave, Lady Je—Lady Ravenscar?'

She tried not to sound meek, but this household was definitely having an effect on her.

Lady Ravenscar turned her black eyes on her.

'He has quite a viper's sting, doesn't he?'

Lily hesitated, searching for the best answer. She gave up. 'Yes, Lady Ravenscar.'

'That was my mistake. I merely wished… He misunderstood me, of course. About his father. Please do not begin to call me Lady Jezebel as well, like my irreverent grandson. It was my mother-in-law, the Dowager Marchioness, that insisted on continuing to call me Lady Jezebel even after my marriage and of course everyone did as she demanded. If you must indulge your penchant for the informal, I prefer Lady Belle. My mother and sister called me Belle. Jezebel was my father's idea. He named my sister Rahab.'

'Good lord!'

'Precisely. Not a pleasant man, my father. Very much like my husband. I was just barely turned sixteen to Lord Ravenscar's forty-one when we were wed. Sit down a moment. Then I dare say you should go after my fool of a grandson before his body catches up with his vanity and he falls into the lake and drowns.'

Lily sat down with a thump. Sue, the timid but gossipy chambermaid who always stuttered when Lady Ravenscar addressed her, was sixteen. A plump puppy of a child. She tried to imagine her married to the type of man who named his daughters after whores and seductresses.

'Precisely,' Lady Ravenscar said again, though Lily hadn't spoken. Apparently her expression spoke volumes.

'Well, it's a pity your father and husband couldn't have married and left you out of it. They clearly deserved one another.'

Lady Ravenscar stared at her, her pale blue eyes wide with shock. Then her gaze seemed to move inside her, her eyes losing focus, and for a moment Lily worried she might be having some sort of attack, a thought reinforced when the old lady suddenly choked. Lily reached out for her but dropped her hands when she realised the choke was actually a laugh. A very creaky and unused instrument, but a laugh none the less.

'So they did. You are quite shameless, Lily Wallace. Your parents have a great deal to answer for.'

'Most of all for leaving me far too soon. For all their faults, they set high standards—they accepted me as I am, flaws, foibles and all. I wish I could have done the same for them while they lived.'

'Yes, that explains a great deal. But husbands are not parents, girl. They needn't answer to the same standards of absolute acceptance. My grandson is not an easy man, but he is nothing like his grandfather, thankfully. I hope you will manage better than I.'

Lily took a deep breath.

'Lady Belle, I realise I made a grave mistake, but any decision to marry will be made by myself and your grandson. Alone.'

'Some decisions in life are made for us by circumstance, Lily Wallace. Now run along. I am tired. He will probably be down by the willows on the lake. And take that hound with you.'

It didn't take her long to find him. She didn't know how Lady Ravenscar was so certain he would be by the lake, but she wasn't surprised when halfway down the path she saw him through the willows overhanging the embankment, seated on the marble bench with his back to the lake, his elbows propped on his knees.

She slowed. It wasn't her role to coax him out of the sullens. She had her own problems and right now he was the most serious among them. She was not fool enough to believe she was qualified to mediate the murky waters of the Rothwell family.

She sat down on the other end of the bench, but he didn't look up, his gaze fixed on the willow branches draped picturesquely over a low stone wall. Beyond the cavern of the trees around them everything glistened as the sunlight cast a sweet glaze over the damp grass and reeds. It was a perfect, restful setting, except for the man radiating fury by her side.

'Did you know your great-aunt is named Rahab?' she asked the willows.

His scowl didn't lessen and he showed no signs of listening.

'After the harlot of Jericho,' she prompted.

Nothing.

'I dare say if your great-grandfather had had another daughter, he would have named her Athalia or Delilah or some other sinner's name. At least those are pretty names. Rahab is horrid. Even Jezebel is better. Your grandmother told me her mother called her Belle, which is quite nice. Never in her father's presence of course. Clearly she was another downtrodden woman. And Rahab was Ray. Belle and Ray. Until she was married off at sixteen to your grandfather. Do you know how old he was when they wed?'

Nothing.

'Forty-one. Now admittedly he might have been a very nice forty-one-year-old. In fact, forty-one is often preferable to twenty-one. One has experience, and perhaps even patience, but in his case I don't think age improved any of his qualities. One is tempted to wonder whether his nastiness might have some mitigating explanation like another nasty Rothwell before him, which by the sound of the Dowager Marchioness might very well have been the case, but the fact remains he was a vile man and made your grandmother's life a misery even before she blessed him with your father.'

'Is this chatter ever going to end or shall I go elsewhere?'

Lily thought lovingly of the mace at Hollywell House and folded her hands in her lap.

'I am done.'

The lake gleamed pleasantly, scarred down the middle by the wakes of three ducks making for the willows at the other edge. She liked willows. If she ever had a house of her own, she would have willows and she would put a table and chairs under them and take her books there and read near the water. Perhaps one day when…*if* she had children, while she read they could feed the ducks and sail little boats among the reeds and…

'So you expect me to feel sorry for her?'

Lily started and gave up her daydreams.

'Yes. You are supposed to feel stricken by remorse that you have been too insensitive to perceive her life was one of miserable domination by a brutish fiend and you will go down on bended knee and beg forgiveness for your callousness.'

A muscle tightened in his cheek and she watched the telltale line beside his mouth curve. The memory of touching that line while he was ill tingled in her fingertips and she turned back to the ducks and willows. She shouldn't enjoy teasing him out of his sullens and she shouldn't be allowing herself to become all warm over thoughts of touching a man's cheek.

'Knee bending isn't a strength of mine. I am afraid I've exhausted my chivalric impulses rescuing a very ungrateful damsel from her own folly.'

'I wasn't in distress. Besides, I did some rescuing of my own. You would most likely have fallen off your horse into a muddy ditch and drowned. All you did was complicate matters.'

'Well, matters are about to be simplified. Marriage has a way of cutting things down to size.'

'That need not be the case. Whatever your grandmother says, we may yet avoid a scandal. Neither of us wishes to be trapped in a marriage of form. You want your freedom and I want a family, which you admitted you have no interest in.'

'You have been spending too much time with lawyers, Lily, you are beginning to sound like one. You can throw as many clauses and sub-clauses at this, but the basic facts cannot be avoided. We were two days together, alone. In my experience scandals of these proportions are impossible to bury and I won't have the ruin of a young woman added to my list of sins. So I suggest you accept your fate with equanimity. You needn't worry I will make any unpleasant demands on you or your fortune. I had never intended to marry, but if it can't be helped, it can't. At least you are an intelligent woman, and I think if we establish the ground rules, there is no reason we can't make the best of this. Speaking of lawyers, I suggest you send for Mr Prosper and have him help you compose a marriage settlement you find adequate to your needs. He will probably explain to you that once you marry, your husband receives all your inheritance outright, barring any landed property for which he would receive only the income. Since I don't want a penny of your money and I have no interest in your father's mines, Prosper will have to be creative about creating a settlement that will provide you with an amount in pin money that would allow you to pursue whatever activities you wish, business or otherwise. I will sign whatever you want so you may do with it as you see fit.'

It was a generous offer. It was certainly far more generous than Philip Marston's, at least with regards to her inheritance and her personal freedom. In her discussions with Marston he had promised her a generous allowance in pin money as well as a substantial jointure, but she doubted he would let her dispose of her assets or decide how she would live her life. Philip Marston wanted a mother for his heirs and a socially adept wife to further his ambitions.

But as generous as Alan's offer was, it could not atone for what he wasn't willing to offer her. She had never expected Marston to care for her, not in any deep way. She had come to accept the fact that she was not lovable, since none of the men who had wanted to marry her had seemed swayed by any strong emotion other than avarice and she certainly had never cared for any of them. But she knew she would love her children and hopefully they would love her, and that, Philip Marston was more than willing to give her. He clearly loved his daughter, but he wanted what his own wife had been unable to give him, a large family, preferably with a few sons, and in the end this was what Lily wanted as well. It didn't matter that Alan had breached walls inside her she had not known existed and awakened needs she had not imagined could exist. In his own way he was generous and honest, but he wanted nothing to do with her dreams and she had no power to change him. To live in the expectation that she could would be to invite disaster.

'Nothing to say, Lily? You were talkative enough before. I should be gratified you aren't arguing, but I worry most when you are silent. It makes me want to check over my shoulder for the descending axe, or, in your case, a mace.'

'When I do next wield a mace at your head, I won't do it behind your back, Alan Rothwell.'

He smiled suddenly, demolishing her defences further.

'I almost hope you do. I would like the opportunity to disarm you. Disrobe you, too, but that will have to wait a few weeks, unfortunately.'

She gasped. There was no other way to describe the sharp intake of air that her body forced upon her at his words. She should have just laughed at his absurd response to her absurd suggestion. After all, she had wanted to infuse a little humour into the impossibly difficult situation they were trapped in and she should be happy she made him and Lady Ravenscar smile. But his voice had lost the rasping edge of the fever and regained the sultry sensation of rough velvet dragging over her nerves. It shoved her back against a mental wall and stripped her.

She stood abruptly. This marked the end of the unevenness in their power play his illness had introduced. He was no longer a patient but a clever, experienced rake; he was back in control of himself and she had better do the same if she was to remain in control of her fate.

'Running away again, Lily?'

'I'm standing, not running.'

'You're contemplating it.'

His voice as smooth as heated syrup and his gaze black as burning coals and hot as Hades. She knew it was a taunt, aimed at the precise opposite result. He wanted her to take him up on his dare and she wanted to. Not because it was a dare, but because she wanted to stay right there and see what happened.

'Are you daring me?'

'You seem to thrive on dares; it's hard to resist tossing them your way.'

'You're just doing this because you're upset I saw you flat on your back and weak as a kitten. If this is an attempt to recapture your sense of manhood, it is rather puerile.'

'You're wrong. That's not why I'm doing this.'

'Then why? Because I witnessed that scene between you and your grandmother?'

He shook his head and moved towards her.

'Wrong again.'

'Then because of Hollywell House. Is that it? Because I didn't want to sell?'

'No. That's also not why and you know it.'

She swallowed and stepped back, but he continued moving towards her.

'That was three guesses, but I'm feeling generous, so you get one more. If you guess right, I'll stop.'

Oh, unfair. That was no incentive to guess right. But the words came anyway, because she needed to see if they were true.

'Because you want to?'

He stopped.

'It is usually the simplest answer that's the correct one, isn't it? So what now, Lily? Shall I stop or do you forfeit your win?'

It isn't that simple, she wanted to say. Not at all simple.

'Here?'

The black fire flashed in his eyes again and he took her hand and pulled her into the shade of the willows. Nothing so tame and cosy as the tea and books she had imagined. Nothing so profound as the children playing, at least not profound for him, but she was afraid it might be for her. There was certainly nothing tame or cosy about the harsh handsome face looking down at her, scored by the lacy shadows of the willow branches that closed about them like a cage. She had stumbled into a wild animal's lair, a panther, dark and sleek and stalking her. He raised his hand and very gently skimmed his knuckles down her cheek, coming to rest just below her mouth, his eyes following his movement with an intensity that burned the caressed skin as much as his touch. She could believe he had read her thoughts, that he knew precisely what she had wanted to do to him as she watched him on the bench and he was paying her back for her foolishness. But then his thumb gently settled on her lower lip, its pressure daring her to open her mouth, to signal that she was ready and waiting for something more.

'Lily...'

She needed to breathe. She couldn't help it, her mouth opened, sucking in his scent, deeper and warmer than the green around them.

'That's right,' he murmured and bent to meet her invitation. 'Open for me.'

His lips brushed hers, gently shaping them, sliding between them only to slide away, lightly tugging and releasing. With each sweep, the urge to cling, to force him to press deeper, harder, grew.

She knew he was playing with her, taunting her into reacting, into making a demand. There was something more, much more, and he was actively withholding it. She resisted, not wanting to give him the satisfaction of begging for what she needed, but it was wearing her down, the friction and his breath soothing and warming and promising.

When he stepped back, she just stood there, disbelieving. Was he so unaffected? Was it only she who was thrumming, singed below the skin, needing…?

'You can't have something for nothing, Lily.' His voice wasn't as confident as his actions; it was rougher than usual, bordering on an accusation.

I don't want something. I want everything. You.

He was right. She wanted to give, not just take. She might have said the words out loud if he hadn't moved towards her again, but just as his fingertips brushed her shoulders he stopped, his gaze focusing on a point behind her.

'Not here. Let's go…somewhere else.'

He grabbed her wrist, but her eyes had followed his and her haze of expectant heat was cleaved through with shock as she realised what he had been staring at while seated on the bench. How hadn't she noticed the tombstone before? Perhaps it was because it was so modest and the same colour as the wall directly behind it. She moved towards it without thinking.

"'Richard George Brisbane Rothwell. 1798–1802,'" she read slowly. Eighteen years ago.

Rickie. The echo of his fevered voice, tortured and foreign, sounded in her mind. She turned to him.

'You had a brother as well. He died when your parents did.'

'We don't speak of him.'

'I realise that. Why?'

He was under control again; even the familiar mocking smile was back. Both passion and pain might never have been there at all.

'House rules. Some people don't like being reminded of their crimes. Certainly my grandparents didn't. They hadn't even known Rickie existed until my parents died; he was born after we came to Edinburgh. At least they had the decency to bring his body back, but not enough to bury him in the Chapel with my father. I used to resent that, but not any more. This is a better place. Someplace he might have played if he had lived here. My grandparents never came down to the lake, too frivolous. That's why I like it here. I can meditate on my sins and my failure in quiet. Until you showed up.'

'Sins plural and failure singular. Why?'

'Must you pick at everything?'

'It's not a question of must. Who did you fail? Your brother?'

'What a tortuous little brain you have.' He smiled at her grimly. 'There were other failures, but he was the most monumental. At least the men who died under my command were there by choice and they knew what might happen to them. Rickie was four years old.'

'Catherine said your parents died of the fever. Didn't he die of the same cause?'

'Yes. Disease and carelessness. The disease wasn't my fault, the carelessness was.'

'You were just a child.'

'So what? Do you know in the mill I won at cards five years ago half the workers were under ten years old? They and their families saw nothing peculiar about that. When I told the families we would no longer be employing children, we nearly had a riot on our hands until we found alternatives. I might have been twelve, but I was still responsible for him. My parents were ill, the whole city was in a panic at the epidemic, people closed down their houses and stores and ran for the hills. I was too ashamed to fetch the doctor again because we had nothing to give him. I actually thought I could care for him myself. My only consolation was that they died before they realised he was dead. Foolish, isn't it? They would have died anyway. What difference would it make if they knew?'

Lily remembered that night watching over the housekeeper's tiny bloodstained baby on the island. Nothing anyone had said, could say, erased her guilt. But this had been his *brother*, in his care while his parents lay dying and his sister and nanny close to death themselves, caught in a city of chaos and without resources. She could imagine nothing more lonely, more terrifying. He was no fool, he probably knew his brother would have died anyway, but the doubt would never disappear.

She crouched down and laid her hand flat on the cool stone, just below the name. How deep did his little skeleton lie?

'It makes a difference to you,' she answered. 'One less burden for you to bear.'

'A burden I will never willingly bear again.'

She shivered and stood up. He had said as much before, but she hadn't realised this wasn't simply a preference for his chosen lifestyle, but a deep rejection of what she held dear. He would do what was proper, marry her, and then she would truly be alone.

'That makes no sense,' she protested, unwilling to accept the verdict. 'What happened with

Rickie wasn't your fault. You cannot go through life blaming yourself for something you had no control over.'

'This isn't only about blame. I watched Rickie die. It took days, but I saw the precise moment. For four years he had been the most wonderful thing to enter our lives, the first thing to bring real joy to my parents' lives for as long as I could remember, and he ceased to be in a second. I couldn't even tell anyone because there was no one coherent enough to understand. I've watched quite a few men die since then, but by some mercy I've been spared watching another child die. If you think I am mad enough to risk that pain again... Just spare me your self-serving lectures, Lily, and disabuse yourself that either of us still has any choice in the matter—you are going to marry me, and if you want children, you will have to do what any other married woman in the *ton* does when she needs something from a man and her husband won't oblige. I don't know what fairy-tale idea you have of our society, but though we are unforgivingly brutal about young women's reputations before they wed, and demand discretion of them once they do, the *ton* is littered with other men's children—why should I be any different?'

Her jaw ached with the weight of his loss, but

the image of her future his last words conjured made her ill. She shook her head. She would never, ever go down that path, no matter how much she loved Alan and wanted to be with him. But the very fact that he could make such a suggestion dragged out the devil in her. She wanted to hurt him as much as he was hurting her.

'So you would have no problem if I seduced another man and brought him to my bed, if I undressed for him...'

'Damn you!'

He was panther swift and just as frightening as he grabbed her, but she wasn't scared he would hurt her, not in body. Part of her refused to believe he could really contemplate such a future, for her or for himself. She heard the pleading note in her voice as she tried to reach him.

'But that is precisely what would happen if I accepted your generous offer, Alan. I would be damned to a life I would hate.'

He let go and turned away, his breathing as tense as her body.

'This is the way things are, Lily.'

'It doesn't have to be.'

'You've a softer heart than you like to accept, don't you, Lily? You absolve your parents, transform my grandmother into Lady Belle... Well, don't strain it on my account.'

She gathered herself up again at the cold warning in his voice. He was at least decent enough to point out her figurative petticoats were showing. What had she expected? That her emotion would trigger his? She wasn't so naïve. But she wouldn't stand down from her own truth either.

'I'll strain my heart over whatever I want, Lord Ravenscar.' It was a challenge, not an admission. At least she hoped not.

'You should watch that soft flank of yours, Lily. That is how battles are lost.'

She shrugged and brushed her hands on her pelisse.

'You may crow from your perch all you like, Raven. At least I know I am still warm and breathing.'

'Do you find me cold, Lily? Even in light of our little interludes? I must have been doing something wrong.'

'That's not warmth.'

'I agree. It was quite a few degrees hotter than warmth. Shall I remind you?'

She stepped back but stopped. She would not run. She didn't want to run. Oh, blast. She *was* asking for trouble. She was a fool, but at least she knew that now. At least the pain that was to come wouldn't be a surprise.

He smiled and touched her cheek.

'Standing your ground can be as much an offensive move as an outright attack, you do know that, don't you? Of course you do. This vixen is more accustomed to standing and fighting than she is to running after all.'

'Careful you don't get bitten, then.'

'Right now I'm willing to risk it.' His voice dropped and he closed the distance between them. 'More than willing.'

His hands could be so gentle. She could feel the tension in them, the leashed power, but they moved over her skin so lightly, drawing her towards him, skimming over her lower lip so that it shuddered against his fingers.

'Are you willing, Lily?' His voice was also gentle as he bent to replace his fingers with his mouth. The words moved over her, encompassing her with liquid heat. This was how it would feel if they were swimming together in the warm tropical waters of the bay in Isla Padrones. She was swimming with her own shark now. She was exposed and he was lethal. At least to her.

Yes. With his lips just poised over hers, promising, she was willing to risk anything he asked.

'Yes… Alan…'

He drew away, his hand closed around her nape, his thumb pressing up against her chin. The lazy seduction in his eyes was gone. She wasn't prepared for the blaze of fire in them now, or the surge of painful heat that echoed through her in response. He pressed her back against the trunk of the willow, sheathing them in the long green darts, a cocoon of shadow.

'There's no going back now.' His voice was rough against her, impatient and demanding like the hands that brought her against him. She didn't argue, just slid her arms around his neck and let herself go, raising her head and pressing her lips to the warmth of his neck, desperate to feel him, recapture his scent.

A groan ripped through him as she nuzzled the soft skin below his ear, his arms painful around her, but she didn't care, she pressed as close as she could, her hands teasing his hair, loving how she felt against him, how her whole body was lighting, filling, becoming alive, waiting for his touch.

'God, Lily, I want to take you here, with your hair spread like a sunset on the grass. I can't stand much more of this. Do you have any idea what you're doing to me?'

She couldn't have answered even if his mouth hadn't finally caught hers, kissing her hard and deep, demanding a response. He held her, his fingers deep in her hair, gliding against her scalp, shaping the sensitive curve of her ears, sinking lower over her shoulders and down her back, curving under her behind, sliding the soft muslins against her skin as though he could rub them off like moisture with a towel, baring her against the silvery bark and the grey-tinged leaves.

He found and lit bursts of pleasure in places she had never associated with sensation, let alone this restless-seeking joy. Somehow he knew and would linger there until she was shaking, trying not to shatter. Her hands and mouth were trying to do the same to him by their own volition, seeking and touching as he did, shivering as he groaned when her fingers stroked down the ridged muscles of his back beneath his coat. His hands tightened on her behind, pulling her hard against his arousal as he bent his head and nipped the sensitised flesh of her neck.

'We have to stop. Any more and I'll take you right here.'

'Yes…' He stifled her moaned invitation with his mouth, but his words were as damaging as his hands, filling her mind with the promise of what was to come. They flowed against the skin as he kissed her, his mouth moving down her neck, tasting the slope of her shoulder, the rise of her breast.

'No. When I show you what you are capable of, I want you where no one will interrupt us. Where I can lay you bare and kiss you inch by inch, from your ankles, the soft skin on the back of your knees, over every soft slide of your thighs. I want to spend an hour on your amazing behind...' he spread his hands over it, kneading and raising her against his erection, his hands contracting as she shuddered in response '... then I will turn you over and kiss this soft skin right here...' he arched her back to trace the slide of her abdomen, from her ribs to her navel and down '...until I come home, right here, where you're waiting for me...'

His fingers curved down, skimming but not settling there. She didn't even realise what she was about to do until she felt her hand on his, pressing him against her. Her eyes rose to his, shocked at her audacity, meeting the silvered storm in his.

'That's right, Lily. Take what you want... Don't be afraid.'

She wasn't afraid, she was terrified. The exhilarating terror of clinging to a ship's mast in a storm, watching the waves gather for the next pummelling. Any second now she would shatter into nothingness.

With a cry she pushed his hand away and instantly his hold stilled, softened. They stood for a moment longer in the cage of willows, the quacking of the ducks as they flapped their wings on the lake a reminder of where they were. Eventually Alan stood back, resting his hand on a willow branch and looking out over the lake, his eyes retaining the shimmer of light reflecting off the water.

He didn't stop her when she left, but she was weak enough to wish he would.

Chapter Twelve

'**W**hat is wrong with the boy? How on earth are people to give any credence to a courtship between you if he won't show his face?'

'He is very busy, Grandmama…' Catherine said.

'Busy doing what, precisely?'

Catherine's eyes dropped before Lady Ravenscar's and Lily couldn't determine if Catherine didn't know or didn't want to tell. Either case wasn't reassuring.

'It has been two days since your return and you have not seen him for more than five minutes if that, have you, Lily?'

The interlude by the lake had been a little more than five minutes, but after that…

What had she expected? That he would dance attendance on her and woo her? The man felt he must wed her and he clearly wanted to bed her, but he had his own life and he meant to keep it that way. This was a fine introduction to the life she would lead if she wed him. She would have all the freedom she wanted, but very little else. She should be grateful that he was making her choice so very clear, but she could no more stop the hurt and the yearning that hummed inside her than she could stop her heart from beating or blood from flowing.

'Who precisely are you accusing, Lady Belle?' Lily asked. 'Lord Ravenscar or myself? Or both?'

She was saved from Lady Ravenscar's response by Partridge's appearance.

'What is it, Partridge?'

'Mr Marston, my lady. For Miss Wallace.'

'Hmmm…bring him in, Partridge.'

Lily stood.

'No, please, Partridge. Could you show him to the library?'

After a pause, Lady Ravenscar nodded and Partridge departed.

'It is hardly proper for you to meet with Mr Marston in a tête-à-tête, Lily. Especially under the circumstances.'

'We had not reached any formal agreement, but I owe Mr Marston the courtesy of explaining matters myself and in private, Lady Belle. Please respect my wishes on this.'

'Oh, very well. Ten minutes. Thorns are best withdrawn swiftly and decisively, Lily Wallace.'

'I will ignore being compared to a thorn in the flesh, Lady Belle, but I agree in principle.'

Philip Marston turned from his contemplation of the garden and smiled as she entered. He was a good-looking man, with light brown hair and blue eyes and a bearing that spoke of a man used to command, but he looked different than when she had last seen him, less imposing, which made little sense. Lily hoped the answering smile on her face didn't look like a grimace or reflect anything of her inner turmoil.

'Miss Wallace. You look radiant. Clearly time away from me agrees with you.'

'Thank you, Mr Marston, pray sit down. I trust your daughter is well?'

His light brows twitched closer, but his smile held and he sat on the green-striped chair opposite her.

'Very well and very excited about meeting you.'

Oh, no.

'She wanted to accompany me today, but she is still a little fatigued after the trip. You look a little pale, Miss Wallace... Lily. Have you been unwell? I have heard there have been quite a few cases of this fever in the environs.'

She was tempted to fall back on this excuse; guilt was rumbling inside her like a poorly digested meal.

'Not unwell, Mr Marston. It is a little more complicated than that. There is something I must tell you and I ask that you wait until I conclude my tale before you comment. Please.'

She didn't wait for his permission. She wished she was wearing gloves so she would have something to do with her fingers. Instead she held her hands tightly together and told him as much as she dared about her escape to Hollywell and forced proximity with Alan, stopping short of admitting to any intimacies between them.

'I know we had never reached a formal agreement, Mr Marston, but that there was also an understanding between us to consider a...closer relationship and so I felt it only right to explain to you as openly as I can why that is no longer possible and to express my regrets that I should have caused you any distress or embarrassment.'

'Why is it no longer possible?'

The question was so calm it took her a moment to understand it.

'I... Because... I explained what happened.'

'So you did. It was unfortunate and perhaps

you will later explain to me in greater detail precisely why you felt the need to arrange this solitary retreat to Hollywell House. However, if I understood you correctly, at the moment the only people who know you were alone with Ravenscar are his immediate family, his groom who drove the carriage over and possibly Lady Ravenscar's butler.'

'Probably. The man who brought the horse handed him the note I secured in the saddle. Apparently it was smudged, but he has seen at least some instances of my handwriting when I posted letters to my lawyers over the past weeks.'

'I see. That was two days ago?'

'Yes.'

'Have you heard of any gossip regarding your escapade as yet?'

'No, but…'

'Well, then, you might be luckier than you deserve and this shall remain the domain of a very few.'

'Mr Marston…'

'Philip. I believe we can dispense with formalities, Lily. We have known each other long enough, surely.'

'Philip, then. You do realise what I am saying—for almost two days and two nights I was alone, unchaperoned, with a man. If this were to be known, I would be beyond the pale. No man of breeding could consider marrying me.'

'My life is peppered with "ifs", Lily. My business prospers because of them. You have been a very definite "if" from the day I met you at your father's house six years ago. I think I am capable of encompassing one more, within reason. All I am saying at the moment is that we not hurry into decisions we might regret. I admit to being surprised. I briefly saw Ravenscar earlier today on some mutual business of ours and he gave me no intimation whatsoever of any of this, but then he was always a cautious fellow.'

Alan? Cautious?

'He did mention you owned a mill together,' she prompted, hating her curiosity.

'A little more than that. My strength is in shipping, but it exposes me to all forms of merchandise. When I see extraordinary demand for particular products, naturally I become curious and sometimes I dabble in new ideas. Several years ago I became interested in the new power looms being built and sold to cotton mills and that is how I became acquainted with Lord Ravenscar. We share a strong interest in the new machinery and its effect on the costs of production. And apparently now in you, of course.' He smiled politely and for the first time she saw the steel under the calm urbanity.

'I see.'

'Do you? I have the advantage of knowing both you and Ravenscar for quite a few years, certainly longer than your brief acquaintance with each other. Perhaps I shouldn't be surprised that when someone did finally breach your carefully constructed walls it would be someone not dissimilar from your father.'

Lily opened her mouth to speak, but he raised his hand.

'Allow me to finish, Lily. Then you may correct me if I am wrong. When I came to your father's house six years ago, I admit I was fascinated with the workings of your mind. Your father and I both had the cross to bear that our wives bore us only a daughter, but I remember thinking, if Penny could grow up to be as poised and intelligent as you, I would not be disappointed. Had you been a man you could have run your father's businesses as well as he, that was clear. But despite your intelligence there was something walled-off about you. During my visits to Kingston over the years, I watched different men react differently to your defences—some stormed the battlements and were predictably repelled and some admitted defeat before firing the first shot. Since my Joanne was alive at the time, none of this was of any significance, but I admit as I came out of mourning and realised that I yet could have the chance at a male heir for my legacy, it was not long before I thought of you. There are only twelve years between us, which is hardly an insuperable divide. Unlike most young women, you have a keen understanding of my world and, despite your superior lineage, I do not believe you find my more humble origins despicable. When I discovered the unfortunate nature of your father's will, it became clear to me that here was a golden opportunity for both of us and so I approached you. Everything we discussed that day in Kingston is still applicable. You wish to have a family and some financial freedom and I would like a male heir, most preferably an intelligent one who would one day be able to assume my responsibilities. I believe given our joint cerebral gifts any child we bear is most likely to fulfil my highest expectations. It is as simple as that.'

She should probably say something, but nothing came and Philip Marston continued.

'I am not surprised that Ravenscar has the power to fascinate someone like you, Lily, so you needn't feel guilty about some natural confusion. I was very fond of your father—he was a charming, intelligent and generous man and he loved you dearly, but he had a fateful need to see himself reflected in those around him, especially women. I broach this subject because it was evident you were fully aware of his weakness. I am not implying that Ravenscar is a mirror image of your father, there are distinct differences, but there are also distinct similarities. He is a man who was rejected by his family, rebuilt himself on his own terms and is, in vulgar parlance, a rake and very used to going his own way. From the little you disclosed about your mother I could tell that aside from your love for her there was also contempt for her willingness to accept half a loaf and sometimes less. I suggest you think well and long before you allow yourself to be forced into a similar alliance without even the love your parents did share and your mother's significantly more accepting nature. You deserve better.'

Her fingers were plucking at the tiny pearls nestled in the hearts of the flowers embroidered on her skirts. She stilled them, but that was worse because they were clearly shaking. Had he stepped inside her head and found that list of fears and objections prepared by her inner lawyer? She didn't know if she deserved better, but she wanted more. From Alan. But Mr Marston… Philip…was right. At least her mother had accepted her father's limitations and learned to live inside their boundaries. She could never be her mother. She would never accept Alan's infidelities and his unwillingness to give her the family for which she yearned.

'What shall I do?' Her voice shook and his hand settled on hers, trapping her fingers against her thighs like a glass placed over bees. She wanted to fling his hand away, but she kept still. If he told her she should go ahead and marry him, she would scream.

'Wait. For the moment. Most likely the threat of exposure will clear like the skies cleared after the storm. Believe me, as a father to a young woman about to take her first steps into society I am well aware of what is at stake for you, but unless fate forces your hand, this is not a decision to be made without careful consideration of the consequences. So my advice is—wait...'

'Wait for what?'

Lord Ravenscar stood with his hand still on the knob, surveying them from the doorway. By the cold lack of surprise on his face she supposed either Partridge or Lady Belle had told him where and with whom she was ensconced. It was fitting that after disappearing for almost two days he appeared at the worst possible moment.

'Wait for what, Lily?' he asked again, his gaze

moving from the light flush in Marston's cheeks to her as he approached.

'Mr Marston was suggesting, quite sensibly, that I wait before I make any firm decision regarding my future.'

His gaze locked with hers.

'I was under the impression a decision had already been made. A very firm decision.'

'As long as no formal announcement has been made, I believe Miss Wallace should be allowed to consider what is best for her future.'

'For *your* future more like, Marston. Stay out of this. You don't know the particulars.'

'On the contrary, Miss Wallace has been very honest regarding the events of the past few days.'

Lily didn't try to hide from the grey ice in Alan's eyes as she waited for the axe to fall. It would almost be a relief if Alan told Philip everything that had happened between them. It would condemn her and remove the choice from her hands—no man would accept a woman who had all but thrown herself into the arms of another, whether she remained a virgin after the encounter or not.

'Have you, Lily? Honest to a fault, are we?' Lily's eyes fell, more disappointed than relieved by his restraint. He didn't wait for her to answer. 'It changes nothing. Whatever the circumstances,

I was alone with Miss Wallace for two whole days in an empty house and we are now to be married. If you had really wanted her, Marston, you would have pushed your advantage before you went off on business.'

Marston's mouth quirked in a smile, not entirely of amusement.

'Can you really hold it against me that I didn't foresee this particular development? I would have thought you would be grateful to be extricated from an alliance that must at least in part put an end to your free and easy lifestyle, Ravenscar. Unlike you, both Miss Wallace and I most avidly want children. I don't believe I could begin to recall the number of times you told me you have no intention of marrying or having children. I believe the phrase you used was "when hell freezes over". Yet here I am, offering to relieve both of you from an embarrassing situation, and you are baulking. So while I respect your sense of honour, it must be pure stubbornness that would make you stand in the way of what is a perfect solution for all those involved.'

Tension hummed in the space sketched between them. Lily knew Philip's suggestion had merit, but more than anything she wanted Alan to smash it as conclusively as he had felled Jackson, as inescapably as he had captured her. But

Alan's voice remained as cool as spring water when he answered.

'I think this is a discussion Lily and I should be having alone.'

Marston half-bowed and took Lily's hand, smiling down at her.

'Of course. I must return to Bristol anyway. I came with the hope of inviting you to a concert being held at the New Music Room on Prince's Street tomorrow afternoon. A very fine Italian soprano, I am told. I thought it would be a lovely opportunity for you to meet my Penny.'

Lily smiled, thankful for his diplomacy.

'I would be happy…'

'I will bring her,' Alan said.

'There is no need.'

'I am certain my sister and Lady Ravenscar would be delighted to attend a concert as well. We will meet you and your daughter there, Marston.'

Marston bowed, squeezed her hand and, with a wry smile at Alan, left the library.

The moment the door closed Lily felt the tug of tension pull back her shoulders. She tried to gather her defences around her anger at Alan's disappearance and her painful imaginings of his whereabouts.

'You were rude to him and you had no right.

He had every reason to be angry at me and yet he was extraordinarily civil and kind.'

He walked towards the fireplace, his movements abrupt.

'A veritable paragon. He was still poaching. It isn't done.'

'Poaching? I am not a property and certainly not yours.'

'You are my betrothed. I would have thought the events of those two days sufficiently clear in your mind.'

'Well, you do know what they say, out of sight out of mind. I had begun to hope your prolonged absence meant you had disappeared in earnest.'

'Is that what this is about? Are you annoyed I wasn't dancing attendance on you? I've been extremely busy, but that doesn't change the facts by a hair's breadth. We are engaged.'

'Not yet.'

As he closed the distance between them, she realised she had forgotten how tall he was and how menacing his darkness could be. Every cell in her body was begging her to retreat, but she stood, her head tilted back to meet the storm-coloured glare.

'This isn't an island off Brazil, Lily. One word can destroy your reputation irrevocably and then any fantasy you have of a happy family is just that. You do realise Marston would drop you like a hot coal if he knew a tenth of what happened at Hollywell. You should appreciate that—he is a businessman and he has his assets to consider. He is well aware his birth is merely respectable, which is why he has chosen to ally himself with someone like you, but should you prove to be a liability he will be only too thankful to me for unburdening him.'

Lily had never slapped anyone, but she could understand the urge. Her hands tingled with the need to shatter the cold beauty of his face.

'Are you threatening me, Lord Ravenscar?'

'I am trying to make you see sense. What the devil do you think he is offering you? Your vaunted freedom? You would have no more freedom than your mother.'

'At least he would be faithful. At least he would give me a family!'

She had no idea what he might have said if Lady Ravenscar and Catherine hadn't entered at that point. But there was enough of an admission in the way he turned his back to her.

'There is a musical concert at the Assembly Hall in Bristol tomorrow afternoon,' he told his grandmother without preamble. 'I suggest we all go.'

'Perhaps it is best I stay with Nicola…' Catherine began but petered to a stop at a look from her brother.

'A concert is an excellent idea, Alan,' Lady Ravenscar said. 'Will you be staying for dinner?'

Alan bowed and headed for the door.

'Try to keep me away.'

Chapter Thirteen

Pathetic. You are without question utterly and thoroughly pathetic, Lily Wallace.

Moping like a lovesick heroine from the worst kind of novel. Why, even Radcliffe's Emily was less of a milksop over her Valancourt and at least Scythorp was entertaining. You are merely pathetic. Simply because you have never been in love before is no reason to go all to pieces. People fall in and out of love all the time. Why should you be any different?

Lily raised her chin at the image in the mirror as Sue fussed over the finishing touches in her hair, pulling and tucking strands into a Grecian knot that cascaded in waves to her nape in accordance with the fashion plate she and Nicky had chosen for the occasion. Finally Sue stood back, her chubby face flushed with concentration and worry. Lily stood and smiled encouragingly, wishing she hadn't sent Greene away. She missed her gruff efficiency and unspoken love.

She slipped the ribbon of her fan over her wrist and inspected her dress once more. She wasn't overly fond of jewellery despite or perhaps because of the source of her father's wealth and his many costly and elaborate gifts to her since her mother's death. She had never worn any on the island and she saw no reason to change simply because people expected it of the daughter of the King of Mines, Frederick Wallace.

Tonight she wore only simple teardrop pearl clips on her ears and a mother-of-pearl comb that had been her mother's. Her gloves were of a pale cream satin, with a long row of tiny pearl buttons, and she carried a fan of painted Chinese silk with the image of two black-and-gold birds engaged in either warfare or rather tempestuous lovemaking. When she had bought it in Jamaica, its scandalous nature had pleased her—now both the colouring and the tension between the birds reminded her too much of Alan, just not enough to have her choose another. Finally she picked up her shawl of painted silk.

'Thank you, Sue. I'm ready.'

She was the last to enter the Rose Room and the Rothwells turned towards her and her heart, usually a steady organ, rose and fell. Alan was clearly still angry. Not that she had expected much else after the armed neutrality of the previous evening and his absence again all day. He would honour his obligation, but no more. Before anyone could break the awkward silence, Nicky bounded over.

'Oh, how beautiful! I love orange, or is that called peach? Is that real gold? Oh, they are birds!' She touched her fingers to the delicate embroidery along the edges of the short sleeve.

'Nicola,' her mother admonished, but Lily forced a smile.

'It is gold thread embossed on machine-made net over satin with appliqué birds,' Lily answered, touching the fanned tail of one of the birds. Perhaps the dress was a little dashing for an afternoon concert, but she needed all the armour she could muster. However unsettled her feelings for Alan made her, it was not like her to concede the battle without a single shot. At the very least she would go to the tumbril with her head held high and dressed to the nines and using every ounce of her ingenuity to shape her fate.

'I want a gown like that when I am grown,' Nicky said dreamily, tracing one of the embroidered gold birds. 'Mama, you would look lovely in those colours, much nicer than purple.'

'Lilac,' Lily and Catherine said in unison and laughed.

'You are probably right, though,' Catherine said with a shade of wistfulness in her quiet voice. 'I would like to say I am past the age of such fashionable gowns, but since I never wore anything half so lovely at any age, the words are sticking in my throat.'

'So they should.' Alan finally spoke, his voice terse. 'You're almost ten years out of mourning, Cat. I've sent you enough bolts of cloth to start your own warehouse.'

'It's simply that I have enough gowns already, Alan.'

'Enough *awful* gowns.' Catherine flushed a little and turned to inspect herself in the mirror. Nicky flushed even more. 'Oh, Mama, I'm so sorry, that was horrid of me.'

Catherine caught the girl to her and kissed her rumpled hair.

'It is true, though, chick. Perhaps we should visit the seamstress before you return to school next week so you can help me choose something that isn't completely horrid. In truth, I am tired of purple. All shades of purple. It is such an unsmiling colour. Still, I am a widow.'

'Yes, but you're not *dead*,' Nicky replied, and

after a stunned moment Catherine burst into laughter, hugging her daughter again.

'Oh, my dear, you are so wise. That must be from your father. Now upstairs with you.'

Nicky hugged her and then turned to hug Lily, surprising her.

'I am so glad you are to be my aunt, then I will have new cousins to play with.'

The moment of stunned silence was broken by Lady Ravenscar.

'Nicola Sayers! Listening at doors is a very bad habit!'

Nicky turned at her great-grandmother's rebuke.

'I wasn't, really I wasn't. I heard you and Mama talking as I came in, I promise. Besides, I shan't tell if it is a secret yet. I can keep secrets. But I can be happy, can't I? I hope you have a little girl so I can give her my dolls and toys. I don't have much for boys, but I could buy them balls and toy soldiers.'

Catherine was watching her brother and she made a gesture with her hand as if to stop Nicky, and it shook him from the silence that followed Nicky's words.

'You are getting ahead of yourself, Nicky. Marriage is no guarantee of children.'

Nicky turned to him, oblivious to the tensions and to the unusual pallor on his face, almost dancing in excitement at her own plans for their future.

'Oh, but of course you will have children, so you can teach them to ride like you taught me when we came to stay with your friend Lord Hunter. But you must have lots because it isn't quite as nice to be just one. I could read to them like you did to me, Lily, though they would probably like you to do it because I can't do all those funny voices, but we could all sit by the fire and you could read my fairy-tale books except that I suppose they wouldn't sit still if they were very little, especially the boys, they would be climbing on things like my friend Anna's brothers. Do you think they will have black hair or red hair? Not that your hair is really red...well, reddish brown, I suppose, but it would be lovely to have a little girl with hair that colour and I could teach her how to braid it.'

'If those braids are any example, then no, thank you,' Alan finally interrupted. 'Now, it is time for us to leave, so upstairs with you.'

'But Partridge hasn't come to say the carriage is out front yet.'

'Upstairs, Nicky,' Catherine said, and Nicky sighed and hurried off, utterly unaware of the tension she left behind.

* * *

Lily pulled her cloak more tightly about her, not because it was cold, for the weather had taken on an unseasonable warmth that was in stark contrast to Lily's mood, but because she could feel the skin of her arms rise in goose pimples under the cold hostility of Alan's gaze as he sat across from her in Lady Ravenscar's ancient carriage. She knew the images Nicky's artless chatter had evoked were as powerful in his mind as in hers, but with very different emotions. Every line of his long lean body was a study in tension and rejection and even Lady Ravenscar seemed cowed. It wasn't until the first buildings of Bristol appeared in the carriage window that the old lady spoke, the words harsh and punctuated with taps from her cane.

'If the two of you intend to continue to behave at the concert as deplorably as you did last night at dinner, I shall order George Coachman to turn about right now.'

Alan didn't look at his grandmother, but Lily saw the anger bubble and hiss, darkening his eyes.

'His name is John, Grandmother.'

'What? Whose?'

'The coachman. John Storridge. He is the second son of the previous head groom. The eldest is in the Navy.'

'I don't see what that has to say to anything.'

'Clearly not. This habit of calling all coachmen by the name of George is convenient, especially when one's faculties are failing.'

'My faculties are as sharp as ever, Alan Rothwell. As is my social acumen despite my preference not to immerse myself in the activities of the local families these past years. You may know the names of the grooms—not that that surprises me given your predilection for horrid pugilism and racing—but I know that if the two of you make your first appearance in public looking like two thunderclouds, we have no hope of passing off any alliance between you as anything other than the outcome of scandal and duress.'

Alan leaned forward and plucked Lily's hand from her lap, turning it palm up and raising it to within inches of his mouth, his thumb strumming the buttons at her wrist.

'Hear that, Lily? Grandmama thinks we can't convince these provincial plods we are enthralled with one other. Care to prove her wrong about our skills as thespians?'

His breath seeped into the buttonholes, tiny licking caresses that spread up and down, sinking under her skin, into her blood, shocking her with the speed with which her body transformed. It was as close to witchcraft as anything could be. All her resistance amounted to nothing the moment he put on an act of passion. There was not even a pretence that this was anything more than a lie, but her body didn't care and her mind was fast losing ground.

'I don't doubt your acting skills, Lord Ravenscar,' she replied. 'I only hope no one looks too closely. Most thespians have the benefit of being at a distance from their audience so their lack of sincerity is less apparent.'

Seeing the anger heat behind the mockery gave her some satisfaction, but not much.

'Perhaps I need a little encouragement to bring out the best in my performance. Think you could encourage me, Lily?'

'Alan Piers—' Lady Ravenscar cut herself off with a thump of her cane, recognising the futility of her protest, but Alan released Lily's hand and sat back.

'Apologies, Grandmama, I was carried away by my passions. Ah, here we are.'

Catherine glanced out of the window at the mean-looking brick buildings outside.

'Where are we? This isn't the Assembly Hall.'

'Nowhere near it. I asked John to stop here for a moment. There is something I must do before we continue. Wait here. I won't be gone above five minutes.'

He didn't wait for them to respond. When the carriage door snapped shut behind him, Lady Ravenscar rapped her cane against the roof of the carriage and the coachman swung off his perch and opened the door.

'Yes, my lady?'

'What is this place, Geo… John Coachman?'

'This is Mead Road, my lady.'

'Edifying! What is this house Lord Ravenscar has entered?'

'I couldn't rightly say, my lady.'

'Couldn't or won't, John Storridge?'

Lily took pity on the coachman and gathered her cloak over her arm.

'Could you help me down, please, John?'

'Miss?'

She didn't wait for any objections, just leapt down lightly on to the pavement, narrowly avoiding a muddy puddle between the cracked paving stones, and hurried into the house where the warped door still stood ajar.

'Miss!'

She hadn't known what to expect. Perhaps a brothel like her father's, or a gaming hell or opium den like she had heard of near the Kingston docks or those frequented by the miners in

Belo Horizonte. Something that would further tip the scales against this persistent pull he had on her. But all those ideas were dismissed in the first steps into the narrow, ill-smelling hallway.

A group of six or so children of all ages were seated on the stairs, laughing at a young man holding two ragged puppets, but they stopped the moment she appeared and scurried up into the dark, dragging staring toddlers in their wake.

To her right a door stood open to a room and several startled pairs of eyes took in her finery. Three of the men were seated in bath chairs, two of them had no nether limbs and the third's head lolled sideways against a cushioned headrest. Two women sat stitching by a fire and beside them several more children were seated playing spillikins on the bare floor, dressed in warm but rough clothes, their hands now frozen in mid-gesture as they stared at her.

'Miss, please!' the coachman hissed behind her, obviously shocked, but she continued down the dark hallway with its damp and mottled walls, pausing before the next door as she heard Alan's voice.

'This should be enough for rent and provisions through the rest of the week, Tippet. If I don't find something by then, it will have to be the Saltford property after all. Jem is overseeing the workers while they assess what will need to be done if we must go ahead. We will still be some ten rooms short, but it can't be helped. We can always accommodate the rest up in Birmingham or London until we find a better solution near Bristol.'

'I know you don't like sending the men and families away from what they know, Captain, but if it can't be helped, it can't. They know anything Hope House has to offer is a damn sight better than the street or the workhouse, which is where they'd go otherwise. The fire was no one's fault but those new gas pipes and we're lucky no one was badly hurt.'

'Very lucky. Have everyone ready by...'

'Are you a fairy, miss?'

Lily raised her finger to hush the little girl who appeared behind her, but it was too late. Alan came to the doorway and the girl hurried off.

'Are you constitutionally incapable of doing as you are told?'

'I sometimes do as I am *asked*,' she replied. 'These are war veterans, are they not?'

'Wait for me in the carriage. I am almost done.'

'Is this what you want Hollywell for? Why didn't you tell me?'

'Would it have made a difference?'

'Of course it would.'

'It is irrelevant in any case. We no longer need Hollywell.'

She glanced past his shoulder at the man behind him. With his grey hair and zigzag of a nose, he looked like an aged boxer.

'Is that true, sir?' she asked the man, and his eyes widened in alarm.

'If the Captain says it's true, it's gospel, miss.' He ventured a glance at Alan, but Alan was watching her, his gaze the blank look he managed so well when he wished.

'Infallible, is he?' Her question won her a sudden grin from Tippet, showing a neat hole where several teeth should be.

'When it counts, miss.'

'Thank you, Tippet,' Alan interrupted. 'Come along, Miss Wallace, we don't want to be late for the wailing Italian.'

As she turned, a scurrying in the doorways and on the stairs marked the careful retreat of whatever spectators had gathered.

Philip Marston hadn't been exaggerating, Penny was indeed an angel, or as closely resembling one as a human was likely to manage. Lily hated being petty, but she would have preferred that the pale gold beauty at least be spoilt or nasty, but in a matter of minutes Lily realised she was not only shy, but quite sweet and more than willing to think the best of Lily if her father so desired.

'This is my very first concert,' she told Lily in a hushed tumble of words as Marston turned to address some comments to Lady Ravenscar and Catherine. 'I'm afraid I don't understand Italian at all. I did try to apply myself, but I simply have no ear for languages, my schoolmistress says. Do you speak Italian, Miss Wallace? Papa says you lived in many exciting places. I do so envy you.'

'Your papa is exaggerating, though I suppose they may seem exciting to others. It is true there were people from all over the world in the mines where my father worked and I learned a little of everything, but mostly they spoke Portuguese or Spanish. Your papa said you are to have your first Season this spring. You must be excited.'

'I am… Oh, good afternoon, Lord Ravenscar.'

'Good afternoon, Miss Marston. Congratulations on having finally put school behind you. Or should I be congratulating your schoolmistress?'

Penny giggled, surprising Lily. She hadn't realised Alan might be acquainted with Penny, but if he and Philip Marston shared business concerns, it was not surprising, though she would have expected Marston to shield his innocent and wealthy beauty of a daughter from a man like Alan with the zealousness of an evangelist.

'I'm afraid I didn't apply myself quite as I ought.'

'Only bores apply themselves as they ought, so that need not concern you. Now you can apply yourself as you wish. As long as you don't apply yourself wholly to what you oughtn't.'

Penny Marston's feather-soft brows drew together in confusion.

'Are you making game of me again, Lord Ravenscar?'

'He is trying to be clever and failing miserably, Miss Marston. Come, we should find ourselves a comfortable place to sit or risk being forced to stand through the wailing Italian as Lord Ravenscar so quaintly titled a woman accustomed to singing for kings and emperors.'

'An excellent idea. Allow me.'

That had not been quite what she intended, to find Alan seated between her and Miss Marston on one of the long upholstered benches arranged before the low stage where the musicians had already gathered. Lily met Philip Marston's sardonic smile, expecting him to sit by his daughter, but as he led Lady Ravenscar and Catherine over by some deft manoeuvre, he sat himself by Lily, with Catherine on his other side, while Lady

Ravenscar was seated on Penny Marston's left side under the rationale that she would thus be furthest from any draught from the windows.

Lily caught the widening of Penny's eyes and turned in protest towards Philip Marston, but he merely smiled and murmured close to her ear, 'Don't worry for Penny. It will do her good to meet a tame dragon and Lord Ravenscar will shield her if need be. He has known her for many years. Here is the programme, Lady Catherine. I'm afraid there aren't enough, so we shall have to share. Do you speak Italian?'

Lily watched in trepidation as Lady Ravenscar began catechising the beauty, but clearly Philip Marston had been accurate and Penny's good manners were finding favour with her even without the threat of intervention from Alan and Lily began to relax, as much as she could seated between the two men.

If she needed any reminder of her folly, her treacherous body was only too happy to oblige. The room was a trifle cold and most women were swathed in shawls, but the whole left side of Lily's body was shimmering with warmth. She knew precisely how many inches separated her thigh from Alan's, three, and her elbow from his, two. If she just shifted a little to rearrange her shawl, she could finally bridge that chasm and...

'Do you happen to know what *strazio* means, Miss Wallace? The first song is in German, which is beyond us, but Lady Catherine and I have been attempting to decipher the Italian lyrics for the second song.'

Lily took the programme Philip Marston was extending to her and stared at the word he was pointing to, her mind untangling itself from shawls and chasms and heat.

'It means…' She cleared her throat. 'Torment. I think.'

'Is it a sad song, then?' Penny enquired.

'It is a song about a woman who is pledged to one man but keeps thinking about another,' Alan answered without inflection. 'Does that qualify as sad or merely a case of faulty judgement on her part?'

'Hush!' Lady Ravenscar said loudly as the singer, an unremarkable-looking woman with dark hair and eyes and a rather pinched mouth, finally climbed to the stage. The buzz and chatter around them thinned and stopped and then the heavens opened. The singer's voice rose above that of the violins, pure and true, the most beautiful thing Lily had heard in years. On Isla Padrones they had believed dead babies' souls were collected by angels who soothed their new charges' ascent to heaven with divine song. The villagers had sung as they took the housekeeper's baby to the little churchyard on the far side of the island, their voices radiating the same joy and hope of redemption. She hadn't cried then, she had been too guilty and too frightened and had not wanted to draw any more attention to herself as she shadowed the procession, but now it took all her effort not to sink her face in her hands and cry out her confusion, like the tired child she had been then.

The room held its breath until the last note shivered and faded and then the applause burst forth. Lily sat with her hands pressed together in a simulacrum of clapping or prayer, holding hard against the need to cry.

'Beautiful.' She hadn't meant to speak, it was hardly more than a breath, but Alan turned to her.

'Lily?'

He bent close to her, his breath smoothing over her cheek and pressing against her ear like a fluttering kiss. She shook her head and felt the careful ringlets Lady Ravenscar's maid had toiled over brush against him and then his finger touched the skin between her sleeve and the edge of her glove above her elbow, sliding down, as soft as a feather, the shawl concealing the contact. His voice was as soft, hardly a whisper.

'Don't. I'm sorry.'

Luckily the singing began again and the pain eased, but not the thudding of her pulse or the need to lean against him. She abandoned all attempt to remain in the room, letting everything fall away but his proximity, facing the truth. She had slept with her cheek against his chest, her hand in his. She knew the rhythm of his pulse. He probably didn't even remember that, but it was part of her and now her body was drawn to his as to a lodestone. Her tiny universe had expanded during those days at Hollywell and it now included one very unrepentant rake. She still had a choice, but it would require a more brutal act on her part than she had wanted to believe.

Chapter Fourteen

He had sunk low indeed. Bringing tepid lemonade to his grandmother at the Bristol Assembly Hall was not something he would have considered a possibility just a week ago. Once fate sank its talons into you, it did so with a vengeance.

'Where has Lily gone?' Lady Ravenscar hissed between clenched teeth as Alan handed her the glass. His own jaw tightened as he turned to view the room.

'Nowhere, Grandmother. She is with Cat and the Marstons.'

'Not any more, I saw her by the back door and that is not the direction of the withdrawing rooms. Why the devil is that man still fawning over her? I thought she sent him packing.'

'Lily is hedging her bets, Lady Jezebel.'

'And you are going to stand for that?'

He didn't bother replying. Anything he said

at the moment would probably not end well. He had been stoking his anger at Lily for the past two days. It was a useful countermeasure to the persistent desire that pulsed through him like a remnant of the fever. It kept him focused on duty and action and away from the unsettling reactions to this impossible girl. Like that moment at the end of the first song when she had been leaning forward, her lips parted as if she had been the one singing. The candles had raised her warmth to fire, her hair shimmering with copper and gold and amber and her skin reflecting the blush peach of her dress. He didn't know what the taut, almost tragic expression on her face had meant, but she had been close to tears for a moment. It had been impossible not to reach out and touch her, however briefly, and even that tiny gesture had cost him, reminding him how much more he wanted than a chaste caress of her arm. Giving a sip of water to a man with a raging thirst was more torture than relief.

In a saner world he would have been able to take her hand, lead her out of this stifling room and…

He frowned and scanned the clusters of people talking and fanning themselves at the back of the room. On impulse he stepped into the hallway that separated the assembly hall from the smaller meeting rooms of the guildhall and glanced up the carpeted stairs guarded by a rather sad-looking Roman bust on a pedestal.

'Female troubles, too, Agrippa?' He patted the balding head as he moved towards the open door of the guild meeting hall across the hallway and paused in the doorway. A still figure stood looking up at the large painting commemorating the Battle of Trafalgar, all taut sails and thrashing waves and bursts of cannons. The room was cold and only the light from two high windows touched the lighter colours with some life.

'What are you hiding from now?'

She whirled around, her skirts billowing like a fluted flower.

'I am not hiding, I needed to think. Then I saw this painting and was curious.'

He was tempted to ask her what she had been thinking about, but he doubted it would redound to his credit. After Nicky's devastating discourse about children he didn't want to talk about anything profound. He looked at the painting instead.

'Decent, but inaccurate. The storm came after the battle was won, and the *HMS Sandwich* didn't even take part in the battle.'

'Let me guess, Nelson was a hero of yours and you know all the names of all the ships and whom they took as prizes.'

'Of course. I was fifteen. My friends and I were masters of naval strategy even though none of us had set foot on more than a barge. I would have joined the Navy when I left Ravenscar, but luckily by then I wanted Napoleon's head, so I enlisted with the Rifles instead.'

'Why luckily?'

'I get seasick.'

'Really?' Amusement warmed the gold in her eyes and some of his tension eased.

'Not really, but I definitely don't enjoy the thought of spending months at a stretch in a small space with a group of rank-smelling men eating weevil-riddled hard tack.'

'I can't imagine anyone does. Jackson, my groom, was pressed into service as a boy until my father took him to work with him. He had some horrific tales to tell. But the war must have been just as horrible. I saw those men today.'

'Peace has been just as hard on many of them. We had a purpose during the war and a family of sorts. All that went by the wayside when they returned to England, some less than whole in body or mind, and found they had no livelihood. A great deal more than vanity rides on a man's pride. Come, we need to return.' He hesitated. 'What were you thinking about?'

'Precisely that. Those men. Why didn't you

just tell me you wanted Hollywell as a home for war veterans? I cannot understand why that is a secret.'

'Ah, the ferret is back. It isn't a secret, but it is private and no one's concern but ours. This is not a topic for a musical evening.'

'Why not?'

'Because. Besides, I told you we are no longer interested in Hollywell.'

'Yes, you are. You were telling Mr Tippet that Saltford is too small. If I am willing to put Hollywell at your disposal, why not take it?'

'What do you mean put it at our disposal?'

'Precisely that. I won't sell it because I understand from Mr Prosper that landed property is the only kind of property a married woman retains any form of control over, however truncated, but I will provide you with an indefinite lease at a symbolic cost and that way you could use the purchase price for any adjustments you need to make to the structure and for whatever other needs arise. I would have one stipulation, but it is a small one and we needn't discuss it now. I can speak with Mr Prosper tomorrow and you can begin bringing people there immediately.'

The words poured out of her, establishing facts and setting up barriers, and all the tension and anger he was trying to push aside returned, as hot and immediate as the desire she evoked in him so effortlessly.

'If this is some form of sacrificial apology because you think you can weasel your way out of this engagement, let me tell you…'

'It is an offer, pure and simple. Do you know that if you had a modicum of trust in people, we might have resolved this issue at Saltford and none of this would have happened? Let that be a lesson to you to be less secretive and distrustful in future. You forgo golden opportunities.'

'Is that what happened? Most people would argue that what happened is quite the opposite.'

'Oh, yes, I'm aware what a golden opportunity my inheritance is…'

He grasped her shoulders as she started moving past him.

'I actually wasn't referring to your three per cents, but to other assets altogether. But this is hardly the right place for me to clarify my meaning. Or perhaps it is, at least if we are interrupted, you won't be able to hide from your actions. This isn't a game and Marston and I are not two dolls on a shelf for you to choose from, so it is time to abandon the delusion that you have a choice here. You gambled with your fate and you lost—that is life. I suggest you stop all this soulful flirting with Marston and start honouring the hand you dealt yourself. In a week we will announce our engagement to friends and you can begin planning your bridals.'

'How could any woman resist such a sweetly phrased offer?'

She tried to pull away, but he held firm, moving in.

'Is that what you want? Once I have you somewhere we are less likely to be interrupted, I will show you precisely how hard it will be to resist a sweetly phrased offer. Stop acting like Andromeda being offered as sacrifice to some damn sea monster. And Marston is no Perseus.'

He was too angry to be conciliating, but instead of matching his thrust she withdrew in one of her disconcerting surrenders that always left him far more vulnerable than victor.

'I know that. If anyone is the sacrifice here, it is you because this is all my fault. You must think me terribly ungrateful and spoilt. But that is precisely the point, you see. I don't want anyone to suffer because of my mistakes. I've not only ruined your life, but also brought this strife between you and Philip when neither of you are to blame. It is so unfair.'

He should tell her that right now it didn't feel at all like a sacrifice. Not with her looking up at him with that mix of contrition and compassion, her lips soft and parted, just waiting for him to taste them again. Right now the only thing that felt like a sacrifice was the weeks that would have to pass before he could finally do something about this aggravating, aching need. He felt perilously close to that sea monster, focused on mindless devouring.

He needed to take her back into the main hall, he needed to keep his footing in the shifting sands around her, he needed…

He pressed her back, bringing her up against the door.

'I'm not concerned with fairness at the moment. Just stay away from Marston. Understand?' He didn't give her a chance to answer. His body moulded itself against hers, his mouth finally lowering to find the moist warmth he was thirsting for, filling with her scent and taste. It was hopeless. He *needed* this. This wasn't the passion and pleasure he knew so well; it was like drinking the finest cognac after years of warm ale. He wouldn't be able to go back even if he wanted to and he didn't.

He felt her shiver between him and the door and he gentled the kiss and pulled away, cupping her face in his hands. Her eyes opened slowly and he waited out the inevitable burn of heat that struck him at the half-lost softness there.

His once-clear vision of the future was lying in a shamble at her feet and he had no idea where he was heading. He had made wealth, he had found purpose and, until he had walked into the library at Hollywell, he hadn't wanted or needed anything else.

But everything precious came at a price. He had never thought he would have to pay this one.

He breathed in, twice.

'Come. We must return to the others.'

'There you are, Miss Wallace. Ravenscar,' Marston said as he and Catherine intercepted them as they entered the assembly hall. 'Lady Ravenscar asked Lady Catherine and myself to find you. She said she had already sent you, Ravenscar, but perhaps you were feeling unwell, Miss Wallace?'

Lily raised her chin at the censure in his voice.

'Everything is quite all right, Mr Marston. Lord Ravenscar and I were merely discussing my offer to lease Hollywell House to his war veteran foundation.'

Alan couldn't help smiling at Lily's diversionary tactics. By the look on Marston's face it was a surprise attack worthy of Wellington.

'I… What?'

'The Hope House foundation, Mr Marston,'

Catherine's calm voice poured soothing oil on the rising waves as she explained the nature of the foundation and Alan's original plans for Hollywell before Albert's death. 'I think that is very generous of you, Lily,' she concluded. 'So is it settled then?'

Alan ignored his sister's double entendre.

'Not quite. I explained to Miss Wallace that though Hollywell House is the right size, we would need to make structural adjustments to it that she might not be willing to countenance.'

'And I explained to Lord Ravenscar that I will not object to adjustments as long as they respect the spirit of the original structure.'

'Could you not find a structure in Bristol?' Marston asked.

'Not of that size and with grounds where we could construct a manufactory to employ the men. We have found they mend better when they have gainful employment. Believe me, I have looked high and low this past week. We are about to lease a property near Saltford—'

'Which is inadequate by your own admission,' Lily interrupted. 'I suggest you swallow your pride and send your men to inspect Hollywell tomorrow, Lord Ravenscar. Now, we should take our places for the second act. Lady Ravenscar is beckoning.'

* * *

Finally it was over. Lily kept her smile firmly on her face and tried to listen to Lady Ravenscar, Catherine and Marston dissect the singer's skills as they moved along with the crowd towards the entrance, but her whole concentration was on the man behind her. As she was edged aside by a portly couple, her shawl caught on the arm of a chair placed against the wall and she paused to untangle it.

'Allow me.' Alan brushed aside her hands and took the shawl.

'I can do it myself, thank you.'

'Yes, I know, but it's done. Here, turn around.'

She met the challenge in his eyes as he held the swathe of silk, aware of the flow of people. To quarrel would only attract attention and more censure. She turned.

'Relax. You're as stiff as a sail in the high wind,' he murmured as he draped the shawl over her shoulders. His breath whispered along her exposed nape, stirring the soft hairs there, preparing her flesh for the kiss she knew could not follow. Then his fingers fell away, just skimming the length of her arm as if arranging the silken folds. 'Birds of paradise. Very fitting... You looked like one in this flock of pigeons and hens. Fire and light and completely out of place. And very hard to capture.'

His voice sank to a whisper and she shivered, a clammy cold skittering under the heat his words and touch were sparking. She wasn't hard to capture; she was snared, utterly. Her legs were shaking and she felt ill with the need to turn to him and either slap him for what he was doing to her or beg him to take her out of there, with him. He had hardly touched her, but just that soft brush of his flesh on hers and she was on fire again, it was staining her cheeks, as corrosive as acid. She could hear her own pulse, sharp convulsive gasps of her heart as his fingers curved over her elbow, taking her arm to guide her towards the door and another step towards her fate.

Chapter Fifteen

$\sim\!\!\sim\!\!\sim$

Alan watched the bemused group of men trail along behind Lily as she pointed towards the shuttered windows of the north wing of Hollywell. They stopped and Tippet scribbled on his pad while the two masons stood elbows akimbo, heads cocked to one side like two curious sparrows trailing an exotic bird.

He should have known it was a mistake to concede even as much as this examination of Hollywell, because the masons and carpenters had already decided it would be easier to modify to their purposes than Saltford and had said so in Lily's presence, leading to disastrous results. She had commandeered Tippet and the masons, left Catherine and Nicky to inspect the contents of the linen closets and marched off, leaving Alan with the carpenters and workmen to inspect the roofs. Tippet hadn't even asked for

Alan's approval to disappear with her, the traitor, Alan mused as he watched the mutiny disappear around the corner of the north wing.

He didn't know if he had it in him to turn down her offer. He should. If he knew one thing about Lily by now, it was that she needed the safety of an island of her own, which was precisely why she had run here when she had wanted to think. This made her willingness to sacrifice it all the more touching, but for her sake he should keep Hollywell inviolate for her. He should have thought of that before and warned the masons and Tippet to offer all forms of reasonable explanations why Hollywell was inappropriate, but he hadn't been prepared for her insistence on overseeing them like a little general.

He sighed. It would lead to another battle royal, but it was unavoidable.

'Is this what you asked for?'

Alan turned to face the tall man striding across the stable courtyard, the sun striking gold in hair the colour of late wheat and a flash of silver in the deep-set eyes. He was always happy to see Stanton, but the extreme degree of relief he felt at seeing his friend was a sign of how low he had sunk since his arrival in Somerset.

He took the extended document and clapped his friend on the shoulder.

'Stanton! Damn, it's good to see you, man. I didn't expect you to bring it yourself.'

'I'm afraid my curiosity isn't equal to the challenge of sending a deputy when one of my two best friends requests I procure a special licence from the Archbishop of Canterbury. Especially when that friend is you. What on earth has happened and who is Lily Wallace?'

Alan tucked the licence into his coat pocket.

'Straight to the crux of the matter as usual. Come, we need some brandy to make this comprehensible. At least I do.'

'That bad? When I warned you that if you ever fell you would fall hard, I didn't expect it to be on your face, Raven.'

'I was actually happy to see you for a moment there, Stanton. Would you mind saving your compliments until I have a glass in my hand?'

'Not at all. So you managed to secure Hollywell from the new heirs after all? Your last communication wasn't so promising. What did you do, threaten to set your grandmother on them?'

'No, compromise them. Lily Wallace is the heir.'

Alan had rarely seen Stanton, the master of diplomatic finesse, bereft of words. He closed the library door and went over to the cupboard where Albert had kept his brandy. He was just handing Stanton his glass when the door opened and Lily and Tippet entered.

'Lord Ravenscar, Mr Tippet and I were wondering… Oh. I'm sorry, I didn't mean to interrupt, but I'm afraid the masons need to know whether we plan to open the wall in the north wing.'

Alan subdued his various warring reactions to her appearance and tried to make sense of her question.

'Why on earth would we need to do that?'

'For the bath chairs. I thought that if we convert the north wing to bedrooms for those who cannot climb the stairs, we should still ensure those men can enter and exit the house without encountering stairs. Like a gangway. A paved one. The north wing is lower lying than the south wing and the mason said we could transform the blind wall at the end of the corridor into another door leading directly to the back courtyard.'

Her voice slowed as they remained silent, as if explaining something to the very dim. Stanton recovered first and moved towards her, hand extended.

'What an excellent idea. Good morning, Mr Tippet. I will save my graceless friend the bother of making introductions because you must clearly be Miss Wallace. I am Lord Alexander Stanton. What a pleasure to meet you.'

Alan waited for the inevitable reaction almost all women had when confronted with Stanton. When he bothered to charm them, which was rarely, they fell like ninepins. When he employed that smile, the effect was often catastrophic.

Lily took the extended hand and smiled and Alan relaxed. He knew the shades of her smiles and this one was friendly, curious, but definitely not bowled over.

'Ah, the least wild of the Wild Hunt Club. You are in the Foreign Office, correct?'

Stanton's smile widened.

'Correct on both counts. The gangway is an interesting idea; I wonder why we never thought of it.'

'I will treat that as a rhetorical question, Lord Stanton, since any answer I give is likely to offend. Are you here to help?'

'I admit I did come here to help, but I see my offices are absolutely unnecessary.'

Lily's eyes narrowed and she pulled her hand away from Stanton's lingering clasp and looked past him to Alan.

'Shall I tell them to make the measurements, then, Lord Ravenscar?'

He nodded, unequal to arguing with her at the

moment, and she smiled at both of them and left, Tippet at her heels.

They both stood watching the closed door for a moment.

'I'm losing my touch,' Stanton said. 'And you've either lost your heart or found your senses. That was not what I was expecting.'

'Lily is not what anyone would expect.'

'No details until I have a glass in my hand. I'm parched after driving all the way on my mission to save my best friend from being forced to the altar against his wishes.'

'Can you?'

'Even if I could, I am not certain I would. I like her. A paved gangway. Since when is she part of the Hope House effort?'

'Since this morning. Or rather since yesterday when she offered us Hollywell. I hadn't realised my tentative agreement to consider Hollywell included allowing her to shadow Tippet and the masons and to set my sister and niece to cataloguing the linen, but to be fair it is her property.'

'A young lady accustomed to command. Interesting. Tell me about her.'

Alan handed him a glass and told him.

'If you laugh, I'll do some damage to that perfect face of yours, Stanton,' he concluded as his friend's smile hovered on the edge of a grin.

'I won't, I promise. I'm as worried as hell. I never would have placed odds that you and Hunter would both become tenants for life within two months of each other after a lifetime of evading that fate with such religious zeal. My faith in my abilities to predict the future actions of men or nations is sadly shaken. But did she have to be an heiress? You know this will just give credence to all those tales about the dispossessed rake. Does the fact that you have been allowed back into the Hall mean you are now restored into your grandmother's good graces as well?'

'Since she isn't restored into mine, I neither know nor care. We are in a state of armed neutrality and I am staying at the Hall merely to ensure our courtship, such as it is, has credibility. I don't need Jezebel's money and you know it.'

'Still, if you are going to marry and have a brood of children, you will need a home.'

'Marry, yes, children, no. And I have a home. Two of them.'

'A house by a manufactory in Birmingham and a bachelor's residence on St James's Street most certainly do not qualify as homes. But you cannot still be serious about not breeding. Even if that young woman believes this is merely a marriage of form, she cannot be so naïve not to know you are likely to bed her. I saw the way you were watching us. You were ready to drive a carriage between us if need be.'

He shrugged. He wasn't ready yet to put into words his chaotic thoughts and feelings.

'Wanting to bed a woman and willingly making a pact with the devil are two different things. You know I swore never to have any children.'

'You swore never to marry and never to cross your grandmother's threshold, too, so forgive me for not being impressed with your record.'

'This is different.'

'I agree, it bloody well is. You cannot possibly mean to marry that delectable girl and keep that resolve.'

'I am perfectly capable of bedding a woman without leading to conception, I have been doing so quite successfully for almost half my life.'

'Yes, but this would be your wife, Raven. Surely she wants children?'

Alan went to refill his glass and Stanton continued.

'How long are you going to punish yourself? This makes no sense.'

'I am not punishing myself. Quite the opposite. Having a child would be the ultimate punishment.'

'So you would condemn her to a life without offspring merely because you are a coward.'

Alan winced, though it was the truth. The rushing river of fear, pain and need that had coursed through him at Nicky's excited babblings about children had still not quieted. The images clung—Lily reading aloud, with a little red-haired girl leaning on her and on her other side, more shadowy, a little boy, dark haired, small hands curved around a ball.

He made a last effort to cling to the vision of his fate he had presented to Lily by the lake.

'I won't stop her if she wishes to…go her own way. As long as she is discreet, she is welcome to conceive as many children as she can bear, literally and figuratively. The *ton* is littered with other men's offspring anyway. I don't see why I should be any different.'

Stanton shook his head.

'My God, you're even more cold-blooded than I thought. No wonder she is considering Marston's offer. Are you purposely trying to drive her away?'

'No. I am merely trying to ensure she isn't disappointed.'

Stanton stood up. 'If you set the bar any lower, she won't have any choice but to step over it, Alan. Now, as much as I would love to continue observing the details of your downfall, I've left my poor horses out there and it's been a long drive. I'll rack up at the Pelican in Bristol, so come pay your respects before I drive back tomorrow.'

'Busy?'

'Very. I'm off to Vienna to discuss how far south the Austrians can go in Italy. I told Hunter I'd come and save you if need be, but if I couldn't, it is up to him and Nell to hold your hand during the ceremony.'

'They might not have to follow your directives after all if Marston gets his way. As for you, try not to get kidnapped by pirates or shot by princes this time. I might be too busy in the near future to come to your rescue again.'

'To be fair I had already escaped when you and Hunter came to rescue me from Derna and it was the veiled bride who was my saviour of sorts on Illiakos, so I think I shall survive even if you are too busy lying to yourself about how much you are the captain of your fate, Raven. I wish I could delay sailing just for the pleasure of watching your expression as you sign the register under the parson's beaming smile, but I promise to try to be there for the christening.'

Alan watched the curricle disappear down the drive and turned to inspect the façade of the house. A little sunshine, however weak, made any house seem more welcoming and Hollywell was no exception. They had done nothing yet and already it looked more like the home he remembered from Jasper and Mary's days. It only reinforced his conviction that Lily should not relinquish her sanctuary. He might not need a home in the sense that Stanton just mentioned, but Lily did and he knew what this place symbolised for her. If she gave them Hollywell, she would have nothing that was truly hers. All her money amounted to nothing more than a banker's draft waiting to be withdrawn by whoever married her. Hollywell had come to mean something different for her, and if he took that, too... In a fair world this should be her home, someplace she could be safe and build her own world. Have the family she wanted. Not as his mistake or as Marston's property.

Could he do it? Let go that last vow and risk the pain. For her.

She would be a good mother. Both stronger and more vulnerable than his. He could see how his mother had never known how to navigate the barriers set by his grandparents. Lily would probably have put his rigid grandfather to flight and tamed his grandmother just as she had these past weeks. All that pain and need inside her only made her strong. What was she asking for in the end? A child. So what if it felt like she was the guardian of hell asking for his soul? Perhaps this was his punishment, to risk that pain again.

This was the real choice—release her to marry Marston or tell her he would marry her on her terms.

No, the real choice was whether he was willing to allow her into his life. Or whether he was capable of letting her go. If so, he had better do so sooner rather than later because with each passing hour that thought was becoming more unacceptable.

The rumble of wheels alerted him and he turned at the top of the steps to see a carriage approaching. He cursed under his breath and waited for the carriage to draw up and the footman to lower the steps.

'Hello, Marston, Miss Marston. Welcome to Hollywell. To what do we owe this pleasure?' He stood back to wave them up the stairs into the house, wishing them at the devil.

'Penny and I decided to take advantage of the fine weather to pay a visit. Lady Ravenscar's butler informed us you were all at Hollywell. Since our visit is partly motivated by some news I have heard which might be pertinent for your effort here, we decided to join you.'

He paused as three figures appeared at the top of the stairs and smiled.

'Good afternoon, Lady Catherine, Miss Wallace. And this must be your beautiful daughter, Lady Catherine. We apologise for the intrusion.'

'You are always welcome, but I'm afraid Hollywell isn't ready to receive guests, Mr Marston,' Lily said as she descended. When she was in her social mode, Alan found it hard to gauge her thoughts, but the very fact that she had withdrawn into her cool shell was telling. She was nervous and alert. He had no idea if that boded ill for him or for Marston. 'But the library is almost habitable, so we should proceed there. Unless Tabby and Grim have laid it to waste again.'

'Who?' Penny asked curiously, and Nicky launched into an animated recounting of the haunting which Lily had shared with her and Catherine. Mr Marston watched his daughter with Nicky for a moment and smiled.

'Together they look like that child's tale my daughter used to love, *Snow-White and Rose-Red*. She would imagine she had a sister like Rose-Red, dark haired and lively.'

Catherine smiled. 'That certainly describes Nicola.'

'You mentioned a proposition, Marston?' Alan interrupted.

'Ah, yes. I was in a meeting with the mayor regarding the planned installation of lock gates on the river and overheard a discussion regarding the Grantham Road Workhouse I believe you might find interesting. Apparently the Parish is in financial difficulties and will have no choice but to sell the property which has been standing empty since they acquired it a year ago. This is not yet public knowledge and I asked the mayor if we might have the right of first refusal. From what I could see outside it is a little larger than this structure and has the benefit of being on the edge of town with some fields behind it that I believe are also open for purchase at the right price. It is also no more than half a mile from the manufactory you and I were considering.'

'But they no longer need a property,' Lily interrupted. 'They have Hollywell.'

'I believe the Grantham Road building is more suitable for the purpose, Miss Wallace,' Marston replied. 'Do you know the place, Lord Ravenscar?'

'I do, but I hadn't realised they were looking to sell. Are you certain of this?'

Marston raised his brows.

'Of course. The mayor is merely waiting for our response. If you wish, we can proceed there now.'

'Oh, Papa, must we leave right away? We have

just arrived here and Nicola said we could go and meet a ghost dog.'

'Perhaps Miss Marston could stay here with us while you and my brother attend to your business?' Catherine suggested, her eyes questioning Alan, and he nodded, very aware Lily had not said a word. 'Good. We shall take good care of her, Mr Marston. When we are done here, we will have tea at the Hall and meet you there on your return.'

'Oh, excellent!' Nicky clapped her hands and took Miss Marston's hand, tugging her towards the door. 'Come, I last saw Grim sniffing around the old conservatory searching for Tabby, not that it is really a conservatory, just an old parlour. His name is Grim because Uncle Alan named him after the fable of Church Grims, which are black dogs that guard graveyards, and that was where he found him when he was a puppy...'

Catherine laughed as their voices faded.

'Poor Nicola, she has been pining for someone nearer her own age after being isolated with her mama and grandmama. I should probably keep an eye on them or Nicola will not let your daughter get a word in edgeways. Are you coming, Lily?'

Lily nodded, slowly, her gaze moving between Marston and Alan. When the honey brown of her eyes settled on Alan, he felt no warmth there. She was miles away. He had a visceral urge to reassure her, but he knew there was nothing he could say with Marston and Catherine standing there. For the moment it couldn't matter if she saw this as a personal rejection. Lily might not know it, but she needed Hollywell.

'Coming, Ravenscar?'

'Yes. Let me just tell my steward and groom to meet us there.

'Well? More suitable than Hollywell House, don't you agree?'

Alan descended the stairs into the courtyard, where Marston stood waiting.

'Yes. There is no need for you to wait, Marston. We are likely to be a while. I've asked my groom to fetch the rest of the men.'

'Good.'

'I am still going to marry her, though.'

Marston's smile flattened. 'You are entitled to your opinion.'

'Is it pride keeping you in the game or are you finally beginning to realise she is wrong for you, Marston?'

'I could ask the same question of you, Ravenscar.'

'I know Lily a little better than you.'

'By George, you're an arrogant devil. You've known her for all of a couple of weeks and I've known her since she was seventeen.'

'Which just goes to show how wrong you are for her, because in all those years you still haven't got her measure, Marston. She might have managed her father's house like a social goddess, but she is no more a hostess than I am. She has discipline, that is all. There's no passion for the vocation behind it.'

'I'm not marrying her to be my hostess.'

'You're not marrying her at all. But that *was* one reason, wasn't it—you want a cool, socially adept wife to add a cachet to your business dealings. The other and more important reason is to produce the perfect heir for your business. I'll concede that any child of Lily's is likely to be intelligent, not to mention wilful, but you are doubly delusional if you believe you will have the schooling of that child. She'll trump you on every hand. If ever I've seen a woman who will command the love and loyalty of her children without even trying, that is Lily. She won't actively overrule you, but the result will be the same. Her values will win over yours every time.'

Marston faced him, feet apart and arms crossed, but Alan wasn't fooled by his cool, mocking smile. Every line of his rival's body spoke of arrows hitting home. But each arrow struck home with him as well. One piercing him with the image of Lily with a baby in her arms, laughing. Another with her as he had seen her in his fevered hallucination with Rickie, seated by a little boy, reading to him. Of a little girl with her flame-touched hair, running towards him. He clenched his hands against the assault and continued.

'Then there is the price she will make you pay for taking away her freedom because you aren't really about to allow her to manage her inheritance beyond whatever generous pin money you allow her in the settlement, correct?'

'She will have a family to keep her occupied. That is what she wants and that is precisely why she won't have you, Ravenscar, so you are wasting your time.'

'Perhaps. I'm done with my lecture. Just think about whether you want to continue pressing your suit or whether you should be looking for someone more suitable for your plans. You're a good man and a damn good business partner, Marston, and I don't want to break up a very comfortable partnership, but I will fight you over this with every weapon in my arsenal until you drive me decisively into the sea.'

'I suppose I should thank you for showing your cards so openly.'

'I'm hoping you will one day thank me for my advice and for helping you avoid a serious mistake.'

Marston unfolded his arms, shaking his head. 'Are you certain you don't want to consider my Penny instead? If I don't have children, at least I would be sure of being able to leave my legacy in the hands of someone as single-mindedly ruthless as you.'

'No offence to your beautiful daughter, but no, thank you, Marston. My taste runs more towards fire than the ethereal.'

'So be it. It is time I joined my daughter and her charming hostesses. You might have drawn a high card with that unfortunate incident at Hollywell, but I don't know if your luck will continue to hold out, Ravenscar.'

'Any decent gambler knows never to rely on luck alone, Marston. I will meet you back at the Hall.'

Chapter Sixteen

Grim straightened, eyebrows twitching, nose raised. It gave her just enough of a warning before the door opened and Alan entered the Rose Room accompanied by Lord Stanton. Their light and dark beauty was a devastating combination, Gabriel and Lucifer. If Lord Stanton hadn't been dressed in a dark blue coat and breeches, he could have been a model for Apollo—tall and powerful and handsome as a god, the candlelight striking gold and silver in his light brown hair and his eyes the colour of ice floes. She watched as Penny Marston and Nicky stared in shy awe at the new entrant and sighed. Next to him Alan looked even more dangerous and she could see why they practically begged an epithet. It would always be like this with Alan. No wonder he was so sure of himself.

He paused on the threshold, surveying the

group by the pianoforte and nodding to his grandmother, who sat on a sofa where she could watch the keys, her hands folded on the knob of her cane like a strict music master. Then he touched his forehead in a strange salute to Philip Marston, who stood between his daughter and Nicky as they sang to Catherine's playing. After the introductions Stanton chose to sit by Lady Ravenscar, with just the hint of the devil in his smile, while Alan approached Lily in the window seat. She straightened but kept her eyes on the pianoforte, resisting the instinctive pull that struck her every time the blasted man walked into a room. However furious she might be at him, inside she felt just as ecstatic at seeing him as Grim looked. She became a puppet on a string around him, reactive, helpless. She hated it.

'What a charming scene,' he said as he sat down beside her, his knee briefly skimming her thigh as he turned to her. Another seemingly casual trespass on her space. Except that it wasn't casual, not for her. She was already aware of him in every inch of her body, but now her skin felt like brushfire. He snapped his fingers at Grim, who trotted towards him, mouth open and panting with joy. 'I'm impressed Lady Jezebel invited them to stay for dinner and the entertainment. She and my grandfather were not the most sociable of people, but Catherine appears to be right that she has mellowed with age. Marston is fitting in nicely, isn't he?'

'He has a very fine voice.'

'And delightful manners. I presume they included telling you I am making an offer on the Grantham Road property, which means we will not be needing Hollywell after all.'

'He told me.'

'It is better this way.'

'His words exactly.'

'Marston and I might not want you to lease Hollywell to Hope House, but our reasons are very different.'

She folded her hands together, wishing she had chosen a chair rather than the window seat. The velvet curtains kept the cool night air out, but now they mirrored the heat rising in her. Every time he came near her she expanded, all the emotions that should be mild and controlled filling and turning wild and too large for her skin. She had been waiting for him to come and now she wished him gone. Or to be alone with him.

'Aren't you going to ask what they are?' he prodded.

'I am certain you have perfectly good reasons, Lord Ravenscar. If you don't wish to share them, that is your prerogative.'

He leaned back against the curtain, crossing his arms.

'You bear a striking resemblance to Lily Wallace, but you can't possibly be her; she would have skewered me to the wall by now. Or has all this domestic charm finally broken your spirit?'

No, you have.

He shifted, the depth of the window seat providing cover for his hand as he traced his fingers down her spine as softly as the fall of her hair. They lingered on the small of her back, gathering the shiver that ran through her, and she saw his chest rise and fall before he drew his hand away. He might have power over her heart and mind, but she had her own power over him and that was a step in the right direction.

'I'm offering you something I have never offered any woman, or ever thought I would.'

For a moment her mind glided away on the soft warmth of his words, allowing herself the fantasy of what might have been said. If their intimate pressure was an invitation to bring their lives together, to build on those two days of mutual caring, on her instinctive knowledge that he could be so much more than he believed of himself.

The risk was so great, but so was the reward.

'I know you are.'

His hand returned to her hip, almost as if he would draw her towards him, an impossibility in the civilised drawing room.

'Tell him to stay away, then.'

'Is this a privilege you reserve for yourself or am I allowed to tell you who you may associate with as well?'

She turned to him and he folded his arms again.

'Don't be clever, Lily. You aren't going to marry him, so for both your sakes you should send him on his way. You risk hurting him.'

'So this is pure magnanimity on your part? Or are you concerned this might harm your mutual business concerns?'

'Blast it, Lily…'

They had both been speaking quietly, but his words fell into the silence that followed the final chords of the music and they shivered in the air alongside the remnants of the song.

'Do you play, Miss Wallace?' Stanton asked, moving towards them, but his arched brow was directed at Alan.

'I have had the pleasure of hearing Miss Wallace often when she played for her father's guests,' Marston said as he helped Catherine rise from the pianoforte. 'Please come play something for us, Miss Wallace.'

Lily didn't want to play, but she allowed Stanton to lead her to the pianoforte. She spread her fingers on the keys and noticed they were shaking. She had intended to play Mozart, but the moment her fingers touched the cool slide of the keys they shifted, spread, choosing for her. The Scarlatti sonata had been one of her mother's favourites, sent by her father the last summer before she died, and Lily had played it often to the sound of frogs and crickets and the lapping of waves coming in from the veranda. He had sent it with a beautiful emerald necklace as an apology for missing his visit and that had been one of the times she had seen her mother cry. All the confused emotions of a thirteen-year-old had entered the music and ten years later she felt they were still there, a tangle of need and sadness and fury held deep underwater, but under them all such a welling of love it choked her. It was more a love song than any of the ballads Marston and Catherine had just sung.

The music faded to the last chord and she took her hands from the keys. She shouldn't have looked. With Grim by his side and the window-seat curtains casting a shadow over him, he looked like a statue cast in black marble of a guardian of a portal to Hades, unyielding and unreachable. Which made her the poor soul, coins clutched in her hand, delivering herself into his world, and surely a life of watching his infidelities from her golden prison would be a version of hell, at least for her. But so would a life without him. So she would have to fight their demons and hope that in the end she won. For both of them.

She didn't hear the applause or even notice when Marston came to lead her to the sofa, his voice low and warm with appreciation. Penny and Nicky began a game of charades and even Lady Ravenscar entered the fray, but Alan just came and leaned against the side of the pianoforte and watched them, arms crossed.

When Partridge brought in tea for the ladies and something more potent for the men, Lily was surprised to find Stanton choosing the seat next to hers. She caught the tension in the look Alan directed him and the same edge of mischief in the look Lord Stanton directed him as he had sat by Lady Ravenscar. Perhaps she had been wrong that this was the tamest member of the Wild Hunt Club.

'You play exquisitely, Miss Wallace. It must have taken many years of instruction to achieve such a pitch of beauty.'

'Is this flattery in aid of something, Lord Stanton?'

He paused and the amusement shimmered to the surface.

'Actually, it is. Can you blame me for being curious about the woman who will become my best friend's wife?'

'Not at all, I would be curious myself. However, I am certain Lord Ravenscar has told you no such announcement has yet been made. I would appreciate if you respected that.'

'Of course, I can be extremely circumspect. If need be.'

She smiled at the qualification.

'You are quite used to having the world bend to your will, aren't you, Lord Stanton?'

'I do my humble best to ensure it does.'

'Why am I not surprised? Your association with Lord Ravenscar should have warned me and on top of that you are also a politician. A lethal combination.'

'A diplomat, not quite a politician, and apparently not much of a diplomat if you see through my façade so easily.'

'Not at all. I am merely naturally wary. So, have you come to scout the enemy's landscape?'

'No, I came to deliver something of importance to Raven, but you are no enemy, Miss Wallace, quite the opposite.'

'That is politic. However, I know Lord Ravenscar has probably told you all the particulars of our predicament. Surely as his friend you are concerned about his being manoeuvred into an association against his will.'

'Alan rarely does anything that is completely against his will. He is even more used than I to having the world bend to his demands, possibly because he has had to work harder at it. That doesn't mean he is an untrustworthy fellow. I would trust him with my life. Well, I already have, in fact.'

She would also trust him with her life, just not with her heart. Now she would have to trust him with that, too.

'How long have you known him?'

He accepted the change in direction with a slight bow.

'Eighteen years. Raven arrived at Eton halfway through the year and into the middle of a rather bitter war being waged between a group of bullies against a friend of mine and myself and a few others. Raven was already very tall and very surly and they took one look at him and invited him into the winning camp.'

'So you began as enemies?'

'Not quite. He took one look at them and walked across the lines so to speak. When they tried to…reason with him, he broke Crawley's nose. He might have been sent down right away except no one would speak against him. That was that. Well, it took a few months to get him to more than snarl, but by the next year he and Hunter and I became close friends and that was that. Raven always had my back.'

'You are very lucky, you three. To have each other.'

His brows rose, as if surprised. Then he smiled and she smiled back. He had a very nice smile when he dropped his charming façade.

'We take care of each other in a way. Which is why I am naturally curious about you.'

'Of course. Now that you have seen the scheming hussy who has entrapped your friend, are you going to forbid the banns?'

He laughed.

'I believe with a special licence that practice doesn't apply.'

'A special licence?'

'Yes, didn't Raven tell you?' Stanton's attempt at innocence was distinctly unconvincing. 'That is the real reason why I came. He asked me to apply for one with the Archbishop. He is clearly taking his new role very seriously.'

'Does he know how much you are enjoying his downfall, Lord Stanton?'

'Most assuredly he does. He made enough

game of Hunter when he fell in love with Nell, it is only fair he suffer a little of his own medicine.'

She shook her head. Men were sometimes beyond her understanding. They certainly had peculiar ways of showing their affection for each other. She cast a careful glance at where Alan was standing by Catherine and Nicky, his dark head bent to something his niece was saying as her hands danced expressively. She turned back to Stanton.

'Did he ever tell you about Rickie?'

His smile held, but the warmth behind it doused utterly. This more than anything told her precisely how strong the ties between these men were.

'Yes. Not until he was much older. He doesn't confide easily. It clarified quite a few things for us.'

'So you know he doesn't want children.'

'Yes. I know.'

Perhaps she had been hoping for a dismissal or a denial or even another politic qualification.

'Both my best friends lost brothers in tragic circumstances and both have to suffer the pain and, what is worse, the guilt,' he continued. 'We each have our own crosses to bear and I don't presume to be able to understand their brand of pain any more than I expect them to understand mine. I do expect them to accommodate me, though, which is enough of a presumption.'

She plucked at her gloves and he continued.

'It doesn't mean you have to let him win, though. He isn't as smart as he thinks. In fact, if anyone is a damn fool… Ah, hello, Raven. We were just talking about you.'

'Were you? Should I be flattered or should I be searching for the knife in my back?'

'Unworthy, my friend. I was just telling Miss Wallace how pleased I am at your betrothal.'

'No such announcement has been made, Lord Stanton,' Lily repeated and Lord Stanton stood up and bowed.

'Of course, Miss Wallace. I stand corrected. How pleased I am to make your acquaintance, then.'

Alan took the vacated seat as Stanton moved towards the others. He turned to her, every line of his body signalling a threat.

'You two appeared to be quite friendly.'

'Did we? I like him. He is very charming.'

'I know he's charming. Women keep falling over themselves to capture his attention and half the time he doesn't even realise it. Try not to join their ranks.'

She laughed at the absurdity.

'Surely you aren't jealous? That is rather facetious after you yourself advised me I would have to seek what I wanted with other men.'

He shifted abruptly, the mocking distance disappearing from his face.

'You wouldn't. Not Stanton.'

For a moment she saw the twelve-year-old boy who had been sent to Eton within months of losing everything he loved, faced with impossible guilt and impossible choices and still choosing to stand with what he thought was right. She reached out and caught herself, clasping her hands in her lap.

'I would never do that to you. That isn't who I am.'

She watched the tension in the etched line of his jaw and the razor-slashed grooves in his cheeks.

'*If* I married you, Alan, I would be faithful. *That* is who I am. You should put aside considerations of honour and decide if that is what you want.'

Both of them were saved from his answer by Lord Stanton's announcement that he had to return to Bristol as he was going back to London early in the morning. In her own inimitable fashion Lady Ravenscar managed to extend her farewells to the Marstons as well and within twenty minutes the room had been cleared of all guests and Catherine was chiding a yawning Nicky towards the door.

'To bed with you, Nicky.'

'That was nice. I like them, Mama. I hope they come again. Isn't Lord Stanton so very handsome? Just like a prince…'

'Yes, my dear. Upstairs with you.'

The door closed behind them and Lady Ravenscar levered herself to her feet.

'It has been a long evening. I will retire as well. Goodnight, Lily. Alan.'

Lily straightened, the numbness falling away as she realised what Lady Ravenscar was doing. No, she wasn't ready to be alone with him, but the door had already clicked shut and the tapping of Lady Belle's cane faded.

'My grandmother has significantly mellowed if she is willing to lower herself to such manoeuvres to further her ends,' Alan said as he sat down beside her on the sofa. 'This is not something my grandfather would have permitted, no matter how sublime the cause.'

'Goodnight, Lord Ravenscar.' She began to rise, but he caught her arm, pulling her back down beside him.

'We aren't done yet.'

'I am tired, Lord Ravenscar. I wish to retire.'

The dark night shades of his eyes had softened a little, revealing the silver that would flash when his compassion or amusement surfaced. It tugged an answering response from her, but she resisted it. She didn't want to soften right now. She had heard of foxes that chewed through a trapped limb to escape a poacher's snare. She just needed to gather her resolve.

'Yes, I can see that. You are escaping back to your island, aren't you? First we are going to discuss Hollywell. Why don't you just admit you are secretly glad you can keep Hollywell for yourself?' he continued, but the underlying truth in his question opened the floodgates.

'Because I'm not. If I did agree to marry you, I would have a lifetime to be alone because in the end that is all you are able to offer me. I wanted to fill that house with people and children, even if they weren't my own. I wanted to turn the drawing room upstairs in the south wing into a schoolroom and there would be a reading room for them so I could read to those who hadn't learned yet, or who just wanted to listen. I know what you think you are doing, Alan, but you are wrong. This just proves it.'

She gasped as his hands shot out and grabbed her shoulders, forcing her to face him.

'I won't let you marry Marston.'

His obtuseness drove her pain into rage.

She could feel the ebb of her tide, the rise of the destructive anger, but she had been holding back too much that day to stop it from crashing through her.

'Let go of me! I didn't say I would marry him, but I didn't say I would marry you, either. I don't like the terms, Ravenscar. If it means I am ruined, then so be it, I no longer care. This foolish dream I had about coming home to England and living the life I might have had is not worth the price. I shall sell my mother's jewels and go away, somewhere. America, perhaps, where they won't mind a little dust on my reputation in exchange for my wealth. I might even find someone who truly cares about me as I do about him. That strange mythical beast might yet exist out there. I'm not escaping to my island this time, Alan.'

She desperately wanted to shake him, to drag him off his own island, but she watched helplessly as he shut down. It was peculiar that this harsh, cynical look reminded her again how handsome he was, almost unfairly so, giving credence to that Wild Hunt nonsense of a man damned and seductively dangerous. She was beginning to forget his physical beauty, merely seeing Alan, but when he turned coldly furious, it became evident again.

'This is all very edifying, but the fact remains that you will marry me.'

'You cannot force me to wed, Alan.'

'Is that another challenge, Lily? Shall I show it will not take any force at all?'

Yes, please. There was nothing she could do to stem the swarm of blood filling her with anticipation.

'I didn't force you to rush into my arms that night at Hollywell,' he continued.

'I was scared.'

'That wasn't why you stayed there, that wasn't why you opened to me, why you moaned in my arms when I touched you, there…'

His fingers lightly traced a stripe of lace embroidered into her skirt, following the line between her thighs. Her legs shivered against each other and the memory of every moment of the night Grim had scared her rushed through her mind and body, as hot and inescapable as the most virulent fever. In a second her cheeks were throbbing with blood, her mouth dry, her lungs struggling to regulate her breath, and at the juncture of her thighs, an immediate awareness, damp and yearning. If she could have resorted to violence to wipe away her weakness, she would have. But she just waited for the worst to pass before she spoke.

'It isn't proper for us to be here alone, Lord Ravenscar.'

'We are engaged and allowed a little lenience,' he replied, his gaze moving over her face, settling on her mouth. He wasn't touching her, but she felt him, the memory of his taste filling her, and she had to fight the urge to lick her lips, capture that shimmering sensation and prepare herself for more.

She was stronger than this.

'We aren't engaged yet. How many times must I say this? Please leave the room or I shall.'

'Then leave.'

She hadn't expected that. She stood, half-expecting him to still protest, but he said nothing, his attention on a stray thread unravelling the petals of an embroidered rose on the back of the sofa.

'Goodnight, Lord Ravenscar.'

The last of the petals succumbed to a sharp tug of his fingers.

'Sweet dreams, Lily.'

She walked out before she broke utterly. She would concede this battle, but not the war.

Chapter Seventeen

It took an exertion of will over every sinew in Alan's body not to stop her. He twined the pink thread between his fingers, trying to bring to bear all the internal lectures about proceeding calmly and carefully and keep a tight rein on this need to touch her, take her…

Right now all this good counsel felt as effective as sheltering under a blade of grass in a storm. It would take more than a few pithy homilies to calm this burn of frustration. A few more evenings like this and he would do something drastic, like march upstairs and show her why all this fine talk about choices and propriety and anything but the elemental bond that existed between them was as empty as…as his life would be if she married Marston.

Damn her. He was done playing fair.

He shook the thread from his fingers and went

upstairs. He would wait until her maid left and then he would make clear her fate was as sealed as his.

'Sue? Did you forget something?'

She didn't turn as he opened her door, but her arm stopped in mid-brush. Her hair hung long and wavy and lush down her back and over her shoulder and his hands were already mapping their way down its length as he closed the door behind him, turning the key in the lock.

She turned, her eyes widening, taking in his coatless, bootless state.

'You can't come in here,' she whispered.

'I think you'll find I can.'

'Alan…'

'Let me.' He took the brush and stroked his hand down the waves of her hair as they fell over her dressing gown, covering her breasts in a mantle of warmth.

'It's even silkier than it looks,' he murmured. 'Do you know, I fantasise about what it would feel like on my bare skin and spread out on the bed when I am inside you.'

He smiled at the burn of colour that swept the coolness from her skin and wrapped his hand deeper in the auburn waves. He was done waiting and he was done playing by the rules. They never worked for him anyway. Tonight he would break another vow and categorically ruin a virgin and risk his soul into the bargain. It was a fair trade.

'I'll scream,' she hissed, recovering from the shock, but her voice shook and she didn't try to pull away.

'With pleasure. I hope so.'

'You are impossible! You know what I mean.'

He tightened his hand in her hair, bearing her head back as he bent to speak the words against her mouth. 'Go ahead. Scream…'

He smiled at the agonised little moan that met his words. She was his. Right now. For ever.

'Your lips are a little dry, let me help you.'

He caressed her lower lip with his tongue, drawing it into his mouth and letting it slide out, half-catching it with his teeth before releasing it so he could see the moist glimmer on the lush curve. He was going to taste every inch of her, find every flavour.

'One day I will discover what magical spice you use, Lily. I've never tasted anything so delectable.'

'Alan, you can't do this; this is cheating…' she whispered, but he felt her hand flutter against his chest, her attempt to push him away turning into an unconscious caress and adding to the urgent pulsing of blood rushing through him like a swarm of angry wasps. He paid no heed either to her or his body, just to his plan.

'I'm just helping you prepare for bed.' He ran the brush from the crown of her head to the tips of her hair, long, slow, definite strokes. Mirroring them with the slide of his mouth against hers, not penetrating her there, just warming and soothing and teasing until he could almost feel the confused pulsing between her legs in the way her hands were curled into each other, her thighs hard together. Her scent enveloped him, beckoning him with the fantasy of slipping into the warm Caribbean Sea with her, as bare as the elements.

'One day you'll take me swimming with you in your bay, Lily. There will be nothing between us but warm water and no one to hear your intoxicating moans but the gulls.'

He kneeled beside her, ignoring the pressure of his pantaloons on his erection as he trailed his hand down to find the ribbon that secured her dressing gown between her breasts and gently eased it free. Her eyes were on his, but dilated, lost in shock and need. If he were a gentleman, he would give her time, woo her fears away, but he was taking no chances any more with his prize. He would woo her after he secured her. There would be no more talk about America and running away.

'Do you know,' he said as he traced the embroidered pattern along the bodice of her nightgown, sinking into the valley between her breasts, curving under them and raising their weight very gently into his palms, 'this cloth might actually have come from one of my mills? I will take you there so you can see what it takes to make something so exquisite, so sheer I can see every shade of colour, every change in texture.' He marked his observations with his fingertips and her flesh gathered and shook beneath them, her breath mirroring the tremors that he could feel down to where he was leaning against her thigh.

He was shaking as well, with hunger and the need to keep it reined in, with the knowledge that he was finally going to take her, make her unequivocally his, that with each tremor that brought him closer to her his life was changing, opening.

There would be no going back for either of them, no running away. She was his.

Lily watched his hands, dark and hard against the white lawn of her nightgown, showing her the vulnerability of the flesh beneath. She knew what he was doing. She had thrown down the gauntlet and he was merely picking it up. He would win, too, because she wanted to lose. When he looked at her like that, nothing else mattered but that he not stop. She was no better than her mother and at the moment she didn't care. All she cared about was right here, his features hard cut with tension, about to take what she had no wish to withhold.

Her eyelids sank as his fingers pressed gently against her breasts, encompassing them, but when his thumbs brushed up, catching the hard peaks, the whip of pleasure was so immediate and foreign she shut her eyes tight against it, sagging against him with a cry. In a second he was dragging her out of her chair to her feet and hard against his body, his voice hard and urgent against her hair.

'You want this... Tell me you want this, Lily.'

'Yes.' She almost choked on the word, her throat was so tight, her mouth pressed against his neck, breathing him in, filling with him. She was back in his room at Hollywell, but this time he didn't stop. This time she was tasting the silky hot skin, touching her tongue to the rough scrape of stubble along the line of his jaw, seeking his mouth. She was drunk on the need to taste him again.

'I want you...'

His body contracted around her, like the tremors of fever, and that excited her almost more than anything, the knowledge that he wanted her, that he was clinging to his control. She said the words again, like a prayer.

'I want you… Alan…'

His name was caught against his mouth as he dug his hands into her hair and raised her mouth to his. This kiss grew wild fast, capturing, tasting every corner of her mouth before claiming its depth until she lost her boundaries, as much him as herself.

It didn't stop with her mouth and now she would have fought him if he had tried to stop. Her nightgown sighed to the floor and she was as bare as he had threatened and his hands closed on her breasts again and the rough and soft drag of his skin felt as though he had reached inside her, curved over her heart and soul, and was shaping them as he saw fit. He was turning her into flame, setting free some mythical creature like the tales of the people of Padrones.

She wanted to feel him. His image of swimming with him in the bay filled her mind, of sliding her body against his, feeling his hands, his mouth sliding against the softness of the water, finding her… Her hands clenched the warm fabric of his shirt, pulling at it. She had lost all shame, all reason.

'I want to feel you on me.'

He didn't need a second invitation. He dragged his shirt off, pressing her against him, and she couldn't resist rubbing herself against the silky dark hair on his chest. It fed the restless hunger inside her, the pulsing heat gathering at her centre.

'Lily, you were made for me. You're mine.'

She didn't answer, intent on his body, his hands as they pressed her back until she felt the bed against her thighs. She looked up, meeting the naked passion in his gaze. There would be no going back, no escape, he was hers.

She wrapped her arms around his neck as he lowered her on to the bed, bringing him with her, bringing his mouth to hers, raising her hips as his hand traced down from her breasts, his fingers skimmed up and over the soft curls between her legs, gliding between her thighs and sending a tingling cascade outwards from that point like ripples on a pond. Her mouth stilled under his, too shocked to react to the intensity of the sensations. His kiss softened, a gentle brush of his lips over hers mirroring the gentle brush of his fingers on her thighs, up between her legs, finally touching her where she never even touched herself. Before she could even react and pull away, a bolt of lightning struck though her. She sank back, breathless with the shock.

'Hush, don't worry, I know what I'm doing...' His voice was hardly more than a rumble of sound, coursing through her like her own blood, but instead of soothing her it stung, sobering her. Of course he knew what he was doing. He had done this countless times before, would do it again, whether he married her or not. At no point had he promised anything else.

But sanity was a weak weapon against what his hand was doing.

'Let me show you what you are capable of,' he whispered against her mouth before his lips moved lower, trailing fire over the rise of her breast so that her nipple hardened, pushed against the muslin, seeking his touch. His fingers kept sliding against the damp heat between her legs, each stroke tightening the spring coiled about her. It would break, she knew it had to break, and her with it.

He pressed his mouth to her breast, his breath spreading over her skin, its edges reaching the hardened arc of her nipple, making her muscles clench in anticipation about his fingers as his lips approached, her whole body a collection of warring elements vying for the attention of that beautiful mouth, those skilled hands...

The next words were just a lick of heat against the apex of her breast and struck a bolt of agony through her body and her mind.

'Trust me...'

Trust me.

Finally the caged tiger struck, slashing her with the memory. Of her mother running down the path towards the docking boat, like a little girl, excited, ecstatic at her husband's return, uncaring of the fact he had probably come from another woman's bed.

'No!'

The cry of denial that burst from her was so sharp his caressing hands stopped immediately. His hand touched her cheek, his eyes narrowed and questioning. He looked beautiful and dangerous and she wanted him more than she had wanted anything in her life and he scared her more than the hosts of hell. She scared herself even more.

'What's wrong, sweetheart? Did I hurt you?'

The endearment sounded so real it stung like a slap. The worst was that she now had to choose. She knew he would stop if she asked. A choice. What did she choose?

'Alan,' she whispered, wishing she could have

kept that burst of pain inside her. She didn't want him to stop, no matter where it took her. She wanted more of this. She wanted him.

So she clung to him as his mouth captured hers again, shivering as it skimmed over her cheek and down to the excruciatingly sensitive skin of her neck, lingering on the silky consistency of her earlobes, demolishing her. She didn't resist when he took her hand from where it clung to his shoulder and pressed it against the unbearable heat between her legs. She moaned as her fingers slid against the slick dampness, guided by his.

'I want you to see what you are capable of, what you can do for yourself. Someone like you shouldn't hide from her own fire. You shouldn't be afraid to touch yourself. Let me show you… I won't hurt you, I promise.'

Of course, he would hurt her in the end, in soul if not in body, but she no longer cared, as long as he was touching her. She wanted him to show her.

The pleasure was different, more muted but deeper in pitch, subterranean.

His hand moved on hers, pressing, teasing, torturing her. She was shaking with it. He was gathering her like the threads of a tapestry, weaving her into this new body, the finest of textures, from rough to soft, silky and frayed. She was everything under his hands, his mouth, being filled with his beauty. She wanted to be filled by him.

Without conscious thought her other hand reached out and met the hard pressure of his arousal through the fabric of his pantaloons and a sound between a groan and growl ran through him and into her, his hand stilling on hers and she could feel him shaking as well.

Now she could concentrate on every point of contact between them, exploring the geography of their shared passion. They were at the edge of a whole new landscape and he had given her only a glimpse of this new world. There was such a force in her to take what she could right here, right now because it was the only thing she had ever really wanted. She hadn't known what wanting was until she had met Alan. She hadn't known who she was until she had met him. Now she knew.

'God, Lily. You're destroying me. I want to be inside you, disappear inside you… I want to go in so deep I never come out.'

She could *feel* his words, a flame rising where he was touching her, shooting up hot and hard inside her. She wanted him to make them real, to follow that heat and replace their fingers with the rigid muscle pressed against her hand. So deep he would never come out. He was already inside her soul, she wanted him inside her body. She was drowning, the only breaths she was taking were coming from the heat of his mouth on hers.

Then his fingers brushed hers away and set about demolishing her. Each sweep sent shards of lightning up through her body, tightening it unbearably. It was devouring her, but she wanted more, she wanted him with her. She wanted him as torn apart by need, but he was holding back. She could feel the acute tension in his breathing, in the frantic pulse in his blood and his tension where their bodies touched and she knew he was as desperate for the release as she, waiting for some sign from her or from himself to take the step from which there was no return.

'I want to feel you, all of you, take your pantaloons off.' Even to her it sounded like a command. He gave a choked laugh, his hand stilling, then his thumb flicked the nub of pleasure and her body arched up against him in sweet agony.

'Your wish is my command.'

She almost wished she hadn't said anything because she didn't want him to move away from her, not even to pull off his clothes. Like the unveiling of a statue she watched the linen pull away from the sculpted ridges of his chest and shoulders, the silky straight dark hair that tapered down from his chest, the angle of his hip bones as he moved to take off his pantaloons. She pressed her legs together at the sight of his erection, not in rejection but because her body contracted as if he was already inside her. Then he was leaning over her, his hand closing on her cheek and jaw almost painfully, his eyes dark and intent over hers.

'You're mine, Lily. There is no going back.'

She shook her head. She knew that. She had made her choice.

'Touch me. I want to feel you.'

'You will. Believe me, you will. I just hope you don't hate me by the end of this, Lily.'

That sobered her a little. She pressed her own hands to his face, meeting the intensity in his eyes. His words should have frightened her, but they just strengthened her resolve. Somehow she would reach him. Whatever it took.

'I'm not scared of you, Alan.'

He groaned, sinking his forehead against hers, and then he captured her mouth with a kiss that drove every thought and fear from her mind. His hands began demolishing her again, then slid deep between her thighs, parting them, stroking the soft inner flesh until she rose against him, and then his weight was between them, his erection thudding hot and hard where he had been touching her. She heard her voice, soft shuddering moans he muffled with his mouth as he poised himself at her entrance, teasing her to a pitch of need.

'Lily. You're mine.'

The words were all the warning she had before he penetrated her, the pain shooting sharp and hard through her. Her nails sank into his back and they both froze, breathing hard.

'It's over. I'm so sorry. It's over.'

She could hardly hear the words, her ears were ringing, her body torn between pain and the unsatisfied need and the pleasure he had promised. Then the shock centred and she was still there, waiting.

'What now?' she breathed.

His head sank so that his cheek pressed against hers and she realised he was shaking.

'Are you laughing?' she demanded.

'Only a madman would laugh at a moment like this, sweetheart,' he whispered, his breath warm against her ear and cheek, heating her again. 'I'm not laughing, I'm dying. Please, please don't move or you will kill me.'

She could feel the wriggling tension again, the delicate imbalance inside her, waiting for the fall.

'But if I don't move, I might die. What do we do?'

'I'll have to sacrifice myself, then.' He groaned,

his body sinking against hers, shifting her legs further apart, sliding against her, not leaving her, just sliding his hand between them, finding the point of contact between them, and her shudder became an ache. The pressure of his fingers against her unleashed pleasure so powerful it spread through him and back into her, up to her breasts that were begging to rub themselves against the hair on his chest and the hard muscles underneath. As he moved inside her, over her, against her, she forgot pain, fear, the future. There was only now and the twisting, unrelenting joy that was just within reach if he would only…

He closed his teeth over her earlobe, whispering the words against her.

'You are magic. You'll come with me, love. Give yourself to me.'

The coiled spring snapped and joy spread through her, warm honeyed pleasure moving through her body, lighting her from within like a paper lantern, and then she burst and sank back, gasping for breath as his body continued to shudder and thrust against her until slowly he sank down on her, his arms gathering her to him, his mouth against her hair, repeating her name.

Alan eased off the bed. Whether he wanted to or not, it was time to leave her. Tomorrow he would leave as early as possible to sign the papers for the Grantham Road building and then come back and make the arrangements to put the special licence to use. Now that the possibility of a child was no longer hypothetical it was crucial there be no chance of scandal surrounding Lily or their children. He owed her that.

He curled his fingers into his palms against the need to run his hand over the curve of her hip under the cover, down the line of her leg, to wake her and see in her eyes that she knew what had just occurred between them. Not a seduction, but an admission and a pact.

It had not been as he expected. He had no knowledge of deflowering virgins, but he had prepared himself for the worst, to go as slowly as a mule cart and to have to comfort a tearstained and shocked young woman after the act. He should have known nothing that involved Lily would proceed as expected. He also should have known that slow was not an option. It had been impossible to go slowly. She had been so responsive, so alive and unbridled...beautiful in her joy. Tearing through whatever remained of his defences like a cannonball through gauze.

He always did his utmost to give pleasure. It was a mark of pride. But there had been no such consideration here—he had *needed* to see her climax, to watch her melt, soften, tense into that final ecstasy. He hadn't just wanted to give her pleasure but show her she had that capacity herself. It had never occurred to him it would be as satisfying as his own physical release and much more addictive. When she had climaxed a second time, he had been completely caught in the wonder of it, in her beauty, as awe-inspiring as the shifting ocean.

But mostly he wanted to lock her to him, body and soul, as deep as he could go. He wanted to wake her and make her climax a third time while he was inside her up to the hilt so he could feel that beauty surround him, feed on her whimpers of pleasure from within. Become part of her joy.

He had come to both signal his surrender and try to tie her to him and he had only proven to himself how futile and unworthy his resistance was. He should have known that day at Saltford that she was his fate, that she had stolen his capacity for pleasure, for feeling alive.

He bent and tucked a strand of hair behind her ear and touched his mouth gently to the ridge of her cheek, breathing her in. She stirred and moaned faintly and his body clenched around the memory and promise of joy. He would give her a dozen children if it made her happy. Whatever it took to keep her, to see light warm her eyes.

'You're mine, Lily,' he repeated, but she didn't stir and eventually he left.

Chapter Eighteen

Lily pulled at the long willow leaf, stripping it from the thread-thin stalk. The pale late-autumn roses she placed on Rickie's grave were shivering in the breeze, their cream petals stained pink at the tips.

After last night she didn't know what to think at the news that Alan had left for Bristol with his groom close to first light. Nothing, probably. She knew how desperate he was to close on the new property. He had solved one problem, or so he probably thought, and now he was off to solve another. Then he would return and set about sealing their fate.

She pressed her hand to her stomach and closed her eyes in a silent prayer. How did one know if he had practised any of those means to avoid conception? Her discussions with those women in her father's forbidden house had taught her a little about what men like him did to avoid breeding bastards, but she thought she would have remembered if he had used one of the French gloves they had mentioned or if he had… well, stopped in the middle. But she didn't have the experience to judge. Could he have forgotten to be careful? It wasn't like the Alan she had come to know, but perhaps. And if he had forgotten, it meant she might even now…

What would he do if she was?

Those women had also been very clear about the means they employed if precautions failed. They were sometimes dangerous, but as they said, it was that or lose their livelihood. Such slips could mean starvation for them and the child to be born.

No, whatever happened she knew Alan would never make such a demand of her and she would certainly never accede to it. He would abide by his responsibility here, too, and it would either destroy whatever fragile bond existed between them or finally break through to him and the love she knew he possessed.

'But I would still like it to be his choice, Grim. Not something else fate forces upon him. Is that foolish of me?'

Grim yawned and lay down, snuffling at the

grass, and she knelt by him, wincing at the stinging between her legs.

'You agree I should marry him and risk everything, don't you? I can see that you do. But on my terms, at least until he sees reason. You see, I can be as constant as you and much more devious.'

She pushed to her feet, brushing at the grass.

'Are you coming? No. Very well, stay here and watch over Rickie.'

'Miss Wallace. Mr Marston is here to see you. In the Rose Room. Lady Ravenscar and Lady Catherine are not yet awake, miss. It being so early still.'

'Thank you, Partridge,' she said, ignoring the pointed note in the elderly butler's voice. Time to clear the decks.

Marston was standing, hands clasping his gloves, his expression wary as she strode towards him.

'Good morning, Philip. I am glad you came so early, there really is no point to beat about the bush any longer. I think you know what my answer is. You aren't in love with me and I am in love with another man, it is as simple as that.'

Marston drew his gloves between his hands with a resigned smile.

'You are right that I knew what I was coming

to hear today. The tension between the two of you is as palpable as a pea-soup fog. But a word of advice, if I may. Don't let him have his way too easily. You are in a strong negotiating position, so negotiate.'

Lily thought of her total capitulation the previous night. It was imprinted in every inch of her body, in the throbbing sting between her legs and the rawness where his stubble and teeth had grazed the sensitive skin of her breasts; in the yearning of her skin and the occasional echo of pleasure where he had touched her and shown her how to touch herself.

She laughed at the futility of his offer.

'I don't know if I would make it to the negotiating table, let alone stand firm on my demands. I don't expect him to love me, men never fall in love with me, but I do want more than he is willing to offer.'

'My dear girl, I've watched quite a few men fall in love with you. You just never realised it.'

She shook her head.

'That is kind but inaccurate, Philip. Certainly none of them ever said anything to me.'

'Men do need some encouragement if they are to risk themselves, Lily. We are fragile vessels.'

'So are women.'

'True. Well. What will you do now?'

'I don't know… Marry him and see if I can win him over in the end, I suppose. I honestly don't know what I should do.'

She must have looked as lost as she felt because he hesitated and sighed.

'Out of pride I really shouldn't be helping him, you know…'

'You are helping me, not him. Besides, since he might be your brother-in-law one day, I don't think you should antagonise him more than necessary.'

His jaw dropped, but the flush that spread over his cheeks confirmed her suspicion that he and Catherine were rather more attracted to each other than either realised and she laughed, relieved. What a mistake she had almost made. Both of them.

'I assure you…'

'Oh, please don't. I shouldn't have said anything that might send you running.'

'Yes, well, to our business. I find when I make a mistake in negotiations it sometimes helps to make a tactical withdrawal. If you accept his terms outright, don't be surprised if they don't answer your needs. Make him come to you, on your terms.'

'How?'

'Penny is leaving this morning to go to her

aunt in Bath for a few weeks to acquire some polish before I take her to London in the spring. I would be glad if you accompanied her there. She would be happy for the company on the drive and my sister is a very pleasant and easy-going woman and would be happy for another guest, especially one as charming as you.'

'This morning?'

'Yes. I gather Ravenscar is in Bristol to sign the papers with the mayor, so his absence is fortuitous. Could you be ready in an hour or so?'

She pressed her hand again to her stomach. She knew running away was no solution, but she needed to think and she couldn't think around Alan. Well, not very rationally. He would just do precisely what he had done the night of the concert—seduce her and push the decision further and further away from her. And she—she would fold like the frailest of fans because for the first time in her life she felt utterly at home with someone.

But wasn't this precisely what had eventually driven her mother into illness and melancholy and on to her refuge on the island? Why should she trust this conviction that she was as right for him as he was for her and if he only gave her a chance…if she only tried hard enough, he would learn to love her and be content with what they could build together? Was she doomed to relive her mother's fate or was there merit to this feeling deep insider her, this blind belief that Alan was not like her father and much more than he himself believed he was? Because if he wasn't, she would have to be strong enough to walk away, whatever the price.

He would follow her, of course he would, he was nothing if not stubborn, but he could hardly manoeuvre her as easily in a stranger's home in Bath as he had at the Hall. She would recover some measure of distance even if she could never recover her heart.

She raised her chin and answered, 'I could, but… If he hears you were here before my departure, he will come asking questions. I don't want to cause you trouble.'

'I will ignore the slight to my manhood. He might come asking questions, but I am not obliged to answer, am I? I must be quite mad. You are a bad influence on me, Lily.'

'I know. Aren't you glad you discovered that now rather than after we wed? Thank you, Philip. I really do wish you happy.'

Chapter Nineteen

Alan stopped at the sight of his grandmother all but bursting from the door of the Rose Room.

'Alan. Oh, thank goodness you are back.'

He frowned, following her into the room, where she sank into her armchair. She pressed one veined hand to her cheek while her other clutched a piece of paper in her lap.

'What is wrong, Grandmother?'

'Lily. She's gone.'

'What do you mean, she is gone?'

'Gone as in gone. Partridge said a carriage pulled up out front and she hurried out to it with a portmanteau before he could say a word or summon me. She left this.'

Alan took the letter from his grandmother and turned away to read it.

It wasn't long, or informative.

A few weeks…

'It doesn't say where she went. It doesn't say if she will return. What did you do to frighten her away, Alan?'

Given her a promise he had never imagined he would give. Taken away her choice. At least he thought he had, but obviously not. Did she think she would escape him? He would find her if it was the last thing he did and then he would...

He pressed the letter down on the table, smoothing out the edges until the snarl of fury and fear and pain worked its way through him. What more did she want from him? He had risked his heart and soul to give her what she wanted last night only to have her run.

'Could she have gone to Hollywell once more? Or to that Marston fellow? Partridge said he was here this morning to see her.'

Alan turned. 'Was he?'

Her eyes widened further. 'Don't do anything foolish, Alan. A duel with Marston would be ruinous.'

'A duel? With Mr Marston? What are you talking about?' Catherine asked from the doorway.

'Lily has left. We don't know where.'

'But...she couldn't have gone with Mr Marston!'

'And why not? He was here this morning and now she is gone with nothing more than this faradiddle about going away for a few weeks with some friends and she wrote that we are not to worry. Not to worry!'

'I don't believe she would have left with Mr Marston. She doesn't even want him.'

'She doesn't have to want him. She wants what he can give her,' Alan snarled.

'No. I don't believe it. I always knew she wouldn't do it in the end and she wouldn't.'

'Well, she's done something, gone somewhere, and I'm going to find out where. Since you are so convinced she didn't go to Marston, perhaps you have some ideas where she did go.'

Catherine shook her head, her blue eyes damp with tears.

'No, none. I mean…she couldn't have returned to Jamaica or to her island, could she?'

'Literally or figuratively? It doesn't matter. I'm going to find her.'

'Where will you go?'

'I don't know. Hollywell, Bristol, Brazil, wherever I need to.'

'What can we do to help, Alan?' Lady Ravenscar's question was so practical, there was no reason why it should have brought down his defences. He paused in the doorway and looked back at his grandmother. Belle and Ray.

'There is something you can do. The Hall. I

want you to change your will and leave me the Hall. I don't want or need your money, but I must have something to offer her beyond money... I need to offer her a home.'

'I have no intention of altering my will, any of it.'

She met his gaze with defiance and he tightened his hand on the doorknob.

'So be it.'

'Catherine and your cousins will receive bequests, of course, but you are and have always been my prime beneficiary, Alan. I know we parted in anger after Catherine's wedding, but if you imagine I would follow your grandfather's example and write you out of my will, then you never knew me. Your grandfather was a...a horrid man and I hated him with every fibre of my being, though I could never fully admit that to myself until well after his death. I was glad you turned your back on us and I envied you the day you left. Thank goodness you did, because if you had stayed, it would have meant he had already broken you as well. It is true I hoped one day you might return, might even ask me for the only thing of value I had to offer you, but I was proud that you never did. The Hall is and has always been yours, as well as every acre of land and the income from it. I hope you and that impossible young woman will finally make it a home worthy of the name. It is about time a Rothwell made up for all the misery of those before him. I think I shall remove to Bath. I am tired of seeing to the Hall and now that my sister is widowed as well we should rub along quite well. Oh, do stop staring at me as if I have grown a second head and kindly refrain from making any comment, either mocking or mawkish. Reserve your energies for dealing with your concerns. Now go.'

'I was expecting you earlier.' Marston rose from his desk as his butler showed Alan into the study. Alan strode forward until only the bulk of the dark mahogany desk stood between them.

'I apologise for keeping you waiting. Where is she?'

'Not here.'

'You're a lucky man, then, Marston. Where is she?'

'Perfectly safe.'

'That isn't what I asked you. If I ask you again, it will be with my hands around your throat.'

'I don't want to brawl with you, Ravenscar. Believe it or not, my objective is not to punish either of you. Lily and I understand each other tolerably well now and have decided we will not suit. She and Penny have probably reached Bath by now. They will be staying with my sister in Laura Place. She is perfectly safe and will be well chaperoned. I have the direction here.' He pointed to a sheet of paper on his desk.

Alan shook his head, trying to rearrange his thoughts, but they kept stumbling over the emotions exploding in his head like a bombardment of French cannon.

'Why Bath?' he finally managed.

'Because Penny was going there and the opportunity presented itself. I believe Lily needed some time to decide whether to accept your offer without you constantly tipping the scales. She isn't as ruthless as you, Ravenscar.'

'I think this is pretty damn ruthless. I don't need you defending Lily, Marston; that is my role. From now on find someone else to fulfil your procreative ambitions and stay out of our business.'

Marston laughed softly. 'It's a pity you never met her father. I asked him once why he was allowing her to remain unmarried for so long—she was already twenty-one then and had just sent another fellow to the roundabout. He said it was his fault she had built a tower to keep herself safe, so he owed her some leeway and that he hoped one day one of them would actually have the bollocks to storm her castle.'

Alan strode towards the door.

'What are you going to do?' Marston called after him.

'Storm a castle,' he answered before slamming the door.

Chapter Twenty

⚜

Lily looked down at the grave. Four years old. He would have been full of energy, already a boy with opinions and a sense of himself. A person. So much of what he might have become would have been there already. She wondered if he had been shy or talkative. A cautious boy or someone who threw his heart ahead of him. She wondered what Alan had been like as a boy before life had forced him to erect walls about himself. She wished she could reach into the past and shift fate to relieve him of that horrible burden, but she couldn't. All she could do was stand by him now.

'I saw you from the drive.'

She turned as Alan let the willow branches fall back into place, so filled with love she couldn't speak.

'At least this saves me a drive to Bath. Did the carriage break down?'

He spoke lightly, but she knew him well enough by now to hear the grinding mix of emotions beneath the carefully suave question. She pressed her hands together and laid her cards on the table, all of them.

'No. I decided not to go. I didn't want to leave and I don't really wish to negotiate. I want to be with you. I can't force you to love me or to want to have a family, but I do want you to try to make more of this than just a marriage of convenience. I love you, Alan. I don't think I will be able to be with you and keep that inside me. It will be like trying not to breathe. Can you understand that?'

He looked up at the arch of the willows above them, the tendons in his neck sharp with tension, like the painting of a fallen angel supplicating the heavens. Then he moved towards her.

'Don't ever run away from me again.'

'I won't. I…'

He closed the distance between them, pinioning her face in his hand, his fingers hard against her bones. There was anger there, and more; she knew that roiling storm of feelings.

'Don't you *ever* dare run away from me again. You want something? You stay and fight for it and tell me I'm being a bloody fool. But you don't run. Do you understand?'

She nodded as best she could in his steel grip,

the first buds of joy forcing their way through her fear as she began to absorb the truth revealed in his eyes, in the agony etched on his lean face. She stroked her fingers lightly down his cheek and something else appeared through the anger, and when he spoke again, his voice was muted, defeated.

'How could you do that to me? Do you know what I thought? I thought you had gone to him. I couldn't bear it...'

'I didn't. I wouldn't. I just wanted to get away to think. This morning I realised you might have forgotten to...well, to be careful and that I might even now be with child. I knew I would have to fight you for the kind of life I thought was right. For us, not just for me. I wanted to show you I would not let you dictate all the terms, but then as we were just coming into Keynsham I realised I didn't want it to be like that. So I told them to put me down and I went to Mr Prosper and asked him to bring me home in his gig. I don't want to run away from this, from you.'

He stared at her, his eyes narrowed and unrevealing.

'Forgotten? What kind of fool do you think I am? What the devil do you think I was doing when I came to your room last night? Do you think I *forgot* to use precautions like some green fool? That after a dozen years of being cautious it just slipped my mind? For someone so intelligent you are as foolish as a newborn lamb sometimes, Lily. I knew precisely what I was doing, and if you had used half the brain God gave you, you would know what that meant. I couldn't have signalled my surrender more clearly than if I walked in there with a white flag.'

She stared at him. She had been so caught in her own drama she had lost all sight of his. Marston had told her once Alan was cautious. The wildest of the wild hunters was as cautious as a mother hen when it came to things that mattered. He had seduced her knowing full well he might walk out of that night a prospective father and had known precisely what that meant and she had been as blind as a bat and fluttered away just as blindly in her confusion and fear.

He reached out and tucked her against him as if sheltering her from a storm. She clung to him, trying not to cry with the joy that was careening around in her like foolish old Grim had careened around Hollywell.

'You're more than I can bear sometimes, Lily, but I can't live without you. If you leave me again, you will discover just how terrifying the Wild Hunt can be. I'll build a damn tower if need be and lock you in and hide the bloody key.'

She laughed with joy, pressing herself against him. 'You don't scare me, Alan Piers Cavendish Rothwell. Besides, ferrets are good at finding things. Will you marry me, Alan?'

'Damn you, Lily.'

'I think I am by now, damned that is. I probably was the day you walked into Hollywell and teased me into giving you Marcus Aurelius. See the lengths I will go to get my property back?'

'Oh, God, anything I can give you, I will.'

'There's only one thing. Will you marry me and let me love you?'

Her shoulders and ribs protested at the fierceness of his embrace, but she revelled in it, and when it gentled, she raised her head to touch her lips to the tense muscles of his neck.

'That's two things,' he murmured against her hair, his hand sliding down her back, softening, bringing her against him. His other hand slid the pins and comb from her hair, and when it tumbled free, he breathed in, raising a fistful to his mouth before moving his attention to her mouth, his lips stroking hers, gentle and rhythmic, like a warm breeze.

'Will you?' she prompted.

'Yes. God, yes…'

This was the wild hunt she had been waiting for. She could well give credence to dark powers when she found herself stripped of her garments and spread out on the shaded grass in nothing more than her stockings, a dark devil poised above her, his eyes narrowed shards of ice as they scraped over her body before her own shivered shut when he bent to kiss her, drawing her soul into his, his mouth torturing her with a trail of kisses that lingered on her breasts, before descending, making her squirm against him as they skimmed and delved the sensitive skin of her abdomen, coming closer to her aching centre. Too close. She half-raised herself on her elbow to see his night-black hair glistening against the pale moon luminescence of her skin. She was already shaking, half in anticipation, half in fear. Her hands caught in his hair and he drew back and she wished she hadn't stopped him, but she didn't know what to do with all these feelings.

'Alan. Touch me.'

'Oh, I will. Believe me. Down to your soul. Just like you've touched me, my lovely Lily. You're mine.'

His fingers playing gently with the soft skin of her thighs above her garters, sliding his fingers under them, transforming their unravelling into exquisite torture, following their descent with his mouth, whispering his love and precisely how he was going to touch her, love her, make her his.

His voice was a subterranean river of lava, hot, destructive, consuming her as it coursed over her. She answered him but had no idea what she said, maybe just his name over and over, a plea and a command, but he understood, his fingers finally returning to her centre again, filling her with a luminescence that radiated through every nerve in her body, his mouth capturing her breasts again as his fingers massaged and coaxed and tortured her arousal, and when his tongue laved her nipple into an unbearable peak, she stopped thinking, obeying his command to forget everything but him and what he was doing to her, what his body was doing to her.

When he shifted her legs apart, she took him in with a gasp of need, her body arching to envelop him. There was no confusion, and if there was pain, she felt none of it in the throes of her storm. She went wild, her fingers biting deep into his shoulders, her mouth capturing his groans of pleasure as she wrapped her body around his erection, laying claim.

She moved with him, utterly open, taking him deeper and deeper with each thrust, uncaring of the hard ground beneath her, of the cold air on her bare flesh. All she felt was his body against hers, hard and soft, inside her, his muscles shaking under her hands, his mouth on hers, his hand caressing her breast, telling her how much he needed her. Loved her.

She hadn't thought the pleasure could come so swiftly. It caught her like a beast from the dark, sudden and inescapable. She shuddered around him, her fingers pressing into his buttocks, and the shudder spread to him.

This time they sank into the warm waters of the tropics. He was pulling her along with him, deep underwater, and it was warm and she didn't even need to breathe, she became the sea, warm, vast. Joyful. She felt the sweet agony of his climax, the violent shudders as his body closed on hers, but for her this time was a warm welling of pleasure that rose and rose and wouldn't stop, carrying her with it into his arms. Home.

'I should have waited. Of all places to do this… I must be mad. It is November and anyone coming down to the lake could see us.'

He dragged his discarded greatcoat over them and she snuggled against him, her leg sinking between his thighs as he shifted, anchoring her on top of him. Under the weight of his caped coat, his hand sloped down her back, warm and gentle, like sun on the surface of water. She arched into it, absorbing his heat as their bodies cooled.

'We would be truly ruined, then, wouldn't we?'

'It would certainly finally put an end to all your indecision.'

'I knew what I wanted before you did,' she protested, tracing the line of his arm from his shoulder to where it rested on her hip, a landscape of powerful muscle, fine silky dark hair, down to the definite bones of his wrist. When she reached it, his hand turned, lacing their fingers together.

'Damn, I love you. Will you marry me, Lily?'

She stilled for a moment, waiting for the mingling of pain and joy to flow through her and calm again.

'I asked you first.'

'I beg pardon, I asked you first.'

'No, you didn't. You *told* me. I asked you. There is a vast difference. And, yes, I will. Your turn now.'

He laughed, pulling her more fully on top of him.

'When you come off your island, you do it with a vengeance, my lovely vixen. I thought I was good at meeting dares, but you outdo me. You've outdone me utterly. Yes, I will marry you.

This very instant, but Lady Belle would never forgive us if we don't appease the ghosts with some show of pomp and circumstance. Hunter also won't forgive me if I don't at least invite him to come gloat at my downfall so he can pay me back for gloating at his.'

She pulled her hand away and planted it on the grass, raising herself to look down at her fallen angel. Flat on his back. It suited him. She would have to do this often.

'You are certain about this, Alan? You must believe me, I don't want to force you if you don't wish to be married.'

'I'm not as generous, love. I'll not allow you a loophole to wiggle out of. You do realise that I didn't use any precautions just now either? You are now honour bound to make an honest man of me. Now come, up with you before we freeze to the ground and are found here encased in ice like fossil remains. Lady Belle will skin me alive if I allow you to fall ill. She is counting on us to relieve her of the Hall so she can lead a wild life of dissipation in Bath.'

'She… What? Does that mean she has reinstated you?'

He secured his buckskins and shrugged into his shirt as she slid the chemise over her head, then he picked up her dress from the grass, his eyes glinting at her as he gathered it into folds and slid it over her head, turning her to secure the hooks.

'Disappointed? She told me she had never respected my grandfather's wish of keeping me from inheriting. Not that I need it, but just so you know, I would marry you without a penny to my name and bear the shame of living up to your fortune-hunting slurs if I had to. There is no possible way I would give you up over a blasted prejudice.'

She turned back to him, gathering his hands in hers.

'I would also marry you if you hadn't a penny to your name, Alan, and consider myself lucky.'

He pulled her against him, grasping her chin, his expression hardening again, a beautiful forbidding statue. He wasn't smiling, but she could see beyond the harsh tension to the fear and beyond that to the giving love she was so lucky to have reached. She touched his cheek as she had when he was ill, softly, full of love, her eyes burning with tears.

He pulled away, stroking the hair from her face.

'What's wrong, love?'

'That day we returned to the Hall, after you were ill, when we sat here, I dreamed of children playing here, but I never believed it might be true. But I need to tell you I don't need anything else other than you. If you will only let me love you.'

'So will you be disappointed if I tell you I was rather warming to the idea of children? I'm terrified of it, but I don't think I can go back to being the way I was any longer. I was thinking we would start with a daughter, just to ease me in. With your hair. And then a son. Or two.'

She laughed, wiping away her tears and wrapping her arms around him again, rising on her toes to press her mouth to his. A son and a daughter. Everything she could give him, she would. She smiled against his mouth, parting her lips to taste him, loving how the hunger was beginning to rise again, how her body was mapping every point of contact between them and laying out demands for more. What a revelation this man was. Hers.

'Alan. My raven with his broken wing. I do love you. I am so glad you shoved me off my island.'

She could feel the rigid tension recede, revealing his warm, generous core again. His fingers combed through her hair, untangling it and unravelling her all over again.

'Not shoved, coaxed. Now I shall have to coax

you back. You owe me a fantasy. You and I are going swimming.'

She laughed, glancing at the lake.

'You're mad. It is November!'

'Hell, no, I refuse to spend my honeymoon in the English winter. You have been swimming around in my feverish brain since we met and it's time I introduced myself into that fantasy and ousted your fairy-tale prince Rupert. It is very demeaning to realise I was jealous of a manatee.'

She leaned her cheek against him, listening to the beat of his heart.

'You needn't have worried. Vixens and sea mammals don't mix.'

He smiled and he tightened his hands in her hair, raising her face towards his as he brushed his lips over hers.

'Ravens also tend to have a penchant for their own kind—feral field animals. Vixens, ferrets, hedgehogs…'

'Hedgehogs?'

He held her firmly as she tried to pull away, speaking the words against her mouth, his breath tangling with hers. She knew what he was doing—he was baiting her, teasing her out of her lair like the wild hunter he was.

'Small, prickly and with a soft underbelly,' he added for good measure, and she sank against him, opening for him, her outrage giving away to laughter.

'You'll pay for that, Raven.'

'With pleasure…'

Epilogue

Summer 1825

The puppy streaked down the bank and cleared the shallows with a leap.

'Good Gwimlet!' Alexander cheered as the black head strained above the surface towards the bobbing wooden boat. The dark green water shattered into ripples around him, spreading all the way to the grassy island in the middle of the lake connected to the bank by a wrought-iron-and-wood bridge.

Their first summer together Alan had brought workers to construct the island for her as well as the classical temple-like structure at its centre, where they went when they wanted to be utterly alone. Everyone knew no one was allowed on the island when the gate on the bridge was closed.

She looked across and sighed, remembering

the perfect summer morning they had spent there a week ago before he had left for Birmingham.

'Very good Grimlet,' Lily agreed, detaching her daughter's chubby hands from her hair and shifting her to her other hip to allow her daughter to rearrange her hair on the other side.

'Greene is despairing of me, Emma. She thinks you are colluding with your father to keep me in a state of permanent disarrangement. And to think I was once considered fashionable.'

Emma detached her hands and raised them in the air.

'Papa.'

'Yes, Papa. I miss him, too, pumpkin, but he should be back tomorrow.'

'I will show him Gwimlet's new trick,' Alexander announced as he took the wooden ship from the puppy's grinning jaw and stood back to avoid most of the shower as Grimlet succumbed to the need to shake off the lake on his new masters before padding over to stretch himself out in the patch of sun between Rickie's and Grim's graves, his pink tongue with its black spot licking absently at the grey stone.

'Papa!' Emma insisted, squirming, and the back of Lily's neck tingled and she turned in time to see Alan push aside the curtain of willow branches.

'Papa!' Alexander got there first, but Emma made good time on her shorter and chubbier legs.

Alan hauled his children into his arms and Lily met the love in his eyes with a rush of emotion and gratitude that never seemed to dim. When Alexander's stream of news and Emma's tugging at his hair and buttons finally subsided, he noticed the mobile ball of dark fluff frolicking at his feet.

'What on earth is that?'

'*That* is Grimlet. Mr Prosper's housekeeper mentioned her son's dog had bred and invited us to see the puppies. The rest, as they say, is history.'

'Grimlet.'

'Alexander wanted to call him Little Grim, but then he thought Grimlet was better.'

'Do you like him, Papa? May we keep him?' Alexander asked with the sudden seriousness that characterised their son.

'If you can keep him from chewing my boots, he can stay.'

Alexander considered the puppy, now rolling on his back at their feet, snapping at a fly that was hovering above him.

'But he likes chewing things. Besides, you have more boots. There is only one Grimlet.'

'Impeccable reason. Yes, you imp. You can keep him.'

'Gimmit,' Emma added.

'On condition you take him with Nanny up to the house now. Mama and I have matters to discuss.'

'Must we?'

Alan beckoned to Nanny Brisbane, who proceeded to pluck Emma from his arms.

'Yes, Master Alexander. It is time for the puppy to have his nuncheon if he is to grow to be as big and strong as Grim.'

'And I shall grow to be as big and strong as you, Papa,' Alexander announced, picking up Grimlet and marching off in the lead.

Lily walked into Alan's open arms and watched the reluctant cavalcade wend its way up to the Hall.

'Are Catherine and Philip well?'

'Very well. They send their regards and said they will visit as soon as Timothy is old enough to be left with his nurse. I told them they might as well bring him as the Hall is one big nursery anyway.'

Lily laughed, leaning against him. It was ridiculous to be so grateful for his return after a mere week's separation, but there it was.

'Lady Belle wrote from Paris full of complaints about French food and manners, but reading between the lines she and your great-aunt Ray are having as marvellous a time there terrorising the French as they had the inhabitants of Bath. I'm glad you returned early. I thought you were only due back tomorrow.'

'That was the plan, but I was having trouble sleeping, so I told Marston he can deal with the rest.'

She frowned, cupping his face in her hands, warming herself against him.

'Was anything wrong?'

'Yes. The bed was too big. I kept waking up wondering where you were and thinking of you in our bed, all warm and waiting. Not conducive to a restful night.'

'I wasn't in our bed, though.'

His arms tightened around her and he raised her face, his eyes taking possession of her again, bringing her to life.

'No? Did you run away again behind my back? I warned you what I would do next time.'

'Yes, I know, locked towers and the like. I was in the nursery. I couldn't sleep either, so I went to listen to Alex and Emma breathing. We are doing very ill at being apart. We shall have to practise.'

'Right now there are much more pressing concerns that require practice.'

'Now? Here?'

'Jem is under strict orders to allow no one to approach the lake path. This is what we constructed our island for, isn't it? Not that we made it there last time. I've been fantasising about how you looked there last time, dappled in sunlight and your hair like fire on the grass. How clever of you to have your hair down and ready for me. Are you sure you didn't know I was coming?'

'Emma helped.'

'She is shaping up to be as intelligent as her mother. I only wish she had your hair. Maybe our next daughter will.'

'Yes, well…about that…'

The heat in his eyes dimmed a little in shock.

'Are you serious?'

'I'm afraid I am—is that terrible?'

He pulled her against him, laughing.

'I leave you alone for a week and I come back and find you with child and a new puppy.'

'I beg pardon, you were very instrumental in at least one of those developments!'

'So I was, how clever of me. This time it will be a daughter with your amazing hair and tortuous mind. Come, all the more reason to gather our rosebuds while we may before I have to share these delectable beauties again.' His hands curved under her breasts, raising them to brush his mouth over the sensitive swells, and her legs sagged against him as her need gathered, fed by the joy and love he woke in her so easily.

She took his hand and led him to their sanctuary.

'I'm so glad you came home, Alan, my love.'

* * * * *

MILLS & BOON

Coming next month

IN THRALL TO THE
ENEMY COMMANDER
Greta Gilbert

'It is true that I am low,' she began, 'and that I was purchased by the Queen as her slave. As such, I am bound to protect her. But that is not why I do it.'

'Why do you do it, then?' he asked, but she ignored his question.

'You speak of logic. Well, logic tells me not to believe you, for you are a Roman and I have never known a Roman I could trust.'

'You are a woman for certain, for you are ruled by humours and whims,' he growled, aware that his own humours were mixing quite dangerously.

A wave hit the side of the boat, causing it to tilt. To steady herself, she placed her hand over his, igniting an invisible spark.

She glared at him before snapping her hand away and stepping backwards. 'Good Clodius—though I know that is not your name—I would ask that you please not insult my intelligence.'

Her sunny words seemed to grow in their menace. 'I may not be as big as you, or as smart as you, or as sly as you, but believe me when I tell you that I know how to handle Roman men.' She flung her braid behind her as if brandishing a whip. 'If you do anything to endanger the Queen, or our quest to restore her rightful reign, or if your deception results in harm to either the Queen or either of her handmaids, you will be very sorry.'

Her audacity was stunning. No woman had ever spoken to him in such a way.

He refused to give her the satisfaction of revealing his discomposure, however, so he placidly resumed his efforts at the oars, taking care to stay in rhythm.

Still, his troops were in retreat; they had lost the battle. His unlikely adversary had utilised all the tricks of rhetoric, along with the full force of her personality, to enrage him, then confuse him, and then finally to leave him speechless.

Nor was she yet finished. As the great yellow globe shone out over the shimmering sea, he felt her warm breath in his ear. 'Just remember that I have my eye on you, Roman.'

He turned his head and there were her lips, so near to his, near enough to touch.

And in that moment, despite everything, he wanted nothing more in the world than to kiss them.

Continue reading
**IN THRALL TO THE
ENEMY COMMANDER
Greta Gilbert**

Available next month
www.millsandboon.co.uk

LET'S TALK

Romance

For exclusive extracts, competitions
and special offers, find us online:

f facebook.com/millsandboon

◎ @millsandboonuk

𝕏 @millsandboon

Or get in touch on 0844 844 1351*

For all the latest titles coming soon, visit
millsandboon.co.uk/nextmonth

Want even more
ROMANCE?

Join our bookclub today!

'Mills & Boon books, the perfect way to escape for an hour or so.'

Miss W. Dyer

'Excellent service, promptly delivered and very good subscription choices.'

Miss A. Pearson

'You get fantastic special offers and the chance to get books before they hit the shops'

Mrs V. Hall

**Visit millsandbook.co.uk/Bookclub
and save on brand new books.**

MILLS & BOON